Dear Benjamin
Vol. Two

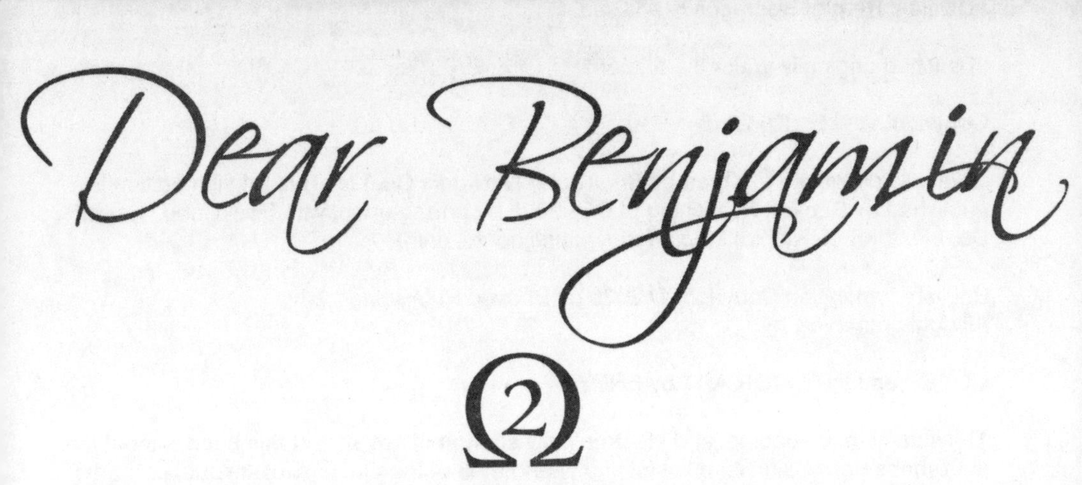

written by
ID

translated by
HJ and CHAEWON KANG

illustrations by
EREYZ

Dear Benjamin is rated MATURE for Intense violence, Graphic sexual content, Strong language, Horror, Mature themes, Blood, Violence, Nudity, Sensuality, and Adult activities. Reader discretion is advised.

Published originally under the title of 디어 벤자민

Originally published in Korea by BookCube Networks Co. Ltd. This English edition is published by BLoved Publishing LLC in 2025 by arrangement with BookCube Networks Co. Ltd. through Rightol Media (copyright@rightol.com).

COVER and INTERIOR ART by EREYZ

TRANSLATION: HJ and CHAEWON KANG
COVER DESIGN: ADDIS
INTERIOR FORMATTING: ADDIS
INTERIOR FLIP DESIGN: RARA
EDITOR: SOFIA ARANGO
EDITOR-IN-CHIEF: ADDIS

ISBN:
HARDBACK 978-1-964533-13-1
PAPERBACK 978-1-964533-11-7
DIGITAL 978-1-964533-15-5

Printed In Canada
First Printing: 2025

10 9 8 7 6 5 4 3 2 1

TABLE OF CONTENTS

Content Warning:

Please be advised that this volume contains extreme content that may not be suitable for all readers. This content contains a nonconsensual sexual scene.

Help is available
Speak with someone today
24/7 USA National Domestic Violence Hotline
1 (800) 799-7233

What is Omegaverse?

While each omegaverse is different, the omegaverse is an alternate universe where people have a secondary biological gender in addition to the traditional male and female roles. This system has three main genders: alpha, beta, and omega. These terms are borrowed from animal behavior research, and each gender has distinct characteristics that influence their societal roles. All these characters are fully human and do not shift into animals!

The Three Genders:

Omegas: Omegas are the most vulnerable gender, capable of giving birth regardless of their primary biological sex. Male omegas can get pregnant, just like female omegas. Omegas experience monthly heats, during which they become extremely fertile and release pheromones that attract alphas. Due to their perceived weakness and low fertility rates, omegas are often marginalized in society.

Alphas: Alphas are the dominant gender in society, often seen as leaders. They have a knot at the base of their penis, which inflates during intercourse with an omega, ensuring a secure "dam" to increase the chance of pregnancy. Alphas can mark their mates through a bite on the neck, creating a lifelong bond.

Betas: Betas are the most "normal" and populous gender, making up around 70% of the population. They don't experience heats or ruts, and they don't have the heightened pheromones that alphas and omegas possess. While they can still form relationships with other genders, they don't participate in the more animalistic aspects of Omegaverse dynamics.

Recessive alphas and omegas: Recessive alphas and omegas spend most of their lives believing they are betas until they eventually present as an alpha or omega. Due to their recessive traits, their pheromones are usually weaker, and their heat cycles or ruts are often uncontrollable even with suppressants—or they may not experience them at all.

Key Terms:

Pheromones: Unique odors emitted by only alphas and omegas that can be perceived by each other.

Heat Cycle and Ruts: Omegas go into heat, a monthly cycle of intense fertility, while alphas experience ruts—periods of heightened sexual desire often triggered by an omega's heat. These cycles play a significant role in mating and reproduction.

Suppressants: Omegas use suppressants to manage their heats, delaying or stopping the cycle. Overusing suppressants can lead to health problems and issues with the Omega's inner spirit. Some versions of Omegaverse also include rut suppressants for Alphas.

Mark: This is a bite on the neck's scent glands that marks an omega as an alpha's mate. Once marked, an omega cannot bond with another alpha. The bond formed by this mark connects the pair physiologically and sometimes spiritually or emotionally.

Scent Glands and Scenting: Scent glands on the neck and wrists release pheromones that convey a person's secondary gender. Scenting is used to mark territory, calm others, or attract mates. Scenting can also be done to objects or people as a sign of affection or protection.

Slick: Omegas produce copious amounts of a sexual fluid called "slick" when they go into heat to make breeding easier. Male omegas often have self-lubricating anuses.

Chapter 1

Something was wrong.

Isaac realized it the moment his team encountered more enemies than expected. The briefing before the mission had stated clearly that there were thirty targets, so they had deployed only twenty men.

A reinforcement unit was scheduled to arrive later, but it was intel-focused, not infantry. That didn't change the fact that the initial team was outnumbered. Their objective was to eliminate a secret warehouse operated by an arms dealer known to be cooperating with terrorist organizations; a mission that was expected to be a minor skirmish.

No one on the team had even felt anxious.

Even during reconnaissance, the area around the suspected warehouse had been quiet. Security seemed lighter than expected—certainly not more than thirty men.

Everything had matched the intel. After all, this was a warehouse no one knew about, hidden on an uncharted island in South America. A place like that wouldn't require many guards.

The issue wasn't the idle men guarding a remote warehouse. The real problem was that the warehouse's owner, Felix Felice, was reportedly on-site for an inspection. That was why Isaac and his team, alongside the CIA, had been deployed.

They hadn't been given direct orders to kill him, but they were expected to disable him permanently, to make sure he'd never walk again. But the moment they arrived and engaged, everything changed.

It turned out that Felix Felice was nowhere to be found.

As time passed, more enemies kept appearing, emerging from wherever they'd been hiding. Worse still, they were heavily armed, retaliating with equipment far beyond what anyone had anticipated.

They may have been special forces, but there were only twenty of them, and their opponent was responding with an overwhelming military power; of course, they'd been caught off guard by such an unexpected response. Within minutes, half the team had fallen, and Isaac was left with no option but to retreat.

Isaac tried to lead the remaining men into hiding, but this was an island—not a small one, but still a tough place to run or hide before the rescue team could arrive. No matter how many radio calls he sent for reinforcements and help, there was no response—just static, as if the signal couldn't get through. The hopelessness grated on his nerves.

"What is going on?" someone shouted. "This can't be right. How could the situation go to shit like this?"

Isaac said nothing. He couldn't. Because they were right, none of it made sense. The mission plans were usually airtight, based on precise data and intel. That wasn't to say their operations weren't difficult, but a scenario so completely different from the briefing? That was unthinkable.

There was only one explanation: the enemy had known they were coming, and the level of response and the sheer firepower proved it. Isaac gritted his teeth. There had been a leak. It was the only possibility.

Fuck!

The headache he'd been having grew worse, pounding harder as he remembered the mission Cole had secretly entrusted to him—a mission that now felt completely impossible. He couldn't focus on anything else, not when he was barely hanging on while waiting for rescue with what remained of his team.

Isaac drew in a shaky breath, forcing his thoughts to settle,

then he rose to his feet. Getting out was the priority now. Whatever it took, even if it meant surrendering, they had to survive first, because everything else could wait. With that thought, he steeled his resolve and set off with his team.

But shortly after, a much bigger problem arose.

His head throbbed with unnatural intensity, a faint fever crept steadily through his limbs, and his breath caught in his throat despite the lack of exertion.

After living his entire life as a beta, Isaac had suddenly presented as a recessive omega at nineteen.

Now, he was entering his first heat.

α Ω α Ω

When Isaac finally came to his senses after hours lost to the fevered chaos of his heat, it was just before dawn, and the sky was still black. Blinking against the gloom, he scanned the warehouse with bleary eyes until something made his breath catch.

The air was thick with a foul, humid stench that clung to everything, from the weathered farming tools leaning in the corners to the scattered haystacks and the dust-covered floor. Light filtered through the cracked, foggy window and barely illuminated the scene, but Isaac didn't need to see clearly—the smell was unmistakable.

It was absolutely obscene.

The cloying mix of sweat, semen, and bodily fluids was overpowering, laced with the sharp, dizzying pheromones of a hyper-dominant alpha, and underneath that, the unmistakable scent of omega pheromones, faint but clearly his own. The riot of smells crashed into him.

His clothes and shoes were tossed everywhere. His entire body ached, each movement creaking with strain, and he was

numb from the waist down, his thighs and ass still soaked in sticky release.

With a thundering heart, Isaac stared at the unbelievable scene, and only then did the memories of the night rush back. A groan escaped him, and almost as a reply, a long, steady sigh sounded behind him.

Isaac's head snapped around, startled. In his daze, he hadn't realized someone was lying behind him, fast asleep, with one arm still wrapped around his waist.

Disgusted, Isaac jerked away. The ache in his battered body no longer registered. All that remained as he stared at the man lying naked beside him was a growing sense of despair.

He had been shocked when he first saw him the night before, but now, really taking in his face in the dim light, a different kind of pressure built in Isaac's chest, deep and insistent. No matter how Isaac looked at him, this man, who was sleeping carefree, had the same face as the photo he'd seen many times before coming here.

The luminous blond hair that practically glowed in the dark; the sculpted, elegant face striking even in sleep; the flawless, lean body stretched out beside him.

There was no mistake. It was Felix Felice, the owner of this island and its arsenal. The man Cole had secretly ordered him to kill.

My God.

Felix Felice. Overwhelmed with despair, Isaac pressed a hand to his forehead. As if it weren't bad enough that his first heat had suddenly started while he was sending distress signals and fleeing the enemy's counterattack—of all people, the alpha who had quelled the uncontrollable fire within him had to be the very man Cole had ordered him to assassinate.

What could be worse than this?

Dragging his hand down over his mouth, Isaac exhaled heavily, then slapped himself out of his daze and scrambled to get dressed. This wasn't the time to fall apart. He had to get out. He didn't even know what had happened to his squad or if they were still alive. His mind had been far from clear when he'd run in here, desperate for a place to ride out the storm raging through his body.

Once he'd hastily thrown on his clothes and gathered his scattered gear, Isaac looked down at the man still fast asleep, and showing no signs of waking. It was remarkable how peacefully he slept in such a place and situation. Then again, the guy had been lounging around in the warehouse since the night before, completely unfazed by the battlefield outside.

But thanks to him, Isaac's heat had passed.

Clicking his tongue, Isaac silently admitted he should be grateful for the man's total lack of urgency; it would be dangerous if he woke up now. Even as he thought that, Isaac pulled a length of rope from his bag.

If the man came to, it would undoubtedly mean trouble. Between the darkness and the camouflage paint, Felix wouldn't be able to recognize Isaac's face, but if he got caught, there would be no escape.

He quickly tied the man's wrists and ankles, but just as he tightened the last knot, the once motionless figure stirred. The man's eyes fluttered open, his thick lashes lifting slowly to reveal the irises beneath.

In the bluish tint of dawn, Isaac's hands froze, his gaze drawn helplessly to the sight before him.

This must be what Sleeping Beauty looked like when she woke up, Isaac thought.

Did that mean the prince who watched her awaken felt the same strange tug in his chest that Isaac felt now? The notion was absurd—yet it stirred an unexpected ache deep inside him, broken only by a voice that cut through his thoughts, low and dark, edged with danger.

"Look here, I'm not into being tied up," he said. "Unless I'm

the one doing the tying."

The words clashed so violently with the man's mesmerizingly beautiful face that it snapped Isaac out of his trance. He jerked his head up, eyes wide.

Their eyes met.

Felix's gaze was cold and sharp despite his casual tone. The lazy drawl in his voice clashed with the murderous gleam in his eyes. Even lying on the floor with his limbs bound, his gaze cut through Isaac like a knife. He looked like a restrained animal, ready to leap and snap Isaac's neck the moment he had the chance, a starving predator catching sight of easy prey wandering alone in the woods. It was the kind of look that made Isaac reach instinctively for his weapon.

Thankfully, Felix was tied to a tractor and couldn't move, at least not easily. Isaac took a steady breath, forced himself to remember that, and swallowed against the dryness in his throat.

"I went out of my way to relieve your heat, and this is what I get in return?" Felix growled, his voice laced with indignation and venom.

Isaac ignored the question and glanced down at his watch. Dawn was already breaking, and time was running out. He needed to finish the job and disappear.

"I'm sorry it had to be like this," Isaac said quietly.

In a way, luck had been on his side. After all, he'd already decided to ignore Cole's secret order—he'd faced bigger problems, like retreating under fire and frantically calling for backup, right up until his heat hit like a bomb. Had events not unfolded as they did, he would never have had the chance to assassinate Felix Felice.

His fingers brushed the knife at his waist. Slowly, he gripped the handle and slid it partway free, steel blade gleaming cold and sharp in the dim, blue light of dawn. Where the warehouse had once been thick with the scent of sex, it now bristled with the weight of killing intent.

Felix's eyes tracked his every movement. He frowned for a second, but then smirked, the corner of his lips curling with palpable scorn.

"My, my," he murmured nonchalantly. "I was all sweet to you because I liked your scent, which is saying something coming from an omega, but now you're sharpening your claws. How adorable."

Isaac's hand paused.

"I'm warning you," Felix said coldly. "Take your hand off that knife."

"You've got a big mouth for someone tied up," Isaac snapped, clicking his tongue at the man's infuriating composure.

Felix chuckled, a low, amused sound that made Isaac narrow his eyes in unease. Then, like a curtain dropping over his senses, it hit him. Pheromones.

Thick.

Crushing.

Drenched in raw alpha dominance.

Pheromones continued pouring over him like a suffocating tide. Instinctively, Isaac's hand shot to his neck, and a gasp broke from his lips as his lungs seized.

"You're an omega," Felix drawled ruthlessly. "Weak-scented, sure, but still an omega. Do you think you can resist a hyper-dominant alpha like me? Don't be ridiculous."

His eyes flashed a dangerous glint of blue, and a second wave of pheromones slammed into Isaac.

Several things happened at once: Isaac staggered, nausea twisting his gut; the floor tilted beneath him, and his vision blurred, black spots dancing at the edges; and his limbs trembled violently, too heavy to lift. He'd never felt anything like it, not even a few hours before, during his first heat.

For a recessive omega who took suppressants religiously like Isaac, the force of those pheromones was monstrous.

"It's hard to overpower an alpha," Felix continued casually.

"But an omega? That's easy."

Felix lay naked and filthy, his hands bound, yet not the slightest bit cowed, smirking like he owned the room. Why would he be afraid when he could crush someone's will with pheromones alone?

As proof of that cruel, effortless power, Isaac couldn't even lift a finger.

The hyper-dominant alpha's pheromones twisted through Isaac's brain like a vise, grinding his thoughts to mush. If this kept up, he wouldn't last another minute, and he'd lose control entirely. His eyes rolled back, and guttural, broken gasps tore from his throat. Saliva slipped from the corner of his mouth, dripping down his chin.

Then his knees buckled, and he crumpled to the floor, trembling and helpless. Through the haze, he saw Felix's blue eyes—serene, smug, victorious. He was wearing an arrogant smile, as if the outcome had been decided before the game began.

Isaac's vision burned under the man's gaze, a wave of disillusionment rising in his chest. No one asked to be born alpha or omega. They were divided from the start, unequal by design. The weight of that injustice slammed into him, hot and unbearable. His jaw clenched so tightly it ached.

Then the blade flashed.

The air split with a vicious *shhhk*, and the sickening sound of steel cutting flesh. For one charged second, the warehouse fell completely still, and a tomb-like silence descended onto the place. The air grew heavy with the stench of blood, which curled faintly through the air, breaking the chokehold of pheromones.

Isaac gasped, dragging oxygen into lungs that had felt sealed shut. The torrent of pheromones ceased. His hand trembled around the knife handle, the white of his knuckles stark against the slick hilt.

A line of crimson slid down Felix's neck from a shallow but visible cut. He didn't move. Just stared, stunned, blue eyes wide in disbelief.

"How did you move?" he asked in a whisper, ignoring the blood trailing down his collarbone.

Everyone knew what happened when an omega was caught in the throes of an alpha's pheromones, especially ones as potent as his. They went mad. Muscles seized. Minds snapped. Resistance became impossible. And it only took an instant.

That fear was why omegas avoided alphas, why even alphas feared the rare, terrifying few born hyper-dominant—the ones who could break betas, omegas, even lesser alphas, just by breathing.

Yet here Isaac was: a recessive omega who broke away from the hyper-dominant alpha Felix's pheromones and brandished a knife at him. Faced with this impossible turn of events, Felix didn't hide his dumbfounded expression and stared at Isaac.

"Don't fuck with me!" Isaac's chest heaved with harsh, ragged breaths as he yanked the knife free from the floor. It had missed Felix's throat by a fraction. Deliberately. The cut was shallow, just enough to bleed, and Felix knew it.

"The only reason I didn't snap your damn neck is because you fuck well enough," Isaac straightened, knife in hand, his legs barely able to hold him.

The pheromones still clung to his system like molasses. One more wave and he'd be down for good. Still, Isaac towered over Felix, whose stunned expression hadn't faded. Then, *crack!* He stomped down hard on Felix's left arm with his combat boot.

"What the fuck?" Felix yelled, panic finally breaking through his carefully curated calm. The steel in his eyes wavered, and anger flared hot behind it.

"Call it payback. For trying to drown me in your pheromones," Isaac said, grinding his heel in for emphasis. "And a warning. *Don't come after me*."

"Don't be fucking stupid!" Felix snarled, teeth bared, just before a sickening snap rang out across the empty space. His scream tore through the warehouse a second later.

"I left your right arm alone," Isaac said flatly, watching as Felix curled in on himself, breath shuddering, beautiful face twisted in pain. Then he turned his back.

"You—*ugh*, you fucking omega bastard! You think you can just walk out of here after this?" Felix's voice cracked with fury and pain behind him, rising in pitch, laced with disbelief.

Isaac didn't stop his uneven, wobbly steps.

"Run, then! Run as far as you can!" Felix howled. "Let's see how far you get!"

Isaac didn't look back, even as Felix's enraged shouts grew louder. He moved toward the exit, shoved the rusted warehouse door open, and slipped into the gray light of dawn. Behind him, the door slammed shut with a metallic bang.

Felix's rage-filled shouts and the crash of debris echoed for a few more seconds, then faded into the stillness. Isaac pretended as if nothing was amiss.

He ran into the thick woods and vanished.

Chapter 2

Isaac still didn't know why he hadn't killed Felix that night four years ago. Somehow, everything had hinged on a single, maddening moment of hesitation.

Drowned in suffocating alpha pheromones, he'd reached for the knife, completely resolved to slit Felix's throat. But by the time his senses returned, the blade had already veered off course. It had only grazed the side of his neck, not pierced it.

Why? Why hadn't he finished the job?

Because they'd spent the night tangled together?

Because Felix was the first man to touch him like that—as an omega?

Because he was the one who'd helped him through a heat cycle he couldn't control?

No. No, it couldn't be for a reason that pathetic.

There was no way he'd develop feelings from a single night, no matter how desperate, how consuming his first heat had been. Acting on a whim was unlike him, but it was the only explanation—a stupid, irrational impulse. Still, not even a day later, regret began to eat at him.

For the first time in his entire career, he had failed to complete Cole's mission. And before noon arrived, the consequences were already crashing down. Search parties were sweeping the island like bloodhounds.

Isaac slipped silently through the dense forest, keeping below sightlines, circling the base of the island in search of his team. The radio offered nothing—not even static, not even a click—just dead silence.

Maybe they'd made it out last night, while I was panting under Felix, Isaac thought bitterly, full of self-deprecation.

It would be fortunate if that were true. Isaac couldn't think of anything more painful than getting his teammates into trouble because of his desertion. If they didn't make it…Then the fallout was his to bear alone. Only his. He wouldn't let his failure drag them down with him.

Sweat dripped from his jaw as he scrambled down a jagged cliffside, fingers digging into damp moss and rock. Somewhere in the distance, the harsh voices of Felix's soldiers echoed, growing nearer. Isaac's breath caught. For a moment, he swore he could see Felix's cold, glittering eyes just ahead and hear his furious voice promising to find him no matter what.

Just recalling that last glimpse of the infamous arms dealer made a shiver down his spine. Isaac shook his head and gritted his teeth. There was no reason to remember! He had to treat that night as something that never happened, and once he got off this godforsaken island, he would bury the memory for good.

He'd make sure of it.

With nothing but that thought to keep him moving, Isaac forced his legs forward and disappeared deeper into the trees.

Early the day before yesterday, during their infiltration, they had hidden their rubber boat and supplies inside a cave at the base of the cliff, and they were still there. Untouched. The fact that neither friend nor foe had discovered the spot made Isaac uneasy, but he quickly shook off the thought and glanced up at the darkening sky, releasing a sigh.

Escaping the island alone would be incredibly dangerous. Crossing a vast ocean in a rubber boat bordered on madness. Even with a motor, there was no telling what lay ahead. The continent was far, and reaching it in a single stretch was unthinkable. He would have to island-hop instead. Most of the islands would be uninhabited, but at least he could pause to reassess before moving on, and if luck was on his side, he might find a way to contact a rescue team on one of them.

No matter what, he had to get off this island!

He had to get away from Felix, who was closing in with every passing second. Isaac looked down the cliffs, where waves crashed violently against the rocks below, then closed his eyes. He would wait for the shadows to deepen. Once the sun set, he would launch the boat.

Until now, his life had been spent on battlefields, braving danger and surviving countless crises, yet few had felt as daunting as this. Could he escape unscathed? He didn't even know what kind of response he'd get if he contacted headquarters and demanded to know what the hell had happened. And what blame would Cole place on him for deserting the team and failing the mission?

Indeed, what awaited him after surviving his current ordeal would be far from favorable. But no matter how unjust the future might be, he had no choice. He would face each challenge, one by one, just as he always had.

Sitting at a lonely cliff, Isaac tried to organize his thoughts, and when the sun finally dipped low and painted the sky red, he pushed the boat out. The roaring sound of crashing waves was especially deafening that evening, amplifying his anxiety about what lay ahead.

In the end, it took over a month for him to return to his homeland, drifting from island to island as he crossed the dark ocean. Prolonged exposure to the elements had left him physically broken, suffering from numerous deficiencies and lingering effects.

Literally on the brink of death.

Isaac, the former Navy lieutenant, now flinched at the mention of the sea, feared the pitch-black night, and suffered from severe seasickness he'd never experienced before. And yet, after enduring all that to make it home, what awaited him wasn't merely unfair; it wasn't even something he could have imagined.

What awaited him made everything else feel meaningless.

First, his desertion was blamed for the total annihilation of his squad. Second, and worse still, he was framed for military corruption and stripped of his rank. Third, his world had fallen apart when he discovered it had all been orchestrated by Cole Patricks, his own stepfather—the man he had trusted and followed.

And lastly, there was one thing that shocked him more than all the rest.

He was pregnant.

α Ω α Ω

Isaac slowly lifted his gaze.

Standing before him was the man he had once spared, defying direct orders to do so. The man—unaware that Isaac was the very omega he despised and was still hunting to this day—looked at him with a gaze that burned.

Isaac had always met those clear, cool Prussian blue eyes without flinching, but this time it was difficult, and his throat dried under the weight of that dark stare. Perhaps it was because he was confronting a past he'd managed to bury, even if only temporarily.

"Are you asking me to clear you of suspicion if you kill someone?" Felix was the one to finally break the heavy silence.

"Yes," Isaac said, nodding once.

"If you're talking about Cole Patricks," Felix said. "Alright. I'll get you out."

"You looked into me?" Isaac wasn't surprised when Felix mentioned Cole. After how easily Benjamin's existence had been uncovered, he'd expected Felix to dig up his past eventually. In fact, the secrets he'd never spoken out loud might all come to light soon.

What kind of expression would Felix make? What would he say when he learned the truth? The question surfaced unbidden, and Isaac rubbed absently at the growing weight in his chest. Imagining Felix's reaction proved impossible.

"Yeah. If you're going to kill Cole Patricks, I won't stop you," Felix muttered, a furrow etched deep between his brows. "I've got my own score to settle with him."

"There's no need. That's enough." Isaac knew exactly what Felix meant, but didn't let it show. He then nodded and turned to leave. There was no time to waste. But as he moved to pass Felix, a strong hand gripped his arm. He looked up and met Felix's blue eyes.

"An exchange always has to be equal."

"Is there something you want from me?" he asked with his usual detachment.

"I don't care who you kill, or how you do it," Felix said quickly, tilting his head as he gave Isaac a curious look. "Do whatever you need to. I can pull the strings to clear your name. But—" He abruptly stopped, his mouth snapping shut as he stared hard, those deep ocean eyes dragging Isaac under like a tide.

A sudden thirst rose within him, like being lost in the middle of the sea, surrounded by endless blue, yet unable to take a single sip. His throat was bone dry. Isaac broke the silence, unable to wait any longer, "But?"

"But you can't get yourself hurt," Felix finished, frowning as he stepped closer. "You can't get yourself killed. Promise me that. Whatever happens, you put yourself first."

"Those are your terms?"

"Yeah."

That's unexpected, he thought.

Felix's name rose to his throat but never left his lips. With a quiet sigh, Isaac lifted a hand and brushed it against Felix's cheek.

A long time ago, Isaac had nearly killed this man with that very hand. If he had gone through with it, what would his life

be like now? He would've never run into him by chance at a flower shop in San Diego, and his identity might never have been exposed. Maybe Benjamin and his mother wouldn't have been taken by Cole.

But…he would have never experienced this subtle, elusive feeling—one that ached quietly in his chest while making his heart beat softer. He would have never known such a strange emotion. If they hadn't met, a flower wouldn't have bloomed in the wasteland he once called life. A flower named Benjamin, who transformed his arid world into something bright and beautiful. Isaac would have gone on believing that the bleak, barren desert around him was all the world had to offer.

And Felix?

He hadn't expected to feel this way about this man. That was what made it hurt even more. Isaac lowered the hand that had been gently resting on Felix's cheek.

"I'm asking you to get me out because I *need* to live," he said. "I can't leave Benjamin alone."

Or you.

He swallowed the unspoken words.

"Yeah, whatever," Felix said, offering a bitter smile. "As long as you don't get hurt or killed."

Isaac listened to the soft cadence of his voice before taking a decisive step forward. It wasn't the time for sentimentality. He couldn't afford it. Gritting his teeth, he forced himself to leave the oddly endearing Mickey Mouse room without looking back.

"Are you leaving now?" Felix didn't try to stop him again. Instead, he asked the question evenly.

Isaac paused, one foot already past the open door. "That's my intention."

"Take my private jet."

The offer caught him off guard, but Isaac found it difficult to refuse.

Chapter 3

The moment Isaac stepped out, Felix's phone rang, right on cue. His gaze lingered on the space Isaac had just vacated as he answered the call.

"Speak." His voice was low and sharp. A man answered on the other end, and Felix listened quietly, a small, sinister smile gradually forming at the corner of his mouth. "I'll be right there. Wait."

That was it, a brief call. Felix slipped the phone back into his pocket and exited the room. The hallway was empty. Isaac was already gone. But Felix wasn't looking for him. No, his steps were purposeful, unwavering.

Not long after, he arrived at a run-down warehouse near downtown San Diego. With Jack in the hospital from a gunshot wound and Tony busy escorting Isaac to the airport, Felix had a different driver and bodyguard today, but he knew their names and faces well enough. When the car pulled up, they quickly opened the door and guided him inside.

The sun had just begun to set, but the windowless interior was already cloaked in darkness. Without the faint flicker of a few old, stained bulbs, nothing would have been visible at all. The air was thick, damp, with a pungent scent of mold, blood, and decay. It was sickening.

Yet Felix walked in without hesitation, the echo of his footsteps hollow in the cavernous space. He drew a revolver from his pocket, absently spinning the cylinder. Every so often, he preferred the weight and simplicity of a classic revolver over an automatic gun. Today was one of those days.

A row of burly men lined the far wall, and in the center of the room sat a man tied to a chair, his body soaked in blood. His face was so battered it was nearly unrecognizable, but his eyes were still intact. When he caught sight of Felix approaching, casually spinning the revolver, he flinched violently and began to shake.

"Boss! Boss! Spare me! I was threatened!" The man's voice shook, warped by blood, broken teeth, and tears. His words were thick and mangled, heavy with pain and fear.

Felix stopped just a step or two from where the man sat and clicked his tongue. Mangled as the man's face was, Felix still recognized him—he'd once been high-ranking, someone privy to their inner workings.

"If you didn't want to die," Felix said, voice casual but razor-sharp. "You shouldn't have done something worth killing you for."

His tone was nonchalant, but the cold glint in his blue eyes was terrifying.

"B-But—"

"Why do you think I came all this way? To hear you out? To let you live? Keep dreaming."

"B-Boss…"

"I came here for one reason. To look at the bastard who sold out Isaac one last time."

The man trembled violently under Felix's gaze. He didn't even try to say "Boss" again. His bloodied lips moved, but no words followed. Just raw fear.

"Honestly, the more I think about it, the more pissed off I get," Felix muttered, brow furrowed slightly. "You dared sell Isaac's information?"

"I-I-I was threatened! I had no choice, I swear!"

With a crisp click, Felix loaded the revolver he'd been spinning. The man paled, his already battered face turning ashen.

Felix felt sick just looking at him.

"How many bullets do you think are in here?" The words were spoken like a joke, but his face remained cold and unreadable. He raised the revolver and aimed it squarely at the man, who froze. The man's eyes widened in horror. His jaw worked, opening and closing, but all that came out were garbled, desperate noises.

"The answer is—" Just as Felix murmured in a low voice, two shots rang out from the revolver in his hand. The man went limp, his head punctured by the bullets; dark red blood began to pool at his feet. Felix glanced at the scene with disinterest before slipping the revolver back into his jacket pocket.

"'Fully loaded,' right? Why would you ever leave a chamber empty when you're planning to kill someone?" Clicking his tongue, he sneered at the corpse that already lay still.

From the very beginning, Felix had been suspicious about how Cole had learned about Benjamin so quickly. The information regarding Benjamin was heavily protected, layered with security measures that couldn't be breached by ordinary means. No matter how skilled their intelligence network was, they couldn't have surpassed Noah's capabilities.

While they were transporting the unconscious Isaac back in the car, Felix had given orders to find the leak. If it wasn't an external breach, then the source had to be internal. And lo and behold, Tony's men had found the culprit within the day, apprehended him, and forced a confession. Just in time, before Isaac left.

The thought alone made Felix grind his teeth.

If this filth hadn't sold Isaac's information to Cole, Benjamin wouldn't have been exposed so easily. He and Jessica would have moved safely to the estate, his men wouldn't have been killed, and Isaac…Isaac wouldn't have collapsed from the shock of losing his child and sunk into that pit of torment.

Regret didn't bring anything back, but knowing one of his own men had caused all this? It made Felix's fury burn white-hot. If he'd had more time, he would've drawn out the execution—

slow and merciless—until the bastard begged for death. He was almost disappointed it had ended so quickly.

"Clean it up." He tossed the command over his shoulder and turned on his heel. There was no time to linger, not when Isaac was out there, hell-bent on killing Cole. Felix strode toward the exit with purpose.

Then a sharp ring pierced the air.

Felix stopped and turned, eyebrows cocked. If his men had any sense left, no one here would dare let a phone ring in his presence.

He could have ignored it, but Felix paused, tilting his head toward the source of the ringing. The sound came from the dead man's chest, where his head now lolled uselessly. Felix's eyes narrowed—a bad feeling stirred in his gut.

"Bring it here." His voice was low and heavy. The men who'd been about to drag the body away froze, then quickly obeyed, handing the phone to Felix.

On the screen: *Unknown*.

He answered it without hesitation.

"What took you so long?" came a man's irritated voice.

Familiar.

"Sorry to tell you, but your buddy just died," Felix said dryly.

For a second, there was only silence. Then, a soft chuckle, "Oh dear. Is it you, Felix?"

Of course, the bastard recognized his voice, too.

Felix's lips curled into a cold smile as he tilted his head ever so slightly. A sharp crack echoed through the warehouse—his neck releasing the tension coiled beneath his skin.

"Yeah. It's been a while, Commander Cole Patricks. Or should I call you something more accurate? How about 'child snatcher'?"

α Ω α Ω

On the way to the airport, Isaac stopped at his recently destroyed flower shop. The immediate area had been tidied up since the police left. Instead of broken glass, white cloth now covered the premises, and the metal gate was rolled down, blocking any view of the interior.

But that was all. Nothing else had changed. It surprised him. He'd assumed the scene would have already been cleared and the evidence gathered.

"We asked the San Diego PD to delay the investigation for a few days," Tony said, catching Isaac's confusion.

"Is that even possible?"

"What isn't possible?" Tony replied, unfazed.

"I see," Isaac murmured, staring at him.

Then, without further ado, Tony moved to open the metal gate as if it were routine for him. Isaac blinked, baffled. *When did he obtain the keys?*

Just as before, Tony caught the look and shrugged. "I've been holding onto them."

This time, Isaac said nothing, just nodded. Tony slid the key into the lock with ease and rolled up the gate. The metal grating echoed loudly in the silence.

With the windows draped in cloth, the flower shop was cloaked in shadow. The sun had already set, making the darkness feel heavier. Inside, broken vases, shattered furniture, and cracked walls gave the room the eerie atmosphere of a haunted ruin, so much so that a ghost could materialize in front of them, and it wouldn't feel out of place.

Just a week ago, he'd spent quiet days here, tending to flowers and trees. Now it all felt like a distant dream, blurred by smoke and gunfire. Isaac quickly suppressed the creeping feeling and turned away from the wreckage; there was no time for nostalgia. He moved swiftly, gathering his things.

There weren't many personal effects left, but he grabbed what he could find: a pair of handguns, a knife, extra ammo, and some

gear he hadn't managed to grab during the chaos. It was a good thing Felix had stalled the police investigation.

With an unreadable expression, Isaac moved efficiently and with purpose. Behind him, Tony sighed. "We've got more than enough weapons, you know."

"I know."

Of course he did. Felix was an infamous arms dealer after all, and he lacked for nothing, especially guns. But these were weapons his hands were familiar with—fitted to his grip, worn in just right. Never mind the weapons, though there was another reason he'd insisted on coming back.

After tossing the half-filled bag onto the counter—now barely recognizable after serving as a shooting target—Isaac headed for the bathroom.

What he really needed were his suppressants.

With Tony shadowing him, it wasn't exactly smart to buy more. That meant making do with what he'd stashed here. There was no telling what might happen next.

As long as he was hiding the fact that he was an omega, Isaac had to be prepared. Always. Danger could come at any time, and he couldn't afford even a moment of vulnerability. He dug into the bottom drawer and retrieved the pillbox, popped the lid, and swallowed several pills on the spot.

Then he looked up.

And stared at himself in the cracked mirror.

A pale-faced man stared back at him from the cracked mirror. As if he couldn't even register the bitterness of the pills sliding down his throat, his features were flat, unreadable. Isaac had never been particularly expressive, but now he looked positively inhuman; cold, unyielding. His black eyes reflected no light, almost glassy.

Lifeless.

He'd spent the past few days exhausted, relentless, spiraling, and still, he'd failed. He hadn't been able to protect his son and mother, the two people he loved the most. Of course, he wasn't all there mentally. Still, the face in the mirror felt distant and wrong, like a stranger's.

He stared longer than he meant to. Then, with a sigh that rasped in his throat, he tossed the remaining pills into the toilet. The flush was deafening in the silence, the small white tablets vanishing into the swirling water.

Isaac straightened, dusted off his clothes, and stepped out of the bathroom. With that, he was more or less ready to face Cole.

Once back in the wrecked shop's main area, his eyes quickly zeroed in on Tony, who was motionless, crouched by the bottom drawer of the counter, staring inside like he'd found a body. His face was pale, his mouth slightly open in quiet shock. Isaac made a point of letting his footsteps echo as he approached.

Tony startled, his shoulders jerking up like he'd been caught stealing. Then, he turned slowly to face Isaac, eyes wide, and his face pale.

"I-I was just trying to grab what we needed," Tony stammered. "Figured this was our only shot, so I was poking around…"

"I meant to return these to you," Isaac said in a flat tone, holding out the luxury watch and ring that Tony had been gaping at. "But I didn't have the chance."

Tony remained frozen as he continued to stare at the familiar objects. They were the same watch and ring that had been taken from him by a disguised thief. It seemed impossible, but as realization struck, Tony's face drained of all remaining color, and he let out a shocked, almost comical yelp.

"Wait, so that robber from before—" Tony blurted, his voice a mixture of disbelief and dawning horror.

Isaac simply hefted the bag he'd left on the counter and moved across the shop with purpose. His briskness was a clear signal that they had little time to waste. Tony, still stunned, scrambled to catch up with him.

"Mr. Sinclair! Wait! Let's talk about this," Tony called out,

his voice tinged with urgency, but Isaac's focus was unyielding. As he turned off the lights and locked up the shop behind them, the distraught Tony could only follow, and before he knew it, they had reached the car. Without so much as a glance back, he climbed into the sedan.

"To the airport," Isaac stated calmly, his tone straightforward.

Tony didn't hesitate. The moment the door opened, he slid into the seat next to Isaac, almost as if to keep him from slipping away. Isaac regarded him coolly, his gaze steady, as Tony panted from the exertion of chasing him. The red creeping into his face spoke volumes about his shock—especially when he clutched the watch tightly in one hand, his eyes still wide with disbelief.

"So, that robber…it was you, Mr. Sinclair?"

"Yes."

"So, you were in disguise, stealing the paternity test results?"

"Yes." There was no need for pretense. Isaac answered Tony's pointed questions without hesitation.

In response, Tony smacked his forehead with a groan and cursed aloud. "Why?"

"I should be the one asking that," Isaac snapped, his voice like ice. "Why did you run a paternity test on my son without my consent?"

Tony flinched as if struck.

"Why did you steal Benjamin's hair and have it tested?" Isaac continued, eyes shooting daggers at the man next to him.

Tony made a strangled noise, guilt catching in his throat. Now that Isaac had confessed to being the robber, he knew there was no wriggling out of it. He had to come clean.

"Mr. Sinclair," he began with a defeated sigh. "The boss might be clueless thanks to his total lack of awareness, but don't you think Benjamin's face raises questions? Anyone who sees the boss and Benjamin side by side would think they're father and son."

Isaac didn't blink. His stare was as unflinching as it was

merciless.

"And? What exactly were you hoping for?" His voice was low, dangerous. "You suspected Felix of being Benjamin's father because of a resemblance? And if the results had said yes, what would have happened then? Has Felix ever gone looking for some secret child he didn't know about?"

Tony's mouth opened, "No, that is—"

"So why were you so desperate to find another father for my son? Without my permission. Without reason. When he's happy as he is." He leaned back slightly, his gaze unwavering. "Benjamin is my son."

Tony shrank under the weight of Isaac's fury, and he felt his mouth going dry, his throat tightening. He tried to speak again, but only choked, the heat of shame and fear prickling across his skin.

Tony couldn't meet those blade-like black eyes. He couldn't even lift his head. God, how could someone so quiet, so composed, radiate such dangerous intensity? Isaac Sinclair was anything but ordinary, as expected of a Navy lieutenant and DEVGRU special ops agent.

"I wasn't thinking. My apologies," Tony muttered, his voice small.

Like a puppy, he tucked his tail between his legs, instinctively sensing that one wrong word might snap whatever invisible thread was keeping him safe. He knew he'd crossed a line. Running that test had been a betrayal, plain and simple.

"Even if you think Benjamin resembles Felix, he is my son. Felix has nothing to do with him," Isaac said, each word clipped, final. "And it's certainly not something you should ever be concerned about. Understood?"

"Understood," Tony choked out, nodding quickly, as the weight of Isaac's stare bore down on his shoulders.

"I won't say anything to Felix about this," Isaac added, voice like steel. "You won't either."

"Of course," Tony whispered, grateful and terrified all at once. He was burning with the urge to ask—to know whether Benjamin really wasn't Felix's biological son—but he knew better than to test Isaac again. So he swallowed his curiosity like a bitter pill. Still, a quiet, frustrated sigh escaped him.

Just what was going on?

Isaac had gone so far as to disguise himself as a robber just to intercept the paternity test results. That level of secrecy and his unbreakable determination to keep anyone from learning the truth only made things more suspicious. There had to be something about Benjamin, who was the spitting image of Felix, and about Isaac, who insisted, almost too fiercely, that he alone was the father.

Tony had a gut feeling, but no proof to support it. And that lack of evidence gnawed at him, left him restless. Yet it was clear. Isaac, the one holding the key, had no intention of ever letting it go.

Was there really no other option but to give up?

The thought of giving up made Tony rub his temples, trying to calm the throbbing in his head. He then stole a glance at Isaac, trying to read him. Isaac was colder than stone, expression locked in place, his gaze fixed blankly out the window. The silence in the car was suffocating. Tony bit his lip, unable to say a word, anxiety coiling tighter in his chest.

Chapter 4

"Child snatcher?" The disapproving tone crackled through the phone. "You exaggerate."

"You sent mercenaries to kidnap a woman and a child. What's there to exaggerate?" Felix snorted as he stepped out of the warehouse without looking back. His subordinates would handle the rest of the cleanup. They were professionals, so he wasn't worried.

Only one thing lingered in his mind.

"It's only natural to be curious about a grandson I've never met, isn't it?" Cole said snidely.

Felix stopped in his tracks and cursed under his breath. For a moment, he was too stunned to speak.

"Oh, didn't you know? Kay is my son. Legally."

"What bullshit," Felix spat. "You're legally his father, so you drove him to the edge of death, kidnapped his son, and threatened him? Even stray dogs have more dignity than you."

"Felix, I know you're as impudent as ever, but you'd best hold your tongue."

"How could mine resist while yours is spitting bullshit as always?" Felix growled, glancing at his wristwatch before resuming his walk. The breeze after sunset would have been pleasant, but Cole had ruined it. If this conversation dragged on any longer, his mood might plummet through the ground.

"No need for chit-chat. I only picked up because I figured it was you and thought I should let you know: the fucker's dead."

"You thought it would be *me*?"

"I have good instincts. Oh, and since we're talking, I should go ahead and say what's been on my mind."

"Felix Felice has something to say to me. What could it be?"

Once back in his car, Felix leaned back against the seat, his lips twisted into a smirk, though his blue eyes remained ice-cold. "Cole, cut the crap," he started. "If you lay a hand on Mrs. Parker or Benjamin, I'll make your life a living hell. Don't think I'm playing nice because I'm scared of scum like you."

His voice, low and laden with threat, sent a chill down the spines of his men in the front seat. The suffocating power and thick alpha pheromones emanating from him petrified his men, and the driver's hands visibly trembled on the wheel, a sharp contrast to the cold confidence oozing from Felix.

Whether he was aware of Felix's murderous aura or not, Cole remained silent for a long stretch, his thoughts unreadable. Just as Felix was about to end the call out of sheer boredom, Cole finally spoke, his tone flat, "What's your relationship with Kay?"

Felix scoffed, unimpressed. "You were busy digging up dirt, bribing my guys, and still haven't figured it out?"

"Just answer the question."

"Oh, why wouldn't I, since you're so curious?" Felix's smirk deepened. "Your son, the one you're so desperate to kill, he's mine."

His smile was so bright it could have blinded anyone standing too close. If Isaac had been there, he might have been in awe of it again.

"None other than Felix Felice, coveting my son?" Cole said, and a strange sound came from the phone, halfway between a scoff and a laugh. "I live to see the day."

Felix's laugh was dry, dripping with sarcasm. "You sure talk like an old man for someone not even fifty."

"But what to do? I have no intention of approving you as my son's partner." Cole's voice was as cold as Felix's, though tension laced every word.

"Are you serious?" Felix tilted his head, smirking. "Were you always this dry?"

"I'm sorry to hear you think I'm joking. Let me be clear. Stay away from Kay. If you interfere with my family again, I'll crush you for good."

"Family? Don't make me laugh." Felix's smile only grew, his eyes glinting with malice. "Fine, I'll spell it out for you, too. Cole, I'm ready to rip apart my future father-in-law and feed the pieces to a dog." Felix chuckled darkly, casually glancing at his watch again. "What do you think of that?"

Cole remained silent, but his ragged and strained breathing was audible through the phone. "Who do you think you are, talking like that—"

"I'm sick of your prattle. Here's the one thing you need to remember. Lay a hand on Benjamin, and you'll find out what it means to live as something less than human."

One time was enough.

One time seeing Isaac break down over losing Benjamin. One time seeing him tear himself apart. One time was more than Felix could stand. He would never let it happen again.

"Fascinating. Why are you more upset than Kay? Let's be real, Benjamin is not your child," Cole muttered, genuinely intrigued.

Felix's frown deepened as his gaze drifted to the darkened freeway outside the window. Past rush hour, the traffic had thinned, and the few cars that passed barely made a sound. It was a quiet, unremarkable scene, so different from the chaos simmering inside him and Isaac.

"That's why I call you trash," Felix responded sharply, his voice low and cutting.

"What?"

"Let me break it down for you. If we flip your words around, you're basically saying that it's fine for me to ignore a three-year-old kid getting kidnapped, just because he's not my kid? I guess

that's how you could justify sending mercenaries to abduct him like it's nothing, huh?"

"Hah, how dare—"

"You seem to have a serious lack of morals," Felix interrupted. "People like you are trash, and it's normal to get angry when a piece of filth pulls this kind of stunt."

Cole's usual arrogance snapped under the weight of Felix's words. He swore loudly, his composure completely unraveled.

Felix, unfazed, held the phone away from his ear, his lazy smile never leaving his lips. As he lowered the window, the rushing air swept back his shiny blond hair. The wind drowned out the rest of Cole's curses, but Felix didn't mind.

"One more thing you don't know, the reason you shouldn't have touched Benjamin," Felix continued casually, though there was an undeniable edge in his voice. Ignoring Cole's fury, he calmly dropped the bombshell, pausing to make sure every word landed. "The Benjamin you took? He really is my son."

"What nonsense!"

"You fucked up." The words were sharp, final. Without hesitation, Felix tossed the phone out onto the freeway. He didn't need to hear another word. The phone was quickly swallowed by the night, certain to shatter upon impact.

Felix raised the window with a satisfied smirk. The wind that had battered his hair and ears was gone, replaced by the silence inside the car. He casually brushed his windswept hair back into place before clicking his tongue in mild displeasure.

The last thing Cole had shouted at him echoed faintly in his mind, *"Don't be absurd!"*

The tone had been frantic, almost desperate.

"What's so absurd?" Felix muttered, a self-assured smile curling his lips. "Once I have Isaac under my roof, Benjamin will naturally become my son."

He snorted to himself, turning his gaze back to the window. The night had fallen quietly, and now everything was cloaked in darkness. Felix wasn't sure when he'd reach that point with Isaac and Benjamin, but he hoped he wasn't too late. His impatience simmered beneath the surface, and with a deep breath, he closed his eyes to calm himself.

α Ω α Ω

Felix slowly opened his eyes when his subordinate announced they'd reached their destination. He looked out and spotted the two familiar faces in front of the building. As he'd expected, they had already arrived and were waiting for him. Felix drew a short breath as the sedan rolled to a stop beside them.

He opened the door and stepped out. The man standing like a statue looked up, confusion washing over his face. Felix's stomach twisted at the sight of how haggard he'd become in less than a week. But when those unaware black eyes locked onto his—stunned, silent—Felix couldn't help the flicker of glee that stirred within him.

"Why are you…?" Isaac murmured, bewildered.

Felix approached, hands in his pockets, smiling. "Isaac, I offered you my private jet, but I never said I'd be sending you alone."

"You're coming with me?"

"Of course. Did you think I'd let you go off by yourself?"

Isaac stared at him, expression unreadable. The way he chewed his lip—wanting to say something but unable to—was infuriatingly attractive.

At this rate, Felix didn't know what he'd end up doing if he continued watching, so he quickly grabbed Isaac's arm and led him into the airport. "You said you don't have time. What are you waiting for?"

"But—"

"I told you, didn't I? From now on, anything you do, anywhere you go, you will be with me." Felix was resolute, reaffirming what he'd said once before.

Isaac swallowed his argument and left with no choice but to follow his lead. The interior of the plane was clean and luxurious. The spacious cabin was modeled after Felix's office at his private residence. On the desk sat an array of computers, tablets, miscellaneous gadgets, and documents. A sofa faced the desk. A minibar lined one wall, and a door behind it led to a bedroom. The jet had everything it needed to serve as a flying hotel.

Isaac settled onto the sofa and looked around before resting his gaze on Felix, who was focused intently on the laptop open in front of him. The way he glared at the screen, brow furrowed and fingers flying across the keyboard, made him look more serious than ever.

In truth, when Isaac had left the manor, he'd found it strange that Felix had let him go so easily. Sure, he'd sent Tony to follow him around, but he hadn't insisted on coming along, nor had he argued that it was too dangerous and that they should find another way.

Even as Isaac had been grateful for the offer of the private jet—and Felix's willingness to step aside—something had nagged at him. He hadn't expected Felix to show up at the airport, but a part of him must have known he would. Smooth operator of the century, this man. Isaac had been upset when he first saw him, but bringing it up now felt pointless. He didn't have the strength to stop Felix anyway.

Giving up easily, Isaac sank back into the sofa. The cushions were so soft, it felt like his body was being swallowed whole.

"We have at least five hours, so get some rest," Felix muttered, eyes never leaving the laptop monitor. Although from the corner of his eye, he noticed the tension draining from Isaac's exhausted frame.

But instead of relaxing, Isaac shook off his sleepiness, and blinked his heavy eyelids.

Their destination was North Carolina. The Joint Special Operations Command that Cole worked for was based in Fort Bragg, and Cole's private residence wasn't far from it. From San Diego on the Pacific Coast to North Carolina on the Atlantic, it was, as Felix said, a five-hour nonstop flight. It was a long journey.

Getting some sleep during that time might help him recover, but it wasn't easy. Maybe he was too tired—his eyes felt like they were collapsing inward—yet sleep wouldn't come. His thoughts were crowded with worry about his mother and Benjamin, about where they were and what they might be enduring now.

"Drink this." Felix held a glass of scotch with ice, right in front of Isaac's eyes, which had been staring blankly out the dark window. He hadn't even noticed Felix approach.

"Thank you." Isaac looked at the glass for a moment, then lifted it and took a swig. The sharp, icy liquor burned down his throat. In his current state, a little alcohol might actually help.

"That reminds me—we haven't had a proper meal," Felix said, eyeing Isaac disapprovingly, as if he were a dried-up twig that might crumble to dust if pressed too hard, before ordering Tony to serve dinner. Only then did Isaac realize he hadn't eaten all day.

Before returning to San Diego, he'd had a light meal in a small town between California and Arizona. But he remembered going two or three days without food during his confinement. Even then, he hadn't really felt hunger.

He didn't feel hunger, fatigue, or sleepiness. Though he could sense his body dragging, the rest of him was numb, as if those instincts had died. Isaac sat pale-faced, then glanced out the tiny window. Beyond the glass stretched the inky night sky.

They hadn't been in the air long. The land below was still sprinkled with yellow streetlights, but soon they would fly over territory where even those would disappear. The pitch-dark sky unfolded like a boundless ocean.

Didn't they say the ocean was the sky's mirror? The ocean had no color of its own; it only reflected whatever the sky offered. In that case, the saying wasn't wrong: the lightless, moonless sky, and the night sea that mirrored it.

As soon as the thought crossed his mind, a shiver crept over his skin. He quickly reached out and closed the shade. Just like his body remembered and became seasick, it also remembered that fear—the fear of absolute darkness.

"Isaac, what's wrong?" Felix asked, seated across from him, watching closely as Isaac wiped away the cold sweat.

At the sudden question, the chill slowly loosened its grip, and Isaac turned his head, blinking. Those deep ocean-blue eyes were fixed on him with concern, so terribly deep he could drown in them.

"Four years ago, I crossed an entire ocean alone."

Perhaps that was why the memory had resurfaced now: not because it had been forgotten, but because it had never been spoken aloud.

"Alone?"

"It had a motor, but I once sailed a rubber boat across a moonless ocean," he said dispassionately, as if the brief phobic episode just now had meant nothing.

Felix frowned and grumbled, "Were you asking for death?"

It was you who drove me into the middle of that dark ocean, Isaac thought. He only smiled bitterly.

"Since then, I've feared total darkness. It's not unbearable, but I shudder whenever I think of it." He glanced toward the closed window and idly twined his fingers together. His expression went blank as he remembered the darkness that lay beyond. "I just felt the same way I did then."

"Because it was dark outside? That's why you closed the shade? I can make the lights brighter, if that helps." Felix's tone was blunt, but the offer was thoughtful.

Isaac shook his head. "No, this is fine. It's more because I

don't have Benjamin with me than because it's dark outside."

He knew himself better than anyone. The spike of anxiety, fear, and tension wasn't just from remembering his scotophobia. No matter how much he tried to appear unaffected, the current situation was pushing him to the edge.

"With Benjamin, I was never afraid, no matter how dark it got. With him in my arms, I had nothing to fear. Isn't that funny? Maybe it was knowing I had to protect my child. Or maybe I was just so happy being near Benjamin that I forgot to be afraid."

Whenever he buried his nose in that baby powder-scented hair, soft as spun gold, with the child warm and squirming in his arms, Isaac would always forget everything else and simply laugh without care. Whenever Benjamin smiled or gurgled a word or two—even when he threw tantrums or cried—every moment was precious. Adorable.

Isaac had begun putting the child before himself in everything he did, and somewhere along the way, he realized he couldn't imagine life without him. He'd long forgotten those early days, when he first discovered he was pregnant and wrestled with whether to keep the baby or not.

The moment Benjamin was born, and he held him for the first time, everything inside him changed direction. He had never once regretted having the child. In fact, he knew with certainty that if he'd chosen differently, his life would have been indistinguishable from drifting alone through a pitch-black ocean.

Benjamin was the only light in his murky world.

Naturally, having that one hopeful light taken from him felt like being thrown back into that endless, dark sea. If he failed to get Benjamin back, he'd sink into that abyss again, and this time, he would never escape. Just the thought of losing Benjamin forever made him shiver. Isaac rubbed his arms.

No.

That wouldn't happen. He couldn't lose him.

Isaac clenched his fists, steadying himself, before lifting his gaze. He was immediately met with Felix's eyes, sharp Prussian blue irises—deep, unreadable, like the sea—churning with emotions Isaac couldn't name.

"Somehow it feels like I'm in some heavy one-sided affair," Felix said, frowning. Then, as if struck by a thought, he tilted his head.

"Hold on, that's strange. You were there four years ago, got betrayed by Cole, kicked out of the Navy, and have been on the run ever since. So when exactly did you have time to make a kid? Did you have a woman before you went underground? What kind of person is she?" His tone was light, almost careless, but his eyes stayed locked, calculating. "There wasn't any record of you being married or even dating. Just that you were constantly deployed like a damn workaholic."

Isaac's guard shot up. He exhaled a tight breath, suddenly wary. It seemed Felix had dug up far more than he expected. Isaac deflected with the question, watching Felix carefully. "How much did you find out about me?"

"Enough, I'd say," Felix answered, shrugging. "I know your alternate identity is Navy Lieutenant Kaysid Patricks of DEVGRU, and that you're Cole's adopted son."

Not just enough—he knew everything. Isaac flexed and uncurled his fingers, calculating.

"That's all you've got?" he asked.

"More or less." Felix's tone was casual, his expression unreadable, but it wasn't an act. There was no deceit—Felix had never been one to play coy.

Isaac felt a small wave of relief. If Felix had uncovered everything, he would've said so. His deepest secret was still safe…for now. Trying to ignore the hammering in his chest, Isaac ran his tongue over his dry lips.

"Then tell me." Felix implored.

"About what?"

"The incident. Four years ago."

With that, Isaac shifted the spotlight away from Benjamin and himself, quietly, but decisively. “Sure.”

Luckily, Felix didn’t seem to notice the shift in Isaac’s tone. He answered with his usual arrogance, eyes narrowing slightly, curious, maybe, about where this was going. Meanwhile, Isaac turned over the questions he had carried for years, the ones that had gnawed at him in silence.

For as long as he could remember, Cole and Felix had been at each other’s throats. It didn’t make much sense on the surface: a Navy commander and an international arms dealer should’ve had a strictly transactional relationship, but they didn’t. Isaac had a vague idea why, though the exact details remained murky.

“Cole stole weapons your company supplied,” Isaac said flatly. “He sold them to a third-world country under the table. No one knew. No one could even imagine it. Not even me, at least not until he had me expelled.”

“But?” Felix prompted, one brow raised.

“But the moment someone traced those weapons back to your company, they blamed you. Said they were from your organization and said you were colluding with terrorists.”

Felix let out a dry chuckle, his lips curling in amusement as Isaac laid out what he knew.

“And that wasn’t all,” Isaac continued. “Cole was taking bribes from several munitions manufacturers. There were higher-ups involved, too. But instead of blowing the whole thing open, they pinned the illicit trade on you. You were the perfect scapegoat. They used the FBI and CIA as a smokescreen to raid your armory, but behind the scenes, there was a special ops unit. Not federal.”

“You know more than I thought,” Felix said quietly, almost thoughtfully.

The ice had melted in the glass of scotch he’d given Isaac earlier. Isaac took a sip, even though the drink had become watery. It still burned all the way down, making his throat feel tight and raw.

"So," Felix said at last, watching him. He set down his glass, the condensation on the sides dripping down. "What do you want to know?"

"Did you really conspire with Cole to traffic weapons?" Isaac asked, staring at him with narrowed eyes. "Then, what? Things went south, and he tried to kill you?"

At any rate, one thing was clear: Cole had trafficked Felix's weapons. Which meant someone on Felix's side had conspired with him, smuggling out inventory under the radar. What remained unclear was whether Felix had known and turned a blind eye or had been kept in the dark entirely.

"First off," Felix started, rubbing his chin. "It's true I trafficked weapons to a third-world country. Illegally. Taxes were too high otherwise. I nearly went bankrupt paying them."

Isaac's brows shot up. The blunt admission still hit Isaac like a slap. He'd suspected as much, but to hear it confirmed so casually left him stunned.

"But," Felix said, wagging a finger with a smug grin. "That was when I was doing the selling."

Isaac furrowed his brow. "Then Cole—"

Felix raised a hand to stop him, his expression sharpening. "Isaac, I'm a businessman—a dealer. My entire reason for existing is to turn a profit. You think I'd just sit by and let some guy steal my goods and undercut my margins?"

Isaac was about to speak, but Felix snapped first. "Not. A. Chance," he snarled, spitting out each word like a warning. "Selling to a third-world country? Sure, I'll do it myself. I don't make trouble like letting someone profit off my wares."

Of course, Felix wouldn't let something like that slide. Knowing his personality, it was almost laughable to think he'd quietly accept someone stealing from him. Still, as Felix gave an answer that was so quintessentially him, Isaac dragged a hand over his face. It was a relief to know Felix hadn't been part of Cole's scheme. But that didn't make the rest of it sit any easier.

Illegal trafficking was still a problem, no matter how casually Felix treated it.

"It was the guy in charge of supplies," Felix said with a scoff. "He's the one who secretly cooperated with Cole. Misappropriated our inventory, little by little. For months, the rat chewed through our assets."

"You had no idea?"

"None. But once we caught him and removed him from the chain, guess who had the nerve to call me?" Felix leaned back, an ironic smile tugging at his lips. "Cole. With a 'proposal.'"

Isaac's posture shifted, spine straightening at the name. His gaze sharpened. He asked, his tone taut, "Cole made you an offer?"

"Yeah. Said he'd raise the rate on my weapons contracts with the Navy, in exchange for me letting him sell them illegally behind their backs." Felix rolled his eyes. "What bullshit is that? Sitting on his throne, thinking he can skim off my product and make a fortune?"

Felix drummed his fingers against the armrest, irritation bleeding through his voice.

"So, did you turn him down?" Isaac asked. "If you'd taken the deal, you could've made a fortune. Higher rates, extra perks. But if you refused, you would be penalized—"

"If there has to be illegal trafficking, then I'll do it myself," Felix interrupted. "But I'm not going to be involved in corruption committed by a bastard like him. How dare he contact me after pilfering my stuff like a rat?"

"That's why Cole has a grudge against you." Isaac rubbed his hands. They were clammy with sweat.

"Probably. Cole started to give me a hard time afterwards. Accused me of collaborating with terrorists or whatever and came at me, trying to destroy my warehouse. It was a joint raid incited by Cole and by folks who were never happy with my profiting." With his arms crossed, Felix drummed his fingers and fixed his gaze on Isaac. "But you see, I have good connections."

Goosebumps erupted at the softly spoken sentence.

What he meant was: he knew beforehand the government was planning to raid him.

"Of course," Isaac muttered despite himself.

The reaction of the island guards back then had definitely been as if they knew everything. They had been prepared and waiting for them to infiltrate. As a result, his team was annihilated.

One side sent troops to destroy Felix's warehouse, while another tipped Felix off. Such was the reality, and the ones to get slaughtered were his teammates caught in the crossfire, when all they did was follow orders.

The more he thought about it, the more bitter the memory became, yet no emotion surfaced. Perhaps enough time had passed for his emotions to be extinguished. Or perhaps he lacked the energy to get angry. He was already at his limit, having to save Benjamin.

"At the time, I was pretty ticked off, and I admit I didn't listen to anyone's reasons and overreacted. I'm still pretending to be tame thanks to that," Felix paused for a moment before starting in a low voice. "In any case, I'm sorry."

Isaac looked up with surprised eyes. He hadn't imagined Felix would apologize for what happened on the island. Yet Felix's eyes, locked on his, did not waver. Feeling almost a burning sensation in his throat, Isaac took another sip of the scotch with its nearly melted ice.

"I had no idea the team Cole sent to crush me was your DEVGRU. Really, who would have thought I'd end up having this kind of relationship with someone who was involved in that shit?"

Angrily, or anxiously, Felix swept back his shiny hair before grabbing Isaac's half-drunk glass of scotch and tossing it back. The watered-down liquor made him grimace, but he lowered the empty glass and continued.

"I heard today you were the only survivor from your team. That's why I'm saying I'm sorry," Felix said woefully, rubbing his mouth.

Isaac let out a scant breath. "It was war."

Kill or be killed. That was war. To them, it had been a chaotic, senseless conflict—but in the end, they lost. For Felix, forced to protect his warehouse and his life, it had simply been self-defense. Kill or be killed.

"And the team getting killed is also my fault."

The biggest issue was that a soldier had deserted his team during battle—and it was none other than the team leader himself. Even if he had no other choice, that was the outcome.

"Don't beat yourself up. I don't know what you were going through then, but seeing you as you are now, I get the picture. Your men died because I went too far." Felix bit his lip, his expression complicated. "It's not your fault. Blame me. It's mine, and I'll take all the blame."

He wasn't the kind to dwell in anguish—but how could he not, after learning that he and Isaac had been bitterly ill-fated all along?

"Fuck, when I heard that an ordinary florist like you had a troublesome past involving being chased, I thought you were talking about loan sharks, not that you were an ex-Navy Lieutenant hunted down by Cole Patricks. And that you and I fought on the battlefield."

"My apologies," Isaac said. "I hid it from you."

"It's not like you had a choice."

Like he said, Isaac couldn't have disclosed everything from the start, not with how poorly things had gone between them before. He had no way of knowing how Felix would react.

Who could have known they'd go from trying to kill each other to standing on the same side, built on trust and support? When Isaac ran into him again at the flower shop, he never imagined it. No one would have.

Isaac rubbed his cheeks with a calloused hand. The shadow over his gaunt face deepened.

"It doesn't matter. What's the use of quibbling over bygones? If you had told me the truth, what would that have changed? I would still be impatient to have you, and I would have taken you by any means necessary." Felix whispered, his darkened eyes consuming Isaac. He continued, "Mark my words, the result would have been the same. Whether you revealed your complicated past or not, I would have still fallen for you."

His velvet voice, melodic in its confession, left Isaac speechless. Then, as if uncharacteristically flustered, Felix leaned back into the sofa and rubbed the back of his neck. "Who cares if you're Cole's adopted son or a Navy lieutenant or my once-enemy? The important thing is that I get hard because of you."

The way he averted his gaze reminded Isaac somehow of a large dog. A husky-like dog tiptoeing around its owner after having done something wrong. Without knowing, Isaac smiled at the ridiculous thought, drawing his lips into a faint curve.

He would have felt the same. Whatever their pasts, he would have been inevitably drawn to that beautiful, arrogant man. What a strange thing destiny was.

"So it is," Isaac nodded. "The result would be unchanged."

He felt the weight he'd been carrying lighten a little bit.

"Didn't I tell you not to smile like that? What are you doing, turning me on at a time like this?" Felix rubbed his forehead and let out a groan, as if he couldn't bear it. "Should have killed that fucker Cole back then," he muttered dangerously, then turned his eyes toward Isaac in a glare. "The moment we retrieve Benjamin, I'm taking every single late fee. You'd better brace yourself, Isaac. I haven't forgotten your breach of contract."

Felix threw the words at him without warning and sprang from his seat before Isaac could respond. At that moment, Tony—who had been anxiously waiting for their conversation to end—emerged from the galley carrying a tray.

Isaac stared after him, unable to call out or demand an answer. Tony was already seizing the moment to set the table for dinner, and Felix, muttering "Go ahead and eat," was already walking away.

Felix had gone a couple of steps when he whipped his head around without warning. "I guess that means that impertinent omega bastard must be dead."

Their gazes clashed midair. Isaac, ensnared by the sharp blue eyes, reflexively gulped. A chill ran down his spine.

"You wouldn't happen to know anything, would you?" Felix asked, wearing an expression full of curiosity.

Isaac was at a loss for words.

Before long, Felix waved his hand as if it were nothing, turning around to resume his pace. "No, never mind, it was a silly thought."

Isaac couldn't take his eyes off his disappearing back until the smell of food on the table snapped him out of it.

The smell stirred something in him, and Isaac let out a breath. Yet his heart, still holding on to the last unspoken truth, beat anxiously all the same.

Chapter 5

Felix didn't come back for a while. While waiting, Isaac finished his soup and ate the meatloaf and asparagus. The mixture of ground meat, vegetables, and bread, roasted together and neatly sliced, was soft and tender.

Had it been just a heavy slab of meat, he might have felt uncomfortable, but this he could force down. The taste barely registered. He wasn't eating because he was hungry, but because he needed to brace himself for what lay ahead.

Felix finally returned and sat down. Isaac looked up, pulled from his thoughts. The soup had long gone cold.

"Did you shower?"

"Ah."

Isaac had assumed Felix had just gone to the restroom, but after taking so long, he returned with damp hair and a change of clothes. His face—already striking—now had the freshness of someone freshly showered.

When Isaac asked why he'd showered at all with an injured shoulder, Felix simply sat there and offered a careless remark.

"I was already pent up, and then you turned me on with that smile. I couldn't hold back," Felix muttered grumpily, pushing the cold soup aside and going straight for the meatloaf with his fork.

Isaac stilled the hand holding his own fork. He asked bluntly, "Did you touch yourself?"

Felix raised his dark blue eyes, still smoldering with intensity. "Yeah. This is the first time I've abstained for an extended duration, and also the first time I masturbated since becoming an adult, so make of that what you will."

"I suppose that's another debt I have to pay," Isaac replied matter-of-factly, unperturbed by Felix growling and stabbing the meatloaf with his fork.

Felix's eyes narrowed further. "Of course. If you didn't look like you'd keel over and die any moment, I would have dragged you into bed already."

"Dear me." Again, Isaac replied monotonously, utterly nonchalant, and kept on eating.

Felix glared at him, clearly offended, but said nothing. He exhaled a long sigh, as if there were no fixing Isaac's heartlessness, and resumed eating his meatloaf in silence.

"So, what's the plan?" Felix mumbled into the meat unhappily, throwing his usual aristocratic table manners to the wind.

"There's no plan." Isaac set his fork down with a sharp clatter, though half his meal was untouched.

Felix's deep blue gaze cut toward him again, sharp as a blade. "No plan?"

Isaac shook his head. "I'm going to give Cole what he wants. I'll hand over the document he wanted and have a talk."

Felix raised a dark eyebrow, surprised. "The document. You're more optimistic than you look."

"Because there's nothing I can do while he's holding the people I care about most hostage. If I can get my mother and Benjamin back safely, I'll do whatever it takes."

"Anything?" Felix echoed with incredulity. "Even if he asks for something outrageous in exchange?"

"It can't be helped." Isaac took a sip of cold water, his demeanor as stoic as ever.

Watching him, Felix's expression quietly crumpled. "Wow, I don't like that plan at all."

Confronted with Felix's grumbling irritation, Isaac set his glass down with a thud and clenched his teeth. He tried to appear composed, but anxiety coiled tight in his chest. "You came this far with me, so I'll tell you."

The only person he could trust now was this man sitting in front of him; the only person who had enough power, wealth, and status to help him. So, of course, he had to hold onto him.

He didn't know what this man would demand as payment this time, but it didn't matter. If Felix could help him bring back his mother and Benjamin, escape Cole, and finally live in peace with his family, Isaac would pay any price. Isaac swallowed dryly, then picked up a suitcase from his side.

"This is the document Cole told me to bring. The reason Benjamin and my mother were kidnapped." Isaac opened the suitcase and offered a thick envelope, his demeanor colder and more rigid than ever. Felix paused mid-chew, his eyes narrowing at the envelope, irritation still simmering beneath the surface.

"What the hell is that? Something dirty on Cole? What's so important about it that he goes around committing atrocities left and right?"

"Proof that he colluded with an inside man to misappropriate and sell your company's weapons to a third-world country. Sales, revenue, dates, distribution—it's all in there. Along with a list of the officers involved, and Cole's own signature authorizing every single withdrawal from inventory."

As soon as Isaac finished speaking, a heavy silence hung in the air. Felix was the one who broke it. "Fuck."

The look on his face as he cursed was contorted in a way Isaac couldn't begin to understand.

"If Cole doesn't let me go, please give the copy of the document to Steve."

"Steve?" Felix asked, a single brow arched up. "Who is Steve?"

"A friend of my biological father, and my benefactor. He used to be a CIA agent, and now he's the deputy director of Naval Criminal Investigative Services, investigating Cole's corruption within the Navy."

"Quite the connection you've got," Felix muttered, eyebrows raised in clear approval. He slid a finger under the flap of the envelope. "Give him enough rope, and he'll hang himself. Took long enough."

He glanced inside, then curled his lips into a smirk, every bit the villain—though one with undeniable charm. Isaac stared, a swell of emotion rising in him until it finally escaped as a quiet request.

"Even if Cole catches me…" The words caught in his throat. Was it because he was looking at Felix? Isaac's throat felt dry, and he took a sip of water before wetting his lips and trying again.

The premise seemed to strike a nerve with Felix—he paused his perusal of the papers and tilted his head. "Should he catch you?"

"You will come and find me." Isaac gazed at him with quiet eyes.

Felix wore a mesmerizing smile. "You know I would."

"Of course. And I know that as a dealer, you wouldn't miss a chance to settle the score."

Felix gave a silent nod, conceding to the truth of the statement. Isaac swallowed hard, his throat dry and burning with unspoken urgency, then continued, "Whatever happens, please put Benjamin and my mother's safety first."

"Isaac—"

"You're the one who always said deals should be fair."

Felix furrowed his brow and tried to voice his complaints, only for Isaac to hold up a hand and cut him off. This was the moment for one final deal.

"If you get Benjamin and my mother back safely—and get me out of this mess, away from Cole for good—then I'll be yours, completely."

"What?" Felix's eyes narrowed.

Isaac's tranquil voice flowed out tonelessly, "I'll be your dog."

Chapter 6

Cole couldn't hide his shock.

He'd brushed it off as nonsense when Felix snarled that Benjamin was his son and that Cole had made a mistake. But the instant Cole saw the three-year-old boy the mercenaries had delivered, a chill spread through him, his blood gone cold.

The child resembled Felix beyond doubt: the blindingly blond hair, pale skin, deep blue eyes, even the pert nose and lips. Anyone would have a hard time calling him Isaac's son when he was clearly Felix's.

As he stared at the child—his eyes puffy from too much crying, peeking out only to quickly bury himself in Jessica's arms—Cole's expression shifted by the minute. His clenched fist trembled. If the person who had tipped them off about Felix protecting Isaac's son had been standing in front of him, he would've pulled a gun and shot them on the spot.

Cole gritted his teeth and paced the room quickly. He couldn't calm down. The child was Felix's. Of all people. How could he make such an absurd mistake! He felt completely off balance, like the rug had been yanked from under him.

Cole knew better than anyone that it was suicidal to provoke the international arms dealer with a big-name mafia executive as his grandfather. Felix Felice was just as bad an individual.

That was why, since that day four years ago, no matter how much of an eyesore Felix was, he couldn't just go and dispose of him. All he could do was be on guard and keep him at bay. Fortunately, until now, Felix had been keeping to himself, and without a point of contact, Cole had been lying low as well.

But what the hell was this?

"Damn it."

The mere fact that Isaac—who had vanished without a trace for years—was somehow connected to Felix was outrageous enough. He could hardly believe his eyes when he saw the photo of the two standing side by side. But learning that the child he thought was Isaac's was actually Felix's, *that* shattered his composure entirely.

He couldn't wrap his head around just what had transpired for Isaac to develop a close relationship with the very man who'd once been his assassination target. Cole had kept his distance from Felix and didn't think he would come into conflict with him again in such a way. Fate truly dealt him a bad hand.

Cole stood in stunned silence, pressing his fingers to his temples, then snapped out of it and walked toward Jessica. Since he couldn't undo his mistake, he had to smooth it out somehow.

Cole sat across the table from her, in an uncomfortable chair of his own, reining in his anger as he spoke, "Mrs. Parker. If you and your son, Isaac, do as I say, I will return you and that child safely."

The middle-aged woman, holding the child in her tense arms, glared at him. "What do you want? What did Isaac do? This child is only three years old! How can you do this to a child?"

"You'd better lower your voice," Cole warned the admonishing woman. "I hate noisy things."

He was already nearly enraged by the fact that he'd taken not Isaac's but Felix's son. He couldn't guarantee what would happen if she continued talking.

Fortunately, Jessica was quick to read the room and shut her mouth, biting her lip. Silence settled over the room, and Cole used the moment to mask his anger with a casual shrug.

"You only need to answer my questions. If I don't like your answer, I will immediately put the child in a separate room. There are many solitary rooms in this place, and no one will hear a child scream and cry." Cole threatened her with a veneer of politeness.

Jessica glowered, yet slowly nodded.

"To begin, are you Isaac's biological mother?"

She nodded again, knowing she had to do as he said if she wanted to keep the child from being sent to confinement.

"Then, whose child is that?"

A thought occurred to him. Why would Isaac's mother be so protective of Felix's child? She seemed too attached to him to write her off as his nanny.

"You took him without knowing? This is Isaac's son."

"So, he is Isaac's son?"

"Yes."

Jessica's firm answer was enough to weigh on his suspicion. Again, Cole stared at the back of the child's blond head with confused eyes. As though he felt the sharp gaze, the child made himself small, and Jessica tightened her arms around him and patted his back.

"And Felix? You're saying Felix is not the child's father?"

"I don't know. Isaac introduced him only as a friend not long ago."

"You didn't know him before that?"

"No."

Cole cradled his spinning head. It was getting harder to figure out what was going on, and he was developing a migraine as a result. Cole scowled at Benjamin's small form for some time before clicking his tongue and getting up from his seat.

He didn't think he would gain meaningful information by asking Jessica any more questions. After all, she had no idea her son had another name or that he was a Navy lieutenant. In other words, Isaac hadn't confided even in his own mother, as expected of a man of few words like him.

"I'll bring you food and rest," Speaking in a low tone, Cole got to his feet. "Like I said, I don't intend to harm you."

He crossed the room in a measured military gait, despite his thoughts being far from measured.

Felix, who threatened retribution for touching his child. Isaac, who said he would do anything to get the child back. The child who looked exactly like Felix, but whom Jessica maintained was Isaac's son. Cole felt he was missing something important. The answer loomed before him, close, but still shrouded. Just out of view

Cole rubbed his chin, deep in thought, when he suddenly stopped in his tracks just before reaching the door. A chilling hypothesis flashed through his mind, freezing him on the spot.

Slowly, he turned his stiff neck and fixed his gaze on the child Jessica was comforting. The little boy, still sniffling against his grandmother, had a head of brilliant blond hair. He was the spitting image of Felix—but Cole could see traces of Isaac too.

"Omega."

Jessica looked up at Cole's blank mutter. And in that moment—when their eyes met, hers trembling—he was seized by a certainty that sent a chill down his spine.

"He's an omega. Just like his father. He'd been deceiving me all along."

Dear God, a faint gasp escaped him. Like his omega father, Keith Benjamin Lee, Kay was also an omega, and he even bore Felix's child. He'd been keeping this secret all along! Cole's eyes bugged out as the puzzle pieces fell into place.

But, when? How did he become an omega? Kay, in his late teens, during the period they lived together before he left for the Naval Academy dorms, was a boring, mundane beta, not an omega like his father. When had he presented as an omega? How had he kept it secret up until now?

The military was swarming with alphas. Omegas were not only rare but virtually nonexistent. Most omegas were physically weaker than betas, and it was rare for them to join the military. And with the problems that arose whenever an alpha's rut or an omega's heat cycle broke out, the military avoided enlisting omegas altogether.

Yet Kay had fared well in that swarm. Not only that, he had more talent than most alphas. He was known as a beta, but no alpha dared to cross him, and his team was always careful to stay in his good graces.

That Kay, an omega?

While aghast at the unbelievable truth, Cole couldn't stop the joy spreading within. All along, he'd thought the puppy he raised was a boring old beta. But an omega? This was nothing if not intriguing. Thinking about it sent blood coursing to his crotch.

Furthermore, somehow, Isaac had Felix's child. So Felix already knew. All the better—he could use that to put the troublesome man in his place. Quickly gathering his thoughts, Cole looked at Jessica and the child and smirked. Then he opened the door and strode off without a word. As he marched down the hallway, a twisted smile deepened on his face. How could he not feel joy, knowing he would soon see his adopted son, the one who stirred such excitement in him?

"Kaysid, I think I have another reason to adore you even more, don't you?" Cole's manic eyes flicked toward nothing, and he burst into laughter. The sinister sound shattered the silence.

α Ω α Ω

When Isaac opened his eyes, it was just past six o'clock in the morning. After eating a bit of the meatloaf, he'd taken a quick shower and checked his wounds. Then he sat down, only to fall asleep without realizing it. Awakened from his slumber, Isaac rubbed his gritty eyes and looked around.

The cabin was quiet, the soft hum of the aircraft engine the only sound. The lights were dim, and a blanket lay gently across his knees. Felix sat across from him, eyes closed.

Seeing him asleep, Isaac felt a heaviness in his chest. He knew Felix could have gone to the bedroom to lie down comfortably, but, because of him, he'd chosen to stay and nap there. The thought left Isaac feeling a mix of embarrassment and unease.

Isaac sat perfectly still, quietly studying the sculpted lines of Felix's face, afraid of waking him. Not long after, the plane rumbled in preparation for landing—they had reached Charlotte Douglas Airport in North Carolina. Only then did Isaac turn to look out the window.

The pitch-black sky that had once filled him with fear had softened into a deep blue. As always, the light had come to chase away the darkness. Isaac watched the dawn spread like watercolor across the horizon and thought of Benjamin, the light of his life.

What was he doing now? Had he slept at all? Had he eaten? Did he cry a lot?

The more he dwelled on it, the more his chest throbbed with pain. In the end, Isaac raised a trembling hand and covered his eyes, as if to block it all out. *Please, let him be safe.* The image of the sobbing child replayed over and over behind his closed eyelids.

As time dragged on, his impatience reached its peak. He didn't feel capable of doing anything in such a state. Isaac gritted his teeth, and forced himself to focus. If he didn't pull it together, he wouldn't be able to accomplish anything.

As the plane descended, his ears clogged with pressure. The sharp pain jolted his scattered thoughts into place, and Isaac drew a deep breath. Then slowly, he lifted his gaze.

His black irises, fixed on the slanted view beyond the window, were as muted and unreadable as ever. No trace of anxiety or impatience remained, only a glacial calm.

"I promise I'll find you and hold you in my arms," Isaac whispered the words—whether to reach the faraway place where Benjamin was, or simply to steady himself—and clenched his fists.

Don't cry. Wait for me.

Chapter 7

Felix looked more uncomfortable than on the plane as he watched Isaac's back leave the airport and head for the taxi stand. An odd discomfort settled in him as he sent him off to Cole, like watching a child edge toward a body of water.

Yet, oblivious to his sentiment, Isaac didn't look back once as he hurried toward the line of taxis. Unable to take it anymore, Felix stepped forward and grabbed his wrist. Only then did Isaac turn, eyes narrowed.

Met with Isaac's questioning gaze, Felix kept the wrist in his grasp while raising his other hand to caress the scar at the side of Isaac's mouth; the rough texture underneath his fingertips sent his heart racing.

He didn't know why he felt so apprehensive. Never in his life had he feared failure. He had always been proud, fearless, and confident in everything he did, so it felt foreign, even unsettling, to feel anything now but. For the first time in his life, he was flooded with fear, tension, and restlessness. Felix ran a hand through his hair and sighed.

"Do you have something else to say?" Isaac looked at him quietly, expressionless as ever, as if Felix were panicking over something as mundane as a walk. The difference in their reactions was so stark that it left Felix feeling slightly ridiculous.

"No," Felix said bitterly, frowning.

Left with no choice, swallowing his dissatisfaction, he slowly let go of Isaac's wrist. Isaac glanced down at Felix's hand, watching it slowly clench and unclench into a fist. Felix lifted his clammy hand and guided Isaac's chin upward. The hollowed face that had been cast downward now met his gaze, dark eyes catching and holding his own.

That was all it took. Acting half on impulse, Felix closed the distance and claimed Isaac's lips with his own.

"Ah—" Isaac's low moan was amplified in his ear. In an instant, Felix lost his sanity. Isaac's cool lips seared against his, and soft, wet sounds slipped between their joined mouths.

Isaac's stony face was filled with surprise. His eyes opened wide, the kiss clearly unanticipated. Yet he remained still, offering no resistance, no refusal. Felix bowed his head and claimed his lips, slow and unrelenting.

He didn't remember how long it had been since their last kiss. What was certain was that it had been far too long, and it felt mind-blowing. The scent tickling his nose, the plushness of the scar-ridden lips, the sweet saliva, and the smooth tongue swirling around his.

Reminded of how sweet kissing Isaac was, Felix encircled his tongue and sucked on his lips like a starving man, but the fervent hunger wouldn't abate, and only grew worse. Perhaps it was a thirst no amount of sucking or licking could quench.

With both hands cupping Isaac's face, he deepened the kiss, the wet sounds between them growing increasingly obscene. Their humid breaths, indistinguishable from one another, mingled as lips licked and sucked with hungry persistence. He felt like he was losing his mind—utterly consumed. He had long forgotten they were standing in the middle of the exit path from the airport.

"Fe-Felix!" Isaac gave Felix's shoulders an urgent tap.

Felix still clung to him, devouring his lips with the desperation of a starving man. His chest was heaving, robbed of oxygen by the frenzied kiss. Isaac let out the breath he'd been holding, panting softly, but Felix still couldn't bring himself to let go. The taste of that sweetness had awakened everything he'd only pretended to give up, and now, he couldn't get enough.

"Hold on!"

In the middle of plunging his tongue deep into Isaac's

breathless mouth, exploring every soft corner, Felix suddenly paused and let out an annoyed exclamation. "Isaac, ah, fuck!"

Only then did their lips part—wet, flushed, and shining with saliva. Isaac lurched back and wiped his lips roughly with the back of his hand.

"What's the meaning of this? In the middle of the street—"

"Isaac, you have no idea how worried I am right now, do you?" Felix burst out, finally releasing the anxiety he'd been holding in. He let out a long sigh and rubbed his cheek. "I've never felt this way before, but my heart is jackhammering like I'm about to die. The bad feeling I have about this is giving me a migraine! If I had my way, I'd be shipping you straight back to San Diego!"

What was that about? The one who had his kid abducted was Isaac, but he was the one who couldn't control his emotions. Felix felt utterly foolish. But he couldn't shake the dread—the terrifying sense that if he let go of Isaac now, he would vanish. Vanish before his eyes and never return. He'd never get to hold him again.

Fuck. Felix swallowed the outburst and clenched his teeth. "Damn, I didn't know I would be like this, either."

How laughable he was, unable to even control his own emotions. Felix raised a hand and covered his eyes. He knew how desperate Isaac was to save his son, and so he said nothing more, but his heart continued to pound wildly, refusing to calm.

"Felix..." A calm voice called his name.

Before he could lower his hand from his eyes, warm breath brushed against his lips. His shoulders trembled. He couldn't speak, couldn't even move a finger. The gentle lick across his lips—and the wet sound it stirred—sent a jolt through him like an electric current.

A blush spread across Isaac's cheeks as he wrapped an arm around Felix's neck and kissed him softly. At first, Felix could only stare down at him in surprise. But when Isaac slipped his tongue between his parted lips and swept it into his mouth, a low growl rumbled in Felix's throat.

He tightened his arm around Isaac's waist. It didn't matter who had started it—tongues tangled, shared warmth deepened, and mixed saliva slid down their throats. The kiss was sweet, yet edged with danger, and it seemed to go on forever.

They paid no attention to the people moving in and out of the airport. For that brief moment, it was as if they were the only two people in the world. And though the kiss had lasted long enough for Isaac's lips to become red and swollen from Felix's hungry nibbling and sucking, Felix still couldn't get enough of those moist lips. He sighed in between pecking him with kisses.

"Have you forgotten?" Isaac whispered, with his arm locked around Felix's neck. "I agreed to give myself to you completely, didn't I?"

The question, asked after such a fervent kiss, almost left him hollow. Felix tightened his hold around Isaac's waist and looked down at him, a bitter smile curving his lips. "Yeah, you did."

"So then, come and find me." The gentle voice dripped with sweetness, almost unbearably so.

It was enough to make Felix pull his hand away, however unwillingly. "Of course I will."

Isaac gave his lower lip one final tug, then turned. As he walked toward the waiting taxi, his back was straighter, harder, more unyielding than ever.

Isaac slid into a taxi, a bag slung over one shoulder, and never looked back. Felix's eyes followed the taxi as it disappeared into the distance, as if trying to etch every last moment into memory.

Felix stood motionless, like a statue, until Isaac's taxi vanished into the flow of traffic. Then his phone rang in his pocket. With a quiet tut, he pulled it out. The caller was exactly who he expected, and right on time.

"Speak," he picked up, his voice void of emotion.

"Felix, we've turned on the GPS."

"Good."

"What held you up so long? You sure are comfortable acting out of character." Noah's lively voice rang out through the phone, a stark contrast to the simmering resentment building in Felix.

Slowly, Felix lifted his piercing blue eyes. "Stop talking nonsense and track him down."

"He's taken the freeway toward the beach," Noah answered with a snicker.

It hadn't been difficult to plant a GPS tracker on Isaac. All it took was a small dose of soporifics on the food he ate, waiting for him to fall asleep, inserting a tube into his esophagus like one would do a gastroscopy, and pushing the capsule inside.

Of course, it might have been easier to ask for his consent, but he'd thought it would be better for Isaac to be unaware. It might have put unnecessary pressure on him, and he needed to get some sleep anyway.

It was agonizing for Felix to see him pale and gaunt yet holding himself up as if it were nothing. Even if Isaac had trained under DEVGRU to stay awake and possessed the willpower and stamina to endure several sleepless nights, it didn't mean Felix wanted to see him in that state.

"And Cole?" Felix recalled the events on the plane for a brief moment before banishing his thoughts and changing the topic. "What about that bastard's location?"

"All in order."

"Send the document to that Steve guy first," Felix gave him one final order, and ended the call without waiting for a reply.

"It's no fun simply dragging a dog down," he muttered to himself. "I'll feel better only if we do a thorough job of killing and disposing of him."

Who knew when—or how—that weed would rear its ugly head again if he wasn't rooted out? Just like what was happening now. If Felix had eliminated him four years ago, none of this would be happening.

Having regrets now changed nothing, but he couldn't help

feeling them. This time, he was going to kill Cole. From the beginning, that had been the only answer to this problem.

With his hands stuck in his pockets, Felix exuded a sinister aura. Tony, who had been on standby, moved to stand beside him.

"I've received word that the mercenaries we hired are ready," he said. "They have already surrounded Cole's private residence."

"Good. I won't tolerate mistakes." Felix's eyes gleamed with focus.

At that moment, a black sedan rolled to a stop before him, and he moved toward it with purposeful strides.

Tony swallowed hard and struggled to speak as Felix yanked open the door of the sedan. "Boss, there is something."

Felix shot a glance over his shoulder at Tony's hesitant figure. Before Tony could say a word, Felix raised a hand to cut him off. His cold voice was firm, leaving no room for argument. "If it's not urgent, save it for later. I don't think I can take in anything right now."

Tony looked at him awkwardly, then closed his mouth on the words he'd worked up the courage to say. A sigh slipped out. After a moment, he simply shook his head and climbed into the passenger seat. Maybe, just as Felix had said, this wasn't the time.

"Cole, I'll make sure I get his precious son back."

Tony heard the chilling monologue as he was trying to placate his heavy heart and fasten his seatbelt. He took a peek at Felix's reflection on the side mirror.

His beautiful face—like something out of a fairytale—was cruelly distorted by a chilling smile. The angelic features were eclipsed by the mask of a demon, one that looked capable of dragging anyone to their doom. Just the sight of it sent a shiver down Tony's spine. He quickly looked away, clamping his mouth shut.

Chapter 8

"Kaysid!" Cole exclaimed. "How long has it been since I last saw you?"

After being forced to surrender all his belongings and frisked from head to toe, Isaac entered the house, where Cole immediately approached him with arms wide. Isaac simply stood still and watched him come closer.

It was always like this. When he faced Cole, Isaac always had to stand at attention, with both arms behind his back and not a single inch out of place. Whether at home or on duty, in front of him, he was always a soldier under his command. Not once had he ever truly been at ease.

Isaac said nothing as he watched Cole approach with a bright smile. There was no greeting, no excuse, no pleading on his end. Then, just a foot away, Cole suddenly raised a hand.

Crack!

With a sharp slap, his head snapped to the side. Had Isaac not been clenching his teeth, the pressure might've ruptured the inside of his mouth. His cheek flushed bright red in an instant. Not letting a single sound of pain escape, Isaac slowly righted his head.

"You ungrateful wretch! Did you think you could run away forever?"

It had indeed been long since he had seen Cole's scowling face, and Isaac stared at him without making a sound. Though now in his late forties, Cole appeared almost unchanged from the last time Isaac had seen him.

As a dominant alpha and Navy commander, Cole Patricks was well-built, strapping, and always impeccably dressed in a suit. At the moment, he was glaring at him with murderous intent, but when he concealed his true face behind a smile, he could appear almost attractive.

Was that why his father had fallen for him?

Isaac thought of his father, who had become this man's partner, but to him, Cole was only ever a figure of terror. It was worse when he was younger. Isaac would think he'd suffocate from the dominating air and pheromones emanating from him. Even after Isaac became an adult, he was still required to follow his orders without question. His mind and body had been brainwashed into fearing him since he was young.

Now, it was different, almost as if Cole were a stranger. It wasn't his looks, *no*. Nothing had changed about his appearance, but to Isaac, it felt like someone completely different was in front of him. He wasn't the same terrifying man Isaac had known since childhood.

Perhaps it was because Isaac had just come to realize Cole was no longer large enough to block the sky. Even his fist—which used to send him flying with one swing—now looked smaller and weaker than Isaac's. Such a thought had never crossed his mind before, and it puzzled Isaac. Why had he feared this middle-aged man?

Cole was already in his late forties. Though he was still in good shape, as good as men younger than him, there was no reason Isaac, a thirty-one-year-old seasoned special ops agent, couldn't overpower a man going on fifty. Yet, Isaac had been afraid of this man.

Cole let out an empty chuckle, "I lost my temper there."

Isaac continued to stare silently at the stranger in front of him. Cole began to drag Isaac somewhere by the arm, and he followed obediently. Cole took him into the dining room, in front of the table.

A light breakfast was set on the table. The plates holding pancakes, bacon, hash browns, and fruit looked appetizing, like

something out of a warm family scene. As Isaac stared at the scene, so jarringly out of place, Cole pulled out a chair and sat him down himself. “I assume you haven’t had breakfast yet?”

The sky, which had still been dark when he got out of the airport, was now fully bright. Isaac glanced outside the window at the cloudless blue sky before glaring at Cole.

“Never mind breakfast,” he snapped. “Let’s get to the point. Where are Benjamin and my mother?”

“No, you must eat first. I haven’t eaten.”

“Then eat by yourself. I don’t feel like it.”

“If you don’t feel like eating, then why don’t you have a glass of the orange juice you used to enjoy every morning?” Cole’s tone was commanding, though he wore a friendly smile as he poured a glass of fresh orange juice.

The glass sat full, untouched—Isaac didn’t lift a finger. In Cole’s territory, he refused to drink or eat a single thing.

Cole paused in the middle of sticking his fork into the bacon and called his name in a low voice, “Kaysid. Are you going to ignore the effort I made to prepare this in time for your arrival?” There was an unsettling gleam in Cole’s eyes. “Drink.”

With hostages involved, Isaac knew he had to cooperate. But Cole’s insistence—his certainty—was too sharp to ignore. There was something in the orange juice, and Isaac was sure of it.

Isaac gritted his teeth. He didn’t know what was in the juice, but it wouldn’t end well.

“I know you’re too suspicious,” Cole said. “But you’ll change your mind when you see this.”

While Isaac was hesitant to move his hand, Cole clicked his tongue and took out a small remote control from his pocket. He pressed a button, and the TV on one of the walls of the dining room turned on. Isaac reflexively turned his head and looked at the screen. And at once, his previously calm black eyes began to waver. The screen was showing a zoomed-in CCTV footage of a small room.

It was his mother and Benjamin.

The small room, which resembled a cell, contained nothing but a bed, not even a window. He suspected it was in the basement. There, his mother lay on the bed, holding a sleeping Benjamin in her arms. Isaac could clearly see his mother was awake, tenderly rubbing the child's back. It was evident she hadn't slept a wink all night.

"I was taking good care of them, since they're your birth mother and son. I gave them sufficient dinner and breakfast, and was thoughtful enough to provide a bed and clothes." Cole said it with a shrug, as if he'd gone above and beyond.

Isaac's jaw tightened at his preening, as though he hadn't just abducted and confined innocent people. Still, Isaac kept his cool and faced him. He spoke as calmly as he could, "I brought the document you wanted. Let my mother and Benjamin go."

Cole ignored him. He pushed the orange juice toward Isaac. "Let's talk about that later," he said coldly. "Drink."

"I will if you let them go."

"I can't do that, can I? Who knows what you'll do after I let them go," Cole mocked him, as if he could see straight through Isaac's heart. "Do you think I'm not aware that the only reason you're sitting quietly is because of them?"

Yet despite his casual demeanor, a razor-edged tension hung in the air. What was he supposed to do? How far was he expected to go along with this man? Isaac sat in silent turmoil, his fists opening and closing beneath the table. Cole tutted, as if he knew exactly what he was thinking.

"Kay, why do you think I showed you your family? Just to let you know they're well? Would you obey if a gun were pressed to her head? Or if a bullet went clean through it? I wonder."

Isaac snapped his eyes up at the callous remark. Cole ordered someone to go inside. It was then that Isaac noticed the wireless earpiece that was connected to a microphone on him.

Isaac whipped his head around, his face petrified. On the large

screen, he could blatantly see the door in the corner of the room open, and a tall man with a pistol enter. He saw his mother quickly sit up on the bed in shock.

Isaac lost composure and jumped up from his seat. The sound of the chair crashing down behind him was deafening.

"Stop," Isaac spoke in a deadened voice, his fists clenched so hard his palms bled.

Across from him, Cole simply sipped his coffee, unbothered. "Sit down."

"*Stop it!*"

"You understand now what will happen if you forget your place and disobey my orders? I will tell you one last time. Drink."

Isaac gritted his teeth at the soft-spoken command. If only he could land a punch across that smug face. But he knew—if he opened his mouth, the man in the room would pull the trigger. He couldn't afford to act on impulse.

Isaac flexed the fists he'd been clenching until the tendons bulged, then finally reached out with a damp hand and grabbed the glass of juice. He downed it in a single breath.

The moment it was gone, he slammed the glass onto the table, the impact sharp and final. He'd never had such difficulty holding back his fury.

"See, you should have listened from the start." Cole watched him calmly over the rim of his coffee cup, a satisfied curl to his lips. Then, without taking his cycs off Isaac, he gave the man on the screen a simple command, "Stay outside." Then he continued speaking to Isaac, "I'll go step by step. You just need to do as I say. When it's all done, I'll let them go like I promised."

Isaac, somewhat calmer, lowered the hand he'd placed over his eyes and glared coldly at Cole.

"Well, promise or not. What I need is *you,* not them," Cole said, snickering over his cup of coffee. "Your mother and son will be a burden if I keep them here, and I can't be bothered with that. It doesn't matter to me if they're in one piece or not. Now, put the document on the table and take a seat."

Cole spoke in a low, menacing tone, making it clear that if Isaac disobeyed, the hostages would pay the price. Obediently, Isaac righted the fallen chair and sat with his back straight. Right now, he had no choice but to do as he said.

Cole cut a piece of pancake and popped it into his mouth, grumbling the whole time as if burdened with some great inconvenience, "Oh dear, it's quite awkward having to check papers while having breakfast."

Isaac shot him a glare, then silently opened the suitcase and laid the documents in front of him without a word.

The thick stack of papers was seamlessly sealed, but Cole used the knife he'd been cutting the pancake with to open the envelope and spread its entire contents on the table. He flipped each sheet of paper and checked if anything was missing, his expression nonchalant, as if he were reading the newspaper or a book.

"Felix didn't say anything?" Cole asked in a casual tone without lifting his eyes from the papers before him. "Surely you must have told him you were coming here."

"He didn't say anything in particular."

"Really? That's surprising." Cole answered dismissively and continued to sip his coffee. After reviewing the heavy stack of papers, he tossed them aside. He acted as if the papers weren't important, but they laid bare the names and deeds of the officers involved alongside Cole in the corruption. It couldn't be anything but important.

Isaac tore his gaze away from Cole's dismissive fingers and finally voiced the question he'd been holding back. "What did you put in the juice?"

"Nothing special." Cole set his cup down with a shrug. He wasn't denying it, and Isaac felt his insides twist. Yet Cole continued to see right through him, smiling crookedly. It was the most unpleasant sight.

"You forced me to drink 'nothing special?'"

"Well, it's nothing special, but it could be something big for you, won't it? Since it's a substance to counteract the suppressants, you surely must have taken it religiously up until now."

Cole's lightly spoken jab knocked the air from Isaac's lungs. His vision blurred. Had he heard that right? He couldn't make sense of it—couldn't understand.

"What did you just…"

"Kaysid, did you think I wouldn't know you're an omega? You had Felix's child, and you're going to deny it?"

"That—"

"The way you, an omega, could pretend to be a beta was because you consistently took suppressants and hid your pheromones, which means you're not a dominant omega. If you were, you couldn't have hidden your pheromones with a few pills."

Isaac could neither reply nor make an excuse. His throat was constricted, and he couldn't make a sound.

"And besides, the child is the spitting image of Felix."

Isaac's gaze drifted unconsciously to the screen where Benjamin lay asleep. The child must have been truly exhausted to sleep so soundly. With his angelic face, bright blond hair, and closed blue eyes, there was no denying who he resembled.

Anyone who sees the boss and Benjamin for the first time will think they're father and son, Tony's firm voice echoed in his ears.

God. He was right. Anyonc who knew Felix would immediately think of him upon seeing Benjamin. Isaac had been too complacent. He tried to stay composed, but the more the thought settled in, the more his gaze trembled.

He hadn't thought Cole would uncover the truth so easily—that he was an omega. But to give him a neutralizer for his suppressants, too? Then that meant the ones he'd taken in his destroyed shop were now useless.

Being exposed as an omega, with his suppressants rendered useless, in front of Cole—an alpha in full control—would be a death sentence. Faced with an unimaginable situation, Isaac's heart began to thunder, and the frozen tips of his fingers trembled. He didn't know what to do. But Cole didn't stop at revealing his identity as an omega, what he said next went far beyond that.

"If Felix hadn't told me himself that your child was his son, I wouldn't have believed it either. An omega performing better than most alphas, it's inconceivable."

This time, his words felt like a literal blow to the head. Isaac's blank expression faltered, then crumpled. "What did you just say?"

"Why? I guess it didn't cross your mind that Felix would tell me this?"

"Felix told you that Benjamin was his son? He really said that?"

"How boastful he was about it, too. Screaming about how I made a mistake touching a hair on his son's head."

Impertinent welp, Cole bit back, seething with anger.

Isaac's pale face turned even whiter. His breathing grew ragged, as if invisible hands were tightening around his throat. Strength drained from his body, and for a moment, he felt as if he might collapse right then and there.

"I was shocked. I took the child thinking he was yours, but here Felix was saying he was his. I wondered if they took the wrong one, but once I saw him, I knew," Cole sounded almost bored as he bit into his bacon. "You're an omega who gave birth to Felix's child."

Isaac fell deeper into a stupor. Being found out to be an omega by Cole was enough to send his head spinning, but hearing that Felix knew Benjamin was his son sent him spiraling.

"Felix..." Felix had known? Truly? All this time, Felix had known Benjamin was his son? But he hadn't shown any sign of it at all. He'd never demanded an explanation. Yet, he told Cole that Benjamin was his son? How?

Isaac's thoughts scattered, impossible to rein in. His mind felt

like it had been bricked over—or stirred violently, like someone churning it with a heavy stick. In the end, he closed his eyes and let his shoulders slump. He couldn't even sit upright.

"I can't make sense of it. You were the one assigned to kill Felix Felice, so how did you end up carrying his child?" Cole spoke with a furrowed brow, his tone full of complaint.

Isaac gritted his teeth, still reeling from the unimaginable news. His voice came out ragged, confronted with a worst-case scenario that had never even crossed his mind.

"And?" Isaac gasped, defiant. "What will you do?"

"What will I do?" Cole sipped his coffee to cleanse his palate, then set his fork down. Slowly, he looked up. "To be honest, I have no intention of messing with Felix's son. Instead, I took steps to hinder his business a little. From now on, the number of arms purchased from him by the U.S. Military will be reduced somewhat. I also added a few caveats."

Isaac blinked, dazed.

"Felix will have seen the notice by now. It'll go off like a bomb over his head, oh dear." Cole checked the time, then continued talking idly, one leg casually crossed over the other. "It'll be a blow to his business. As you know, the military's purchasing power is no small matter. Losing his child on top of that will be too much of a shock, won't it? It's only reasonable to give him a breather."

It might have sounded like he was letting Felix off easy, but the truth was, Felix had become too powerful for Cole to touch. There was a reason Cole hadn't been able to lift a finger against him even after suffering a blow four years ago.

As it was now, it was clear he was unable to sever Felix's supply of weapons completely and could only reduce the amount. Any further prodding and it would backfire on him. If he happened to lay a hand on his son Benjamin to boot, no one could be sure of the consequences.

Felix was working closely not only with the military but also with the government, just like his grandfather had. After all, it was in the nature of the mafia to occasionally collude with the government behind the scenes, and Felix's family was one of the biggest.

If Cole foolishly provoked Felix—who had connections everywhere and could exert his influence anywhere—it wouldn't be a mystery if those involved were found dead somewhere. As a result, Cole needed to maintain a buffer: outwardly disrupting Felix's operations to keep him preoccupied, while quietly presenting himself as generous by releasing the child. He was digging an escape route for himself.

Not that it was certain to work.

Isaac reined in his rampaging heart and evened his breath. Perhaps this was for the better. With Felix having revealed Benjamin was his son, Cole couldn't keep him captive or hurt him. As he'd said, it would be difficult even for a man like Cole to dare lay a hand on Felix's son.

Quickly organizing his thoughts, Isaac slowly lifted his eyes. The obsidian-black eyes, which had been shaking a moment ago, were subdued.

"If Felix personally asked about my son, then you should let him go immediately."

"I was thinking the same. But before that…" Cole eyed Isaac as he got up from his seat. At the sound of the chair dragging, Isaac tensed and swallowed dryly. As he walked around the table at a leisurely pace, Cole's gaze was on Isaac's neck. "You're not marked, are you? There's nothing on your neck. How odd."

"Marked?" Isaac froze at the foreign word, while Cole's gaze remained glued to his neck, that same mocking, unsettling smile still on his face.

"He didn't mark the omega who bore his child. He must have meant to use you once and discard you. Well, that's good for me."

Rigid in his chair, Isaac watched Cole draw closer. He realized then—he hadn't planned for this. It was a problem that hadn't

crossed his mind when he heard Felix knew everything.

Isaac had lived his entire life without understanding what a mark was. What puzzled him most was Felix's act of ignorance, despite knowing Benjamin was his child. He'd never stopped to wonder why Felix hadn't acknowledged him as an omega, or why he'd never once mentioned a mark.

His spine stiffened after hearing Cole's mocking criticism. The image of Felix gazing at him with burning eyes as he promised he would come and find him glimmered before him. Even then, Felix hadn't mentioned the fact that Isaac was an omega or anything about a mark.

Along with it, Isaac remembered his resentment toward omegas due to the incident in the past. Had Felix realized he was that very omega? Was that why? Or was his hatred for omegas so deep that he couldn't even admit Isaac was one? Isaac had no clue as to Felix's intent.

What he could feel, without question, was the dull ache in his heart caused by Felix's unreadable attitude.

"Of course, it's no surprise. Felix is an infamous lecher."

Cole's insult snapped Isaac out of his turmoil. He looked up, utterly tense, but Cole suddenly bent down, put his nose against Isaac's cheek, and sniffed.

The moment the damp breath wafting from Cole's nose and lips hit his skin, Isaac's blood curdled. Especially since Isaac knew he was checking his pheromones. He couldn't move, and only his fists trembled minutely.

"Kay." Simultaneously with calling his name, Cole reached out and grabbed Isaac's black hair, pulling his head back.

Isaac let out a groan and frowned.

"What will I do? You're really asking?" Cole kept his violent grip in his hair, dark grey eyes flashing with lust. "Simple. I'm going to mark you."

This statement chilled Isaac to the core. "What?"

"You still don't understand?" That deep, chilling voice held no trace of humor. "I am going to mark you."

Isaac knew this man never joked, but still, he struggled to believe what he was hearing.

"Are you insane?" Isaac finally burst out with uncontrollable emotion and slapped his hand away. "I'm Keith's son! He was your partner! Legally, I'm your son, too!"

Cole merely followed Isaac with muddied eyes as he flew up from his seat. He was in no hurry. "Yes, yes. That does excite me more," he drawled. "You weren't interesting to me when you were a beta, but an omega is a different story. I'm an alpha who goes crazy for an omega's pheromones, and even crazier for the opportunity to tame an omega."

"What—"

"Even better if the omega is a rampaging stallion. It's fun to domesticate them. Like you." Cole sniggered silently and slowly approached. His eyes remained lit with a crazed glow. "And you being my legal adoptive son adds an immoral flair, doesn't it?"

"You're actually insane."

"I told you before," he murmured darkly. "I have no intention of letting go of the pup I raised. Wherever you run, I'll drag you back. Although that's a big waste of time, I was considering breaking a part of you. But you wouldn't be of much use if you're broken. So, you can imagine how ecstatic I was to learn that you're an omega. If I claim you as an omega, you won't even think about running away from me."

Staring at Cole and his deranged nonsense, Isaac instinctively stepped back and kept his distance. That man was insane. Claiming him…The mere thought repulsed him. Isaac bit out all his unfiltered killing intent. "You didn't think I would kill you before that?"

"Until I let them go, you won't be able to lift a finger against me."

"I will kill you if you mark me."

Cole laughed loudly as if he'd heard something amusing.

"Kay, you're an omega yourself, yet you know nothing about them," Cole said, mocking him as he loosened his immaculate tie and tossed it over the chair. What should have been a mundane gesture felt threatening enough to make Isaac shudder, his shoulders drawing in defensively.

Cole looked Isaac up and down with his gaze and opened his mouth unhurriedly. "You should know an omega claimed by an alpha can't smell or react to another alpha's pheromones. Instead, they become addicted to their alphas. That's why they cling to their alphas whether they like it or not."

"*Shut. Up!*" He bit out. "I don't want to know."

"Do you think you can kill me, then?" Cole ignored him. "Not a chance! You'll become unable to live without me. Every time you smell my pheromones, you'll stick your ass out with your hole dripping wet like a cat in heat. Begging me to give it to you one more time."

With every obscene word he spat out, Isaac's throat grew drier. It was getting hard to breathe. But then Cole said something else unexpected. "Like your father, who clung to me like a whore, I can bet you'll become one, too."

Isaac opened his eyes wide at the mention of his father. "My father? What nonsense—"

"Hmm, I guess you wouldn't know, but Keith always wanted to kill me. Though his body couldn't help but shake its ass at me." Cole curled his lips up arrogantly and snickered. "Poor thing."

Isaac was at a loss for words. He'd wondered sometimes just why his father became this man's partner, but he never knew he wanted to kill him. The father he remembered wasn't the sex-crazed, depraved man Cole described. If anything, he was the opposite—an ex-CIA agent with gender-neutral features and a composed, disciplined presence.

He was always busy, spending more time outside than at home, and wasn't very expressive, but he was also someone who would embrace Isaac and tell him he loved him whenever they saw each other. But hearing his father was claimed by someone he wanted to kill and had no choice but to…

From the moment he arrived, Cole had been unveiling secrets Isaac wasn't ready to hear. The pounding in his head made it hard to stand. He clutched the table with one hand, his breathing ragged. He wished everything were a dream, a nightmare that would vanish once he woke up.

He couldn't bring himself to look at Cole, who was exposing it all—Benjamin, Felix, his own secret, even the story of his father. It was all too much, too unreal.

Hunched over, Isaac clutched his throbbing forehead with a shaking hand. His voice shook with his question, "Then you claimed my father by force?"

"There were circumstances, but you could say that." Cole shrugged, uncaring. "Ah, Keith worried about you terribly. As you're doing for your son now."

"So you took his son hostage—you took *me* hostage—just to get to my father." His chin quivered as he forced out the words, the awful truth sinking in. "And now you've taken my son to do the same to me."

Cole didn't answer immediately, he merely sauntered toward Isaac's panic-stricken form. "I have a taste for men who resist and look at me like they would kill me, only to start leaking and sobbing once I start thrusting."

"You fucking perverted bastard." Isaac squeezed his trembling fists and glared at Cole, who had stopped mere inches away from him. The pits of his black eyes held only revulsion.

Cole grabbed Isaac's chin and yanked it up. "Do you know?"

Isaac couldn't talk.

"It's not only the omega who becomes addicted to the alpha's pheromones. The alpha, in turn, goes crazy only for the marked omega's pheromones and their hole. To stop them from going after other omegas."

Isaac swallowed dryly. His fingertips were frigid. His vision

was fogging.

"Sometimes the alpha loses control during rut, with the result being the marked omega going insane and dying." Cole smiled sickeningly. "But we'll call that an accident."

Isaac was forced by the hand on his chin to meet his eyes. He heard the bloodcurdling words, and his vision momentarily went black.

What was this bastard saying? What did he just hear? The same questions circled his head, never settling into a coherent thought. His mind felt clotted, as if submerged in wax.

Surely, the marked omega who died during the rut wouldn't mean his father.

No, no.

It can't be.

It can't be...

He tried to placate himself, but his heart bucked ominously. His father had been healthy. When Isaac was in high school, he'd been told his father died in an accident. He hadn't been shocked then—the nature of his father's work always carried the unease that death could come at any moment. Isaac knew, as well as anyone, that countless CIA agents met sudden ends in the line of duty.

That was why he hadn't questioned his father's death. If there was a chance that his father's death was because an alpha lost control during a rut, like Cole was boasting about...No, that was too much. He was already about to throw up from knowing his father had been claimed by force. But if his death had been gruesome, if this man had killed him—

"You should be grateful. It means I'll adore you. I'm taking in an omega who gave birth to another alpha's child, Felix's at that!"

Isaac writhed under the vomit-inducing thought.

Cole kept talking, whether or not Isaac was listening, until he suddenly barked his name. "Kay! Are you listening?"

Isaac snapped out of it and looked up, his pitch-black eyes

unsteady on Cole. "It wasn't an accident," Isaac choked out. Isaac hurled the question at him with a knife-like gaze. "You killed my father. Right?"

Cole settled, clearing his throat. The words left his mouth with indifference. "I told you. It was an accident."

"H-How could…"

Surely not, Isaac thought, even when he asked the question. Surely something like that didn't happen to his father. Cole was just saying it happened. But the bastard hadn't denied it—and that was enough to shatter his mind and heart.

His teeth ground until they felt they might crack. Isaac lashed out, swinging a fist without aim or restraint. In that moment, he forgot his mother and Benjamin were hostages. His father's secret—the appalling truth of his death—drove him past the breaking point.

His fist connected squarely with Cole's chin, a loud crack splitting the air. Cole, who didn't have the chance to avoid Isaac's sudden attack, staggered back. Isaac immediately ran after him and threw another punch, hitting Cole in the stomach and sending him crashing to the floor.

"You dare!" Isaac gritted his teeth and charged, radiating pure intent to kill. Pummeling him to death wouldn't be enough to dispel his grief. He landed one punch after another. Cole's nose broke, and blood splattered on the floor.

"Kay, you fucking brat! How dare—" Cole's roar was followed by a flood of pheromones, thick, almost visible, spilling over Isaac. The strength bled from his fist before he could resist.

"*Ack!*" His eyes rolled back. The unfiltered alpha pheromones poured over him from head to toe, reeking. His insides churned at the thick, numbing stench. His vision darkened, and his limbs convulsed.

As a recessive omega, Isaac was simply powerless against the torrent of dominant alpha pheromones. The fight left him, and Isaac curled into himself, drawing in ragged breaths.

"You're signing your death warrant!" Cole snarled. "Do you want your mother and son shot to death?"

Cole came to his senses and, gnashing his teeth, lifted his leg and kicked Isaac in the stomach.

Isaac fell back. He shook his head, clenching his jaw. Yet all he could do was grip the table with a shaking arm and just barely manage to pull himself up. "Ugh, w-what is…"

It was similar yet totally different from when Felix had released his hyper-dominant alpha pheromones. Every person had different pheromones, so naturally, they would be different to receive, but something felt off. Since his first heat cycle four years ago, Isaac had never reacted so violently to an alpha's pheromones—least of all to those from a regular or dominant alpha. But right now, it felt like the raw pheromones were seeping directly into his skin and lungs.

Isaac pushed himself up, gripping the table, only to hunch over again. It was as if the invading pheromones were burning away each and every cell in his body. Cold sweat cascaded down onto his skin, and his breath ghosted over his chin. His vision swam, his limbs gone weak. He couldn't grasp what was happening or why.

With trembling hands, Isaac clung to the table, fighting to keep his sanity. Cole's harsh voice cut in from behind Isaac, "Fuck, only now the neutralizer is doing its work."

Isaac was painfully aware of how wretched he looked.

Blood streamed from Cole's split lips and his bruised, collapsed nose. It was a gruesome sight, but he merely wiped it off carelessly with his sleeve, as if he were numb to the pain. His face was contorted as he directed a murderous gaze at Isaac.

"I told you the substance I made you drink is a neutralizer for the suppressants." Cole bit out the scathing words, then ripped his suit jacket off. "Now that the effects of the pills you took to pass as a beta have worn off, your omega nature will show."

He undid the buttons of his shirt as he approached.

"You bastard—" Even as Isaac spat out curses, he couldn't move. His vision was foggy, and shaking his head did nothing to clear it.

"You didn't realize your omega pheromones were leaking, even if just a little? I had a hard time restraining myself with all the blood rushing to my dick. Now that you've made me bleed, I can't resist."

Cole's bloodied face was an open display of his desire, making him look like a demon. Maybe this was his true nature at last. His brazen gaze clung to Isaac's skin from head to toe, sticky and revolting, sending a shudder through him.

"Don't come near!"

"And of course, you need to be punished for biting the hand that feeds you."

Isaac forced his failing knees to hold him as he backed away. It was hard. His eyes were blurred, his voice mumbled and weak—the opposite of moments ago. He knew there was no escaping Cole like this, and he hated that he was an omega, suffering the same violation his omega father had endured.

"Do you know how much you're turning me on? I almost want to get you a mirror." Cole mocked Isaac before unbuttoning the cuffs of his shirt and rolling them up. In one swift motion, he grabbed Isaac's hair, and in the brief moment his head was yanked back, Cole slammed it on the table with a curse.

Isaac's forehead hit the table, and Cole forced him down against the surface. Plates toppled, food scattering, glass shattering on the floor. The sound reached Isaac garbled and distant, as though it came through water.

Lying on his back on the table, Isaac looked up at the ceiling with bleary eyes. He saw, in the periphery, Cole's lustful face as he grabbed his legs and spread them apart. As he hurried to unbutton his pants, his groin kept jerking uncontrollably against the inside of Isaac's thighs.

The sensation was pungent, and a swear automatically left

the tip of his tongue. It felt like a nightmare. Something Isaac had never imagined would happen before he came here was happening. He expected physical assault, not this sick joke.

No. Perhaps it was his fault in the first place for being unaware that this man was a deranged dog. Perhaps it was Isaac himself, who had become this man's attack dog without knowing what happened to his father, who created this situation.

Isaac bit down on his chattering teeth, trapped in a pit of despair. The sound of pants coming unzipped still echoed.

"Fuck, Kay! Do you know how sweet your omega pheromones are? You smell even riper than your father," Cole said, groaning. "You were hiding it from me all this time?"

Cole buried his nose into Isaac's neck and sucked his flesh eagerly. The way he took his fill of the pheromones flowing from Isaac's neck was no different from that of a shameless beast. Isaac gasped raggedly. His vision was blurry, and his muscles were slack, leaving him limp like a corpse.

Every time he writhed in an attempt to escape, the cascade of alpha pheromones made him black out. Cole expertly pressed down on Isaac with his pheromones as though incapacitating an omega was nothing.

"How sweet will your hole be?" Cole nibbled and licked at Isaac's neck, then pushed his shirt up to stroke his sides. "The anticipation is driving me crazy."

"Fucking dog!"

"I don't care what you call me."

"You killed my father and lied to me! Get off! Don't touch me!" Isaac shouted with all his remaining strength.

Cole only twisted his nipples and smirked. A groan was wrenched out of him. "Yes, yes. It's only fair you take your father's place after he got away, isn't it? You must become my omega in his place!"

Isaac opened his eyes slightly as he took heavy breaths. He was feeling like just giving up on everything. Yet the image of his little Benjamin stayed in his mind, just like Felix's firm voice in his ears:

But you can't get yourself hurt. You can't get yourself killed. Promise me that. Whatever happens, you put yourself first.

Terms that tore at the heart.

Oh, Felix…It was strange how he still thought about him. Isaac paused in his attempt to bite his tongue. Yes, he couldn't stand dying like this. He couldn't let this fucking lunatic gloat.

As he made his resolve, Cole was coveting his body. He'd taken off his pants and briefs and was sweeping his eyes over his exposed lower half. His eyes were gleaming with lust and were disgusting. They appeared doubly bizarre with the dried blood on his face.

"Now, why don't you cry prettily for me? Cry and scream that you'll kill me. Let me hear how lovely your moans are."

While Isaac lay writhing limply, Cole grabbed his cock and squeezed it as if he would crush it. A scream escaped from Isaac's throat. His mind was on the verge of shattering, yet Cole didn't care. He unfastened his pants, drew out his darkened cock, and pressed it against him, rubbing them together.

The heat from the rubbing in his lower body convulsed Isaac. The damp breath that touched his skin as Cole sucked on his neck disgusted him, but the pheromones seeping directly through his mind and flesh rendered him helpless. Isaac didn't know what exactly marking a claim was, but that it was something vile and wretched went without saying.

Cole's merciless alpha pheromones pervaded his mind, his flesh, and his cock, which was forced to rub against the other. Isaac's scent was erased and slowly filled with the alpha's pheromones. At this rate, he felt like his spirit would give out before his body did.

"Your hole is already wet and quivering, did you know?" Cole muttered while gnawing at Isaac's neck viciously. He, too, was intoxicated with the pheromones he drank from his neck, his eyes

unfocused and bleary.

Isaac couldn't say anything beyond his arduous breaths. Wretched helplessness weighed on his whole body.

In the meantime, Cole was laughing and busily stroking their cocks together. The wet sound of flesh rubbing on flesh assaulted his ears, and Isaac ground his teeth.

"Fuck! Off!" He managed to get the words out, but there was no telling if they were conveyed over his gasps.

At last, Cole glanced up from his wear and tear on Isaac's neck, and smiled in derision.

"You have to realize it's no use fighting me. If you continue to deny it after absorbing all those pheromones, it will only become harder for you. Just a little bit more and…" Cole licked his wet lips and savagely spread Isaac's cheeks. "Yes, it'll be perfect once I cum inside you."

Then he rubbed the tip of his angry cock at Isaac's entrance.

"You're mine. You'll never run away from me again!" Cole bellowed, and simultaneously with his mouth clamping down on his neck, the tip of his cock, which had been rubbing maniacally against Isaac's perineum and butthole, pressed heavily into the wrinkled entrance.

Isaac closed his eyes at the unbearable, horrible sensation. His helplessness shattered him; he couldn't let this continue. He refused to live a life forcibly taken by an unwanted partner and going into heat for them just because he was an omega. He couldn't let himself be used by this man, either in memory of his father, who was trying to protect him.

He bit his lip, and blood burst out. Isaac stopped breathing, his heartbeat growing louder in his ears. The metallic smell of blood dripping from his torn lips pierced his nostrils. At that moment, he gathered strength in his shaking hands and moved them up from the table.

Chapter 9

"This bastard is asking for it, huh?" Felix said, frowning.

The report Tony had delivered just now was enough to churn his insides. The act of kidnapping Benjamin and forcing Isaac to return was already unforgivable, but Cole was now trying to mess with his business as well. It was practically a declaration of war.

The report's contents were as follows: they would cancel their recent agreement on new weapons, citing safety concerns, and reduce the number of arms purchased by the Navy. Not only that, but they would also inspect the production lines to ensure the weapons met the standards.

In conclusion—*fuck you.*

"Commander Cole Patricks must have taken power while I wasn't looking, didn't he?"

Felix crumpled up the multi-page notice and dumped it into the trash before standing up. A normal company would have a fire lit under their ass with such a notice. He should make calls here and there, find out what was going on, devise a solution, and prepare for the inspection.

This was undoubtedly what Cole intended—to keep Felix on edge and out of his affairs. But Cole was underestimating him far, far too much.

"Tony." Felix held up his phone as he called Tony, who stood nervously by.

"Yes," he answered at once.

"Call the company and the person in charge. Starting today, we're discontinuing the sales of arms to the U.S. Military."

"Yes. Underst—Huh?"

"If they think I'll meekly comply with this trash notice, they got the wrong person. They're the ones who broke the contract first, so tell them to shut up about it."

"But—"

"Ah, now will be a great time to get some rest. Shut the plant down for the time being. Tell the military to find another supplier. There are other arms dealers out in the world. They'll manage."

Tony was stunned by Felix's nonchalant words. He didn't know what to say. He just stood there like a statue with his mouth half-open.

What kind of solution was that? Sure, Tony knew the inner workings of Felix's mind were different from those of normal people, but not that he would close the business he'd worked hard to build in a single day.

"Are you really going to close the business?" Tony asked with an anxious glint.

"Who says I'm closing it?" Felix glanced up while tapping on his phone and clicked his tongue. "I said I'll be taking a break. Do you think my business will go under if I stop supplying to the U.S. military? Think again. I have rows and rows of customers. It's not one or two that's desperate to buy my weapons."

"Yes, that is so."

"What's the difficulty? I can give everyone, including myself, plenty of time off, and if things don't improve, I can just downsize. But what will happen to them if their supply of arms gets suspended right now? Do you really think it's possible for them to find a new supplier, finalize a contract, and get things moving within a day?"

Felix went back to looking at his phone, tapping the screen rapidly. "Tell them to shove it up their ass," he said saucily. "I'm going on vacation in the meantime. It'll be the perfect occasion to take Isaac to the south of Italy."

"B-But—"

"Tony, why don't you stop worrying so much and start

planning what you're going to do on vacation?" Felix wasn't worried at all, except about the idea of going on vacation.

Tony, who hadn't been on one in years, couldn't help but let his jaw drop at the thought. But then he shook his head and coughed. Tony sighed, his face full of worry. "It won't be that easy."

Felix walked away without a care.

"So what if it's not?" he said, looking over his shoulder. "The worst it'll do is put me out of business. Stop worrying and follow me."

Until a minute ago, Felix had been staring at the map showing Isaac's location. He now pressed the call button, and it didn't ring for long.

"What?" Noah spoke in a surly tone.

"Noah, how did the paper delivery go?" Felix immediately asked about the evidence Isaac had given him, along with the data collected by Felix's team on Cole Patricks and the officers involved in his corruption.

They planned to release the papers not only to the military and the government, but also to the press and it should have been done precisely five minutes ago. The findings were, of course, accurate, reliable, and undeniable. The moment they became known to the world would be their downfall.

While the bastards had their eyes on him, Felix, too, had been watching their every step, to hang them with their own rope. That day was today. And in truth, the papers were merely a front. Cole Patricks wasn't going to face trial or be investigated for corruption because today he was going to die.

That would be the sole outcome.

"They're all sent," Noah replied cheerfully.

Felix lifted his wrist to check the time. It had been thirty minutes since Isaac entered Cole's private residence. There was no more time to waste.

"The status of Cole's residence?"

"Great location in the mountains. The neighbors won't mind when we shoot it up."

"If it's ready, then begin. Kill any and all who resist." Felix continued walking.

Noah was snickering, "Impatient, are we? It's broad daylight, you know?"

"Is there a law that says we can't attack in broad daylight? Don't you know a single minute is enough to kill someone? It's been thirty minutes since Isaac went in."

A pull of the trigger was all it took to end a person's life. He didn't know what kind of shit Cole would try to pull, but Felix had no intention of waiting any longer.

"All right. I'll send you Isaac's location in the building. The alarm system, electricity, and the communication in the house will be cut starting now."

"Do what you will. I'm heading for Isaac. The rest of the team should focus on finding Benjamin and Mrs. Parker."

"Got it."

The brief exchange ended. Isaac had been standing in the same spot for minutes, so he must be confronting Cole. At the thought, Felix clenched his gloved fist.

Felix had long since gotten into gear. He wore a bulletproof vest on his chest, an assault rifle slung over his shoulder, and two handguns at his waist and thigh. He had fitted ammunition into every seam of his vest and knuckles over his gloves. He was ready to fight properly, making it clear he was out to catch and kill.

"Cole, if you value even a quick death, you'd best not play games."

A deadly voice flowed from his pretty lips. Beneath his boots, his heavy steps continued to sound in haste.

α Ω α Ω

Crack!

A small piece of equipment crunched, its shattered debris spattering with blood.. Isaac, who was lying on his back on the table, had to squint his eyes through the spray of blood.

But he didn't stop his trembling hand.

With each frenzied swing of the fork in Isaac's hand, blood spattered everywhere, and Cole squealed above him. Isaac gritted his teeth, brandishing the fork with intent to kill. If only he'd grabbed a knife instead.

"I said…Don't you dare touch me!" Isaac ruthlessly stabbed the short tines of the fork into Cole's face and ear, his dark eyes burning with razor-sharp savagery. His first step was getting rid of the earpiece Cole was using to communicate with the mercenary watching over his mother and Benjamin. That was why Isaac had struck him in the ear.

When the end of the earpiece broke off and fell, Isaac swung the fork down with all his might. It was embedded in Cole's cheekbone before being pulled out and then shoved into his throat. The fork's pointed attack didn't last long, however.

Cole dodged an attack, lifted himself, and caught Isaac's wrist. The captive hand shook in midair.

"Bastard, I'll fucking kill you," Isaac growled through his mangled mouth.

The more he thought about it, the more he clenched his teeth. This bastard had destroyed his father's life and his own, and kidnapped his mother and Benjamin. Isaac regretted the years he spent trusting him and following his orders.

"How are you able to move?" Cole held tightly to Isaac's wrist as he gasped, confusion clear on his face. The fork had pierced his ear, face, and jaw deep enough to reveal bone, but instead of caring for his injuries, he just stared at Isaac.

He was confused because it had never occurred to him that Isaac, who was drenched in pheromones with the marking in progress, would be able to act out. Isaac didn't reply except to wrest his wrist free from Cole's grip and swing the fork again. His wide-open eyes sent a chill through him.

This time, though, Cole didn't accept it passively. He jerked his head away, cursing and roughly yanking Isaac's wrist back. It had been a challenge for Isaac to strike with his weakened, trembling hand, and he fell apart all too easily.

"Kay, how long do you think you can hold out with willpower alone? You should know resisting will only make it worse for you!"

With a twist of the wrist, the fork slipped from Isaac's hand and clattered to the floor. He gritted his teeth and swung with his free hand, but Cole deflected it easily. A resounding smack split the air as Cole struck him across the face. The inside of Isaac's mouth tore, blood spilling over the table—and still, Cole's blows kept coming.

One punch after another instantly covered Isaac's nose and mouth with blood. As his surroundings turned red, Cole wildly flashed his eyes and swung his fists around. Isaac's own fist, which he had held out in a desperate attempt to escape, dropped. His head spun. Isaac couldn't even see Cole baring his teeth and spitting out curses.

"Are you aware that the mark is already showing on your neck? And you try to resist? It's faint, but it's starting to show! You can't escape me!"

Thick pheromones rolled off Cole again. Isaac's gut heaved, and he vomited onto the table, over the blood that already stained it.

Last night, Isaac had only taken a few bites of the meatloaf served on Felix's private jet, so he mostly threw up bile and orange juice. But there was something unusual in the vomit. Had it just been food, Cole might not have noticed—but in the thin, watery mess, it stood out clearly.

"What is this thing?" Cole paused in his assault on Isaac's face to take the small pill-like object in his hand. It was encapsulated,

yet it was clearly a device. Isaac couldn't keep his eyes open; he could only gasp for breath.

"I asked you what this is!" Cole then pulled Isaac up by the hair. "Is it a bug? Did you have a GPS tracker on you?"

As Cole shook his head like a madman, Isaac couldn't say anything. Blood from the tears around his eyes blurred his vision, but more than that, he knew nothing about it. He had a hunch, though.

If someone had unknowingly fed him something, then it could be one person. Isaac pictured him before his foggy eyes, and a faint smile broke out.

"Too bad for you. Looks like Felix cares about me," Isaac whispered, his voice breaking. "More than you think."

"It was Felix?"

"You get it, so fuck off," Isaac replied through ragged breaths before spitting blood onto Cole's stricken face. He wiped it off, furrowing his brow fiercely.

"Don't make me laugh! Just what do you think you can do with this, huh?" Cole struck Isaac across the face again with a loud smack. Leaving Isaac sprawled on the table, he threw the encapsulated device down and stomped it to pieces out of spite. His feet pounded mercilessly on the floor.

The capsule quickly turned to dust. Still, Cole stayed angry, and he forced Isaac's legs apart on the table.

"Even if Felix were to barge in now, it's too late! The claim is in progress, the mark is showing!" Cole bellowed like a lunatic. "You're mine!"

The scream threatened to split Isaac's eardrums, yet under the suffocating haze of pheromones, Isaac could only move his lips soundlessly. Cole clutched his thigh and grabbed his own cock, shaking it in a filthy display that sent bile rising in Isaac's throat.

"I said…*Fuck off!*" Isaac felt his stomach churn again, feeling the cock rubbing against his perineum. He refused to let this happen. Gritting his teeth, Isaac groped around for a stray knife on the table.

Then the monitor showing his mother and Benjamin fizzled out. It was followed by intermittent sounds of electricity being cut off, as every appliance and piece of equipment fell silent.

It was bright and early in the morning, which kept the room from darkening, but the silence that followed the shutdown of all the appliances filled Isaac with unease for a different reason. Cole also paused and looked around.

Something was wrong.

The mixture of bafflement and apprehension was evident on Cole's face as he scowled and muttered under his breath. "What the—"

Loud gunshots fired outside cut off his words. Following the volley of rifles, the sound of glass shattering, and screams filled the premises.

Cole finally released his grip on Isaac's thighs, throwing him down, and straightened himself up. His face was contorted with rage.

"Who dares—" Cole gritted his teeth and looked around in panic. He shouted for someone, but no answer came. Instead, on the blackened TV monitor, an image appeared, and a jingle from a video game started to play.

A round rabbit character was smiling and frolicking, not just on the monitor but on every digital screen. Cole stood in shock at the sight. The pink rabbit stopped running and seemed to face him directly.

"Cole Patricks, your house is surrounded. Come out and surrender quietly, and the property damage and casualties will be minimized. But if you resist, there will be no survivors."

"What in the name of—"

"Oh, and we inform you that as of today, you are removed from your rank as a commander. Your corruption will soon be under investigation and make headlines on the news."

Under the dark bloodstains, Cole's face was clearly paling.

The pink rabbit kept going as if it had noticed.

"You'll never be able to show your face in this country again. And, of course, your sentence will far outlast the years you have left. Don't look so shocked—you reap what you sow. You just happened to sow quite a crop, that's all."

The pink, round rabbit spoke like an old man doing a public announcement. The person behind this has bad taste.

Naturally, Cole's face became further distorted. He pulled out the radio transmitter to call someone. The earpiece and microphone were broken, so he attempted to talk directly into it, but it was as dead as the rest of the house. The system had been hacked for good.

"Fuck! Which filthy rat—" Cole couldn't finish his impassioned outburst.

The racket outside, akin to a battlefield, was growing louder. Yet there was nothing he could do. He was surrounded and shut in. The realization made Cole's face go stark white.

"Kay! Those are the ones you brought? Just who did you conspire with?" Cole demanded, shaking Isaac by the shoulders. "No, it can't be? Did Felix really—"

Isaac, who had been feeling around the table for a knife even as his awareness faded, had to close his eyes as they spun.

"I said I would return Felix's kid!" Cole bellowed, his own eyes bulging.

Then suddenly, with a smash, the previously sealed doors of the dining room broke open. Among them, a tall man appeared. He stepped inside. Each step he took rang gravely throughout the room. The unhurried rhythm of the sound seemed to herald his command over this place, and it was breathtaking.

When he saw Felix enter, fully armed, Cole froze as if he'd seen a ghost. "How did you…?"

His eyes were laughably big, like he couldn't believe he was seeing Felix himself here—the man who was never known to be hands-on.

Felix froze as he took in the scene—Isaac splayed on the table, pants half-down, his crotch exposed, Cole looming over him, his cock hanging from unzipped pants. A dangerous light ignited in Felix's blue eyes. "I should have known when the GPS went dead."

He couldn't tell how many blows Isaac had taken for his face to be so bruised, torn, and bloodied. Cole's nose was broken, his face stabbed with a fork and beaten out of shape as well, but none of that registered.

Felix was fixated on Isaac and the fact that he was reduced to this state so quickly. He ground his teeth and immediately pulled the trigger of his Colt. With a deafening bang, Cole screamed. Felix had been aiming as far away from Isaac as possible since Cole was standing too close to him, and the bullet only grazed his arm. Tutting, Felix reloaded his gun.

He was the one who said a minute was enough to kill someone, but he hadn't expected Isaac to be in this state. No, he couldn't have imagined it. Maybe he had believed in Isaac's abilities as a special ops agent. Yet here was a scene worse than his worst nightmare.

"Get your hands off him," Felix growled and aimed the Colt pistol as he crossed the dining room at a brisk pace.

"This is unacceptable!" Cole clutched at the arm the bullet had grazed while pulling Isaac in front of him. He was going to use him as a shield against Felix's inevitable fire.

"Felix, I don't know what you're thinking, but if you do anything, he will die." Cole looked like a cornered rat, clutching at Isaac's back with an arm around his neck. Though cold sweat was streaming down between streaks of blood, the way Cole was threatening Felix with Isaac in a chokehold made it clear he was backed into a corner.

"Cole, I'm this close to blowing up. Cut the crap if you know what's good for you." Felix lowered the muzzle of his Colt to the floor and warned him in a low voice.

Cole had no intention of listening and merely tightened his hold around Isaac's neck while backing away.

"Is that what a home intruder should be saying?" Cole bared his teeth and growled, making his escape with Isaac in tow. "Behave and leave. I'm the one whose mood is ruined."

Felix could only tighten his grip on his Colt, filled with rage over the dirty move. Meanwhile, Cole dragged Isaac's limp body away. But then, barely a step further, Cole let out a shriek. Isaac had found a knife after all and quietly stabbed Cole in the thigh.

The visceral sound of his thigh being ripped open rang out along with the shriek. Felix didn't waste the chance to run at him like a lightning bolt. He grabbed Isaac, who was drenched in blood and gasping weakly, by the wrist and reeled him in. At the same time, he clubbed Cole in the jaw with the grip of his Colt.

"I told you to get your hands off him!"

There was a deadly crack as the grip of the gun met its mark and broke Cole's jaw. Cole crashed to the floor.

Felix spared no opportunity to fly at him and stamp his boots into his side. "I meant for today to be your last, but I won't let it end quickly. Killing you in one shot wouldn't be any fun, would it?"

Felix kicked him as if he were about to kill. Cole barely managed to roll away and wiped the blood dripping from his mouth with his eyes wide open.

"Felix! If you kill me, then you should know that Kay, no, Isaac will die, too!" Cole's shout was as miserable as his appearance, a last-ditch effort.

It caused Felix, who was adjusting the knuckles on his fists, to jerk and pause. "What kind of bullshit is that? Kick and struggle all you want. It'll only tire you out. I don't know if you've noticed, but this place is surrounded. Didn't you hear the announcement a moment ago? All your deeds have been exposed. To the JSOC, the NCIS, the military, and the press—everywhere."

Felix's eyes blazed like blue flames as he deliberately opened and closed his gloved hands.

Cole trembled all the way up to his chin and couldn't even blink. "Lies!"

"See for yourself later whether or not I'm lying," Felix challenged. "If you can make it that far."

"Felix, you just had to do this!"

In response to Cole's bared teeth, Felix revealed his deadly intent. "Well, you should have taken a course in ethics and learned not to touch what belongs to others."

Remembering the scene that welcomed him when he entered the room, not even tearing him apart would be enough. If he'd been a moment too late…*Fuck!* With the bone-chilling scenario in his head, Felix was about to lunge at him with his fists.

"If I die now, Isaac will die of shock as well!" Cole yelled frantically, and again, Felix's fist jerked to a stop in midair.

"What the fuck are you talking about?" Felix sneered, though the words stuck with him. "You're spewing all kinds of shit because you don't want to die."

The knuckled fist was still suspended in the air. Seeing this, Cole smirked, where before he'd been crawling pathetically on the floor. He was triumphant, knowing he held the last key at the edge of the precipice.

"I was claiming him, to make him my omega! The mark is already visible on his neck, and if you kill me—the owner of the pheromones poured into him—he will die from shock!"

The shit leaving Cole's bloodied mouth was enough for the strength to leave Felix's fists. "What?"

"If you were going to talk so big about him being yours, you should have marked him when you had the chance!" Cole guffawed like a madman, saying whatever came to him. "I thought he was free for the taking!"

Felix frowned. "Omega?"

When he'd broken the door open and entered, Felix had been blind with rage at the bastard's perversion that he hadn't noticed the

alpha pheromones filling the room. In fact, the large dining room was chock-full of thick alpha pheromones. It wouldn't impact a hyper-dominant alpha like Felix, but it was a level of density that an average alpha or omega would struggle to withstand.

But wasn't Isaac a beta? What was this fucker saying?

Felix squeezed his fists, unable to put the pieces together, and turned his gaze to Isaac. After stabbing Cole with a knife, he was lying limp on the table, almost like a corpse, if not for the intermittent spasms.

He wasn't well—broken nose, split mouth, blood around his eyes. But Isaac never faltered over such things; he'd walked just fine after two days locked up. Even when his son was kidnapped, he'd only fainted once from the shock, and when he woke up, he'd been alert and aware.

His physical and mental strength was extraordinary, but right now, he looked different. It was strange he didn't have the barest presence of mind to pull his pants over his naked crotch, helpless and shivering as if he were on drugs.

Omega.

The word Cole threw out instantly pivoted as a blow to his head. Felix rushed to Isaac's side, feeling cold.

"Isaac, *Isaac!*" He tapped Isaac on his bloodied cheek, but the bleary black eyes only roamed about in the nothingness.

Shit. Felix gnashed his teeth as he took Isaac's chin in his grip and turned his head. Behind his car, where his hair could cover it, was a faint mark, proving Cole's ridiculous words to be true.

It was the mark of an omega claimed by an alpha. Still, its progress was slow, likely because of the absence of pheromones ejaculated inside him and Isaac himself rejecting the claim. Realizing this, Felix's eyes shifted from confusion to anger.

"Fuck! Are you really an omega? Are you? Answer me!" Felix couldn't help it. He shouted, feeling a surge of wild energy, pulling Isaac up by the shoulders. "How could you do this to me? How can you be an omega—Isaac!"

Isaac, half-unconscious, couldn't hear and remained limp. It was different from when he'd brandished the knife at Cole.

Felix clung to his slipping form, exuding furor. "What is all this? Isaac! Get up and answer me right now!"

Felix was out of his mind with anger and confusion, shaking Isaac's shoulders. For a brief moment, Isaac gained awareness and stared at Felix with hazy eyes. At that plaintive gaze, that look on his face, Felix's heart dropped with a thud. He forgot his rage, cupping Isaac's cheeks and kissing him.

"Fucking hell! How could you do this to me?" The short, sorrowful kiss broke, and Felix shouted again. "How can you do this to me?"

He didn't notice the tremor in the fingers that caressed Isaac's face. Felix kissed him once more, at the torn edge of his lips—and this time, his own lips trembled.

"Benjamin…"

"I sent people after him. You just focus on getting out of here."

Felix ignored how Isaac had asked for Benjamin, with the little bit of consciousness he had regained, and lifted him in his arms. If Isaac really was an omega and the claim was in progress, then he had to be removed from this pheromone-filled place as soon as possible. Anything else could wait.

First, he had to get rid of Cole's pheromones.

With Isaac in his arms, Felix ran out of the dining room. Cole had hurried off in the meantime, leaving specks of blood on the floor where he'd been. But Felix didn't have the time to go after him.

Isaac—an omega, not a beta—was being claimed by another alpha, and by Cole, no less. Felix's composure shattered. He felt wronged, stunned, and driven to the brink of madness. He'd had no idea Isaac was an omega, and now the revelation struck like a blow to the back of his head. How could he remain sane after this?

He was furious at Isaac for hiding his omega identity from

him, and he was also upset with himself for never having figured it out all this time. But right now, he couldn't sit around dwelling on it. He had to stop the claim that was in progress, and he had to do it before Cole died. Like he warned, if the alpha died halfway through, the omega could go into shock.

Felix crashed into what appeared to be an empty reception room and carefully lowered Isaac's battered form onto a sofa. It was when he was brushing his black hair, soaked in sweat and blood, away from his forehead.

Isaac opened his eyes, took a deep breath, and squeezed Felix's hand. His bloodied grip was ice cold. Felix didn't like that one bit, and he was creasing his brow when Isaac moved his lips.

"Felix, Benjamin," he panted. "Get Benjamin to safety first."

Isaac let the faint words escape, barely able to open his eyes and recognize Felix now that he was away from the suffocation of Cole's pheromones. His voice was feeble, like a candlelight about to be extinguished in the wind.

"I told you I sent the others," Felix ground out, answering the same as before.

But Isaac shook his head. "No, you go. You have to get him. You don't know what Cole will do."

"Isaac! Why the hell would you ask that of me now?"

"He's your son. You'd really leave him to others?" Isaac, with ragged breathing and muddy speech, pressed him with his question, causing Felix to freeze.

"Benjamin is my son? What do you mean by that?" It was as if someone had erased his mind. Felix couldn't understand what Isaac was saying. This Isaac, who was an omega, made him forget to breathe as he stared at him, and Isaac started to look anxious.

"Didn't you know Benjamin is your son?" Isaac asked, and Felix remained speechless. "I thought you knew."

Felix's deep blue, oceanic eyes remained wide open and unblinking. Isaac sensed that something was amiss. His shoulders trembled. "Cole said…you knew…" His trembling voice was almost foreign. "You told Cole he was your son."

Felix still couldn't come to his senses. He couldn't even begin to process the meaning of his words. He stared at Isaac for a long while before cursing and ruining his hair. Everything was upside down. He couldn't have a single coherent thought.

"I told Cole that, but I meant— No, Isaac, say it again. Benjamin is my son? You—an omega—gave birth to my son? When…Oh God, Isaac, be honest with me."

Isaac was as shocked as he was and stared up at Felix with a petrified expression.

At Isaac's stupor, Felix was unable to stop himself from yelling, "Tell me!"

Only then did Isaac swallow dryly and move his bloodless lips. His chin wobbled intermittently. "Y-You really didn't know? That I'm an omega, and Benjamin is your son?"

"Tell me the truth, Isaac. I just learned you're an omega—because Cole, that crazy bastard, told me. And now you say you had my son? You gave birth to him without me knowing? When? Where? How?"

As Felix fired off his barrage of questions, Isaac held his breath. His vision darkened. He didn't understand—Felix didn't know? Then what were all those things Cole had spewed at him? His thoughts spun out of control.

"Four years ago, the omega who went into heat on your island was me. You knotted me, and I had your child. That child is Benjamin. So, go and bring Benjamin to me!" Isaac somehow managed to shout even as he was about to faint completely, shaking Felix by the shoulders. He was completely out of his mind. He had to be out of his mind.

"The omega from four years ago," Felix gaped at Isaac with an utterly flabbergasted expression. "What kind of nonsense—"

"He's your child! He's your son. Go save him." Isaac clung to Felix's arm and sobbed, "Please…"

"Look at you! How can you do this to me? How could you?

You hid the truth that you were that damned omega, and you hid the truth that Benjamin is my son?" Felix shouted loud enough for his ears to ring, and Isaac screwed his eyes shut at the cold front of his wrath. Felix's teeth cracked as his blue eyes darkened. "And I was the only person who had no fucking clue? Do you think this makes sense?"

The chill pierced through his lungs and tore his heart apart. He was almost terrified of what he would do in his anger.

"You agreed that no matter what, you wouldn't kill me," Isaac rasped, his voice slurred and faint. "That you wouldn't hurt me or my family."

Isaac instinctively cowered, his pale lips moving. He wasn't even aware of what he was saying. His mind was in chaos. Silence settled for a moment. Then he slowly looked up, meeting Felix's dark blue, almost black gaze.

"Let me guess, that was in case I found out you were that omega from four years ago? You knew I would be this angry, and still you hid it from me and put it in the contract instead? You expected this from the beginning?"

Isaac's hands started to shake under his fury and unrestrained pheromones. He had no space to run with the arm of the sofa against his back, but he kept trying to back away. Funnily enough, he couldn't bring himself to let go of Felix's arm.

He couldn't let go, even though he was terrified of Felix, who was angrier than ever. Maybe it was because, despite everything, Felix was the only support he had left. Or maybe it was because, more than anything, he was hurt that Felix's murderous stare was fixed on him.

Isaac couldn't shake the feeling that he was being unfair, even underhanded. Still, he couldn't let go of him.

"That's right, I did. I put my own safety before your emotions, in case you found out about everything. It's true, I was only thinking for myself. Everything is my fault," Isaac whispered. "Later, you can take it out on me as much as you want. So, right now, please help."

"Isaac!"

"We had an agreement that you would save my mother and Benjamin first," Isaac said, but he couldn't look him in the eye. "I made you promise me."

If Felix had indeed known nothing about him and Benjamin, contrary to what Cole had said, then all of this would be completely out of the blue for him, and for that, Isaac was sorry. But he had no choice but to act ignorant and shameless. He had no choice but to hold on, especially now that he was in this state.

"Fuck!" Felix's tight fist landed on the back of the sofa with his curse. The dent in the cushion rebounded, releasing a cloud of dust that danced in the air.

Isaac's hand, which had been clutching at Felix's arm, slipped and landed coldly on the seat.

"Take it out on you later?" Felix grabbed Isaac's chin and lifted it, murmuring darkly. "How could you possibly deal with my anger when I'm having trouble myself?"

Isaac gasped as he was forced to confront the inevitable rush of his wrath. "Felix."

"You shouldn't talk so freely, Isaac."

"Felix!"

"Fine. It's a fucking contract, just like you say. I can't hurt you, can't kill you, I have to save your son and your mother first." His voice was low, cold. "All according to the contract, so I'll listen."

Unable to take his chin out of his grip, Isaac swallowed dryly. Then the beautiful, scowling face leaned closer. "But I also said you need to put yourself first."

"Huh?"

"I don't care whether Benjamin is my son. You come first. And you're liable to go into shock anytime soon." Felix gnashed his teeth. "Anyone could kill that fucker Cole outside at any moment, understand? You might die!"

The revelation that Isaac was the omega who broke his arm and ran away from his island four years ago, and Benjamin was the result, had to be put into the back drawer now. He had to tamp down the rage and indignation erupting within him. In any case, at the moment, nothing was more important than Isaac's condition, and he had no time to waste.

"Fucking hell! Everything is a mess!" Felix glared at Isaac with burning eyes and, cursing, lifted his hand to grip Isaac's chin. Yet Isaac simply stared at him blankly, unable to move.

"I'll question you again later about the audacity of acting innocent when you gave birth to my son without my knowledge. You said you'd take everything I throw at you." Felix growled, still shooting daggers at him, but he couldn't berate him any further. "Mark your words."

The claiming mark wasn't progressing because it lacked sexual intercourse, and because Isaac was rejecting it. If it had been completed, he could have just killed Cole and been done with it. But as it stood, there weren't a lot of options. At this rate, if Cole were to die, it would cause problems for Isaac, and so he had to act.

"Mark your words…" As Isaac's head drooped beneath Felix's intense anger, Felix cupped his face with a calloused hand. The touch wasn't rough or rude like before. It was a more careful, almost gentle, caress on his cheek. "You said you'll be my dog, right?"

Isaac looked up in surprise at the unexpected question.

"I don't need that. Say you'll be my omega instead. I'll draw out Cole's pheromones and override them with mine. Say it right now that you'll be my omega. That you'll accept me and won't reject me." Felix's voice was still harsh, but the proposal was honest if unexpected, and there was no hesitation in his blue eyes.

"You want to claim me?" Isaac couldn't give a clear answer. His thoughts were too scattered, and he chewed at his pale lips. Felix simply stared at him coolly.

Since Cole had tried to claim Isaac first and left a visible mark, there were only two possible outcomes. The first was Cole finishing the job and then being killed on the spot—something Felix would rather die than allow. The second was for an alpha with stronger pheromones than Cole's to override the incomplete mark and replace it with a new one.

Luckily, Felix was a hyper-dominant alpha, stronger than Cole, a dominant alpha. He could proceed immediately if Isaac could withstand it.

"You don't want me to?"

"I-I don't mind. But that means you'll be bound to me as well. Isn't that—"

Isaac had just begun to let the question out of his trembling lips. Felix swooped down and captured them. A tongue delved in greedily between their locked lips. Saliva was mixed, tongues were intertwined, and without warning, alpha pheromones spilled.

It went without saying, of course, but his pheromones were stronger, more suffocating than Cole's beyond comparison. The torrent numbed his mind, made his limbs shudder, and tore a moan out of him.

His heart pounded as if ready to explode, while two different pheromones clashed inside him. His fingertips vibrated. His body lurched forward. He could no longer see Felix in the darkness that engulfed his vision. It felt like every part of him was torn apart.

"Hold on."

The pheromones made his brain into putty, and blood erupted from Isaac's nose in between his gasps. He twisted and groaned against the pheromones entering his body unfiltered, but there was nothing he could do. Isaac screwed his eyes shut and clung to Felix's arm, panting.

"Felix, Benjamin... You must—"

Even during all this, Isaac continued to ask after Benjamin. Felix had to let out an absurd laugh. He really saw no way out of this. He couldn't be sure what would happen to Isaac if he didn't

bring Benjamin, so Felix had no choice but to get up.

"Will you be able to withstand it?"

Though curled up and shivering, Isaac nodded in affirmation. Felix brought his hand to rub at his neck. Cole's mark was blurring little by little. A little more, and it would be gone completely, replaced with his mark, if Isaac didn't go crazy before that.

"Isaac, you lied to me and deceived me all this time. I could have killed you on the spot, but as promised, I won't lay a finger on you."

"Uh, ah—"

"So hold up your end of the bargain. You're mine, my omega. Mark *my* words."

Felix kissed Isaac's torn lips savagely before raining his thick pheromones on him once more. Again, Isaac was convulsed with pain. But nothing could be done about it until his mark appeared, and he had to make sure Benjamin was safe before that.

Felix left Isaac on the sofa and strode out. The small reception room, where Isaac now sat alone, was thick with Felix's torrid pheromones. The angry, vicious pheromones sent an unmistakable warning to all alphas, even betas. The powerful and frightening miasma wrapped around Isaac effortlessly and kept everyone at bay.

Only the owner of the pheromones, Felix, would dare approach.

Chapter 10

Felix slammed the door shut and walked down the hallway with menacing eyes. *Fuck!* He swore under his breath. His head felt scrambled, and his heart was racing uncontrollably.

Isaac, whom he'd believed without a grain of doubt was a beta, was actually an omega? That cursed omega from four years ago who, on top of that, apparently gave birth to and raised his child? God. Benjamin was his child. He couldn't keep his head on straight. Even being struck by lightning during sleep wouldn't be this shocking.

He'd never wanted a child, had avoided steady relationships thus, and with hook-ups always made sure to use condoms and other contraceptives. He never made mistakes. Not once had he imagined the existence of an offspring somewhere in the world, but that now turned out to be baseless confidence.

Even if there were the possibility, he'd always thought the mother would bring the child to him. They would have to, if they wanted to extort money from him using the child as an excuse, and most of his one-night stands wouldn't be above that.

To think there was someone who had his child alone and out of sight. To think it was Benjamin, whom he was contracted to protect…

"Hah, this is madness."

His head felt like it was burning from the realization that he'd been completely fooled. Felix stopped in his quick steps and caught his breath. It had all been right in front of him. Omega Isaac and his son. He hadn't even sensed it when he was right beside them. How could he have been so blind?

Felix massaged his temples and clicked his tongue. Soon enough, he calmed his rising anger and forced a blank smile. He remembered the night four years ago when he knotted that arrogant omega. It had been his first and only knot, done on a whim, yet it still could have resulted in impregnating the one omega on his heat cycle who drove him mad.

He was so annoyed by the omega's actions that he forgot about the knotting. But that omega was Isaac, and the knot led to Benjamin. He was confused.

"I'm losing my mind."

Felix curled his lips up. As he remembered that day, the vague image of the omega who dared to maim him gradually turned into Isaac's face. Not only his face, but also his body, his movements, and his moans. And finally, the image of the omega thrashing in the flames of his heat cycle and panting desperately beneath him became Isaac.

A deep groan escaped Felix's throat. He finally understood. The truth was that the omega could only ever be Isaac. If not Isaac, then who else could he be so eager for? Who other than Isaac could make him want to knot?

No one.

No one would be able to drive him crazy with lust like Isaac. The realization made Felix laugh again. His rage melted away like snow. He really couldn't help it. Isaac. No matter what that man did, it only pulled him further under. Their bond was unshakable. He had been his from the very start, and he remained so now.

"Yes. Be patient and wait."

Felix grabbed the assault rifle on his back and flashed a sinister smile. As he jogged toward the chaos, which resembled a war zone, he thought of Isaac, drenched in his pheromones and being claimed. He'd never considered or wanted a claim in his life, and yet it was Isaac who made him act without a second thought.

He didn't have a moment to spare.

α Ω α Ω

After settling down somewhat and arranging his jumbled thoughts, Felix's first move was to call Tony and give him a new order. "If you spot Cole, bring him to me alive. Do not kill him. Understand?"

Tony responded to Felix's urgent shouts with an affirmative, but he was clearly confused. He had good reason to be since the initial order was to kill Cole on sight, but Felix didn't have the time to explain.

Cole's residence was slowly being captured. Inevitable, given its numerical, armament, and expertise disadvantages. Thanks to that, Cole's mercenaries were mostly dead or had fled, and only a few remained. It was chaotic, however—gunshots, screams, and wreckage sounded ceaselessly. Felix turned a deaf ear to it as he stepped out of the hallway and gestured toward his bodyguards, who were on standby.

"You'd better keep this in mind: *do not* kill Cole," Felix commanded as he ran down the stairs. "Bring him alive."

On his way down, he shot any stragglers and headed for the basement, his pace almost hurried.

"Noah, send me Benjamin's location." Felix ran without hesitation as he spoke to Noah. He was wearing an earpiece like Cole's, and the line had been open since he entered the place.

This meant Noah had been listening in on Felix and Isaac's entire conversation, but had kept his mouth shut so Felix briefly forgot he was there. He spoke to him once he collected his thoughts, but Noah stayed completely silent. Which wasn't like the Noah he knew, who loved teasing Felix and digging into people's affairs.

"Are you listening?" Felix prodded the earpiece. He even cast a suspicious glance into the empty air.

Finally, the sound of a throat clearing came from the earpiece. “Sure, I’m listening. A bit too well, actually.”

“Then, why didn’t you answer?” Felix asked irritably.

Noah ignored him and forged ahead with what he had to say. “As I expected, Benjamin and Jessica are in the basement. I confirmed it five minutes ago through the cameras of the guys who made it there. It took them a while because of high security, and they still haven’t reached the two. They’re holding out against the guards.”

“Still? What’s taking them so long?” Felix asked impatiently. “We suspected from the beginning that the two were in the basement.”

“This is fast.” Noah sighed. “We suspected, but it wasn’t like we had the precise coordinates. Well, they might be finishing up now.”

“Get the chopper ready.”

“It is ready. It’s practically parked on top of your head.”

A helicopter was needed to extract a middle-aged woman and a child from this hellscape. However, it would take time, as they were underground.

Assessing the situation in his head, Felix was about to go down the stairs to the basement when Noah’s even voice called his name. “Felix.”

“What?”

“You’d better bring my nephew back safely.”

“What the fuck? Did you think I wouldn’t bring him out safely? And who’s your nephew?”

“He’s my nephew! I don’t want to see your stupid face, but I want to see my nephew!”

With Noah’s emotional, almost tearful outburst, Felix forgot where he was and scowled. “Shut up.”

The fact that Noah had overheard the entire revelation just because he had forgotten about the earpiece was bothering him.

"You fucking bastard. I already knew you were a lowlife, but not so low you didn't know you had a kid! Who knows what kind of hardships my poor nephew faced?" Noah cried. "Bastard! I'm telling on you to Grandpa, you mean bastard."

Unable to stand any more of Noah's weeping, Felix turned the earpiece off. His insides were churning worse than before. He chewed on his lip in vexation.

One of his bodyguards emerged from the back and lined up his rifle, alert. "Boss, this way."

Felix looked up from his thoughts sharply. At the bottom of the stairs, he saw his men in a narrow hallway tensely aiming at a single door. The hallway was splattered with blood and strewn with gunned-down men. The smell of gunfire in the air was thick, making it difficult to breathe.

He understood the situation for what it was. His men must have been eager to drive out Cole's mercenaries, forcing them to hide in the room with Benjamin and Jessica. Only his men stayed outside, pointing their guns at the door.

Felix creased his brow. How the situation had become more annoying, he didn't know. The bastards were obviously still holding the two hostages, which meant it was his side that was at a disadvantage.

"They seem to have fled. What should we do?"

He approached the men and evaluated the situation, but it was exactly as he expected. The door through which the enemy had escaped was securely locked. Whatever they were doing inside, it was silent. The men around the sealed door waited for Felix's command. If they forced their way in while hostages were inside, things could turn dangerous.

"Cole?" Felix asked, glaring at the door.

"We haven't caught sight of him."

"Fucking rat."

It wouldn't be easy for him to leave the premises with his wounds. He would certainly be lying in wait to take Benjamin

hostage because there was no other way for him to weasel out.

"Break the door." Felix made his decision and gave the order.

The men expressed confusion, but with a gesture from a stout individual who seemed to be the team leader, they affixed a small explosive device to the door handle. Bullets wouldn't open a metal door, so they were going to blast it off.

"Those of you who are betas, cover me. The rest should keep far away as soon as the door opens." Felix spoke with determination once the explosive was in place and everyone had backed away. On the last syllable, there was a boom, and the door handle dangled in tatters. The metal door slowly creaked open.

It was before the door opened that Felix dropped the words. "Step back."

In an instant, his alpha pheromones spread over the floor. The stench of gunfire disappeared as if it were swept away in a gust of wind, replaced by the suffocating fog of Felix's pheromones.

No alpha could withstand the rage-filled, hyper-dominant alpha pheromones filling their airways. The ones near Felix were rushing to escape even before the door creaked, covering their mouths, and some of the sensitive betas were inching backward.

By the time Felix kicked the ruined handle of the door and slammed it open, the entire basement was steeped in thick pheromones none could bear. Even the betas flanking him sank to the floor with a yelp.

The inside of the room, which had been locked, wasn't an exception. The pheromones seeped through the gap in the door and filled the air as well. No one was left standing. Most of them were unconscious or rolling on the floor, puking and shaking. A few betas and dominant alphas barely managed to raise their guns, but of course, Felix was faster than their unfocused eyes and unsteady hands. With a few shots, it was over.

It was laughably easy.

It was true that in battle the usage of pheromones gave alphas and dominant alphas an edge—more so in an enclosed space like this—but it was rare that it could decimate a large number in such a short time, and it was rare that an alpha had such an ability.

Having proved he wasn't a hyper-dominant alpha for no good reason, Felix sauntered into the room. It wasn't a small feat for him either to radiate so much at once, and he was a bit short of breath. Cold sweat trickled down his spine, and his heart raced. And yet, not a hair was out of place as he positioned his gun and looked around.

He didn't see a middle-aged woman or a child among the bodies, no matter how many times he looked with narrowed eyes.

Felix held back a swear as it threatened to escape at the scene, which seemed to be mocking him, and carefully examined his surroundings. That was when he noticed a faint mark on the opposite side of the bed. The drywall was slightly dislodged. He ran up to it and kicked it, causing the wall to slide vaguely to the side.

"The crazy fucker pulled out all the stops," Felix muttered to himself angrily and scowled again.

Noah had warned in an offhand manner how the house, which was based on an old castle, might have tricks and traps, but seeing a secret passageway with his own eyes made his teeth grind.

Indeed, Cole wouldn't have just locked up his only remaining bargaining chip. Isaac probably suspected something like this and begged Felix to go after Benjamin himself. The more he thought about it, the more irritating Cole became.

Felix charged into the dark passageway without hesitation, loading the Colt while cursing. Not knowing where it led, he turned on the earpiece, but the underground's depth or some interference prevented him from reaching Noah. All he could hear was static.

Cole, that fucking bastard.

Left with no choice, Felix turned off the earpiece again and kept cursing. But no amount of swearing comforted him. Determined to make Cole's death painfully slow, Felix picked

up his pace. He couldn't have gone far. Cole was injured, and dragging a middle-aged woman and a child would only slow him down. It was a matter of time before he caught up, and Felix wasn't worried about losing them.

What he was most worried about was that the crazy bastard would go off and harm the hostages. The more time passed, the further Cole would be backed into a corner, and there was no telling what he would end up doing.

Felix walked nervously along the dark passageway, gritting his teeth. His heart was pounding in his chest. Then, a sound brushed past his ear, making him stop in his tracks and listen. The sound was coming from nearby, buzzing through the narrow passage: the cries of a child, the protests of a woman, and the irritable barks of a man all spilled out at once.

Felix pressed his back to the wall and made himself inconspicuous as he slowly approached. His palms were clammy with sweat.

"Shut up! I told you to quit bawling!" The man, breathing heavily, lost his temper. He didn't raise his voice too much, fearing he might be heard. Still, the murderous rage in his words and tone was clear.

"He's a child! He doesn't know anything, don't—! *Ah!*"

A slap followed as the woman started to raise her voice at the man.

Naturally, the child's cries grew louder, and so did Cole's shouts. "Shut up! I told you to shut up! Are you deaf?"

Felix's teeth clenched upon hearing the commotion the woman-abusing scum was causing.

"Don't touch him!" The woman suddenly screamed, and the child cried frantically.

The mere sound sent a chill through Felix. He couldn't stay still and broke into a sprint. Just a moment earlier, he had flooded his surroundings with pheromones and revealed his exhaustion, but now it was gone. Instead, a wave of sharp, furious pheromones radiated from him.

"Cole, take your filthy hands off of him!" Felix's angry steps and voice, laced with killing intent, filled the narrow passage. Cole whipped around in shock, coinciding precisely with the moment Felix turned the corner and appeared in front of them.

"How, how did you—" Cole's eyes widened. He was drenched in blood from head to toe, his tone laced with disbelief. Felix came to a halt, breath hitching as his gaze locked onto Cole's hands.

They were wrapped around Benjamin's neck.

The child's face, framed by bright blond hair, was flushed red—his feet kicking weakly in the air, too far gone even to make a choking sound. Jessica, bleeding from a cut near her mouth, was dangling from Cole's arm, herself blue in the face. She was desperately trying to get him to release the child.

Felix froze in place at the absurd sight when Cole shouted and shook Benjamin back and forth. "Don't come closer if you don't want to see your son's neck snapped in two!"

"I didn't realize you were so eager to die," Felix replied, his voice dark, his eyes unblinking. The pressure he exuded was a crushing weight upon the shoulders.

"I warned you not to lay a hand on my son."

For a moment, Jessica, who was tugging on the child, looked up in surprise at Felix's declaration of "my son." But Felix didn't notice her discomfort. His blue eyes were almost black as he stared murderously at Cole.

Even as he was sweating profusely, Cole kept talking. "If you move, I'll—!"

That was when a wave of Felix's pheromones hit him hard. Cole convulsed as if electrocuted and dropped to his knees right there. His hands fell slack from Benjamin's neck, setting him free. Jessica quickly scooped up the child who started to cry.

"Wah! Grandma, Grandma! Daddy!"

The child's sorrowful wails, searching for both his grandmother and father, felt like knives in the heart. Naturally, he was calling

for Isaac, but somehow the word cut through Felix.

When Felix turned, his gaze finally fell on Benjamin, whose eyes were swollen red and shedding pearly tears. The child's blond hair was a shade lighter than that of an adult. It was a bright gold, almost platinum. Felix's hair had been that light when he was a child, too.

The platinum blond locks, the pale, chubby cheeks, quick to flush, the deep blue eyes, the straight nose. To Felix's eyes, Benjamin was still the spitting image of Isaac, but something about his crying face was familiar.

He looks like I did when I was young, the thought flitted past his mind. Then, one by one, Felix remembered the previously unimaginable truths, and his eyes widened in shock. Dear God. His and Isaac's son.

He really is my son.

He hadn't fully grasped it when he listened to Isaac's sudden confession. He'd been too unsettled, and the idea of his flesh and blood had been unclear. Now that he saw Benjamin and recognized a hint of himself in him, his feelings flipped completely.

A storm of unnameable emotions flooded over him. Things he'd never experienced before pierced his heart and caused sharp jolts of pain. Felix inhaled deeply. He might just start to whimper.

He was still out of it, but the certainty that this small child was his shook him to the core. No, rather, his heart was pounding as if it would burst out.

When Isaac revealed that Benjamin was his child, he was confused. It hadn't fully sunk in until now, and his heart raced, his breathing unsteady. It was a nameless, ticklish, but uplifting feeling. Sadly, it didn't last long.

While Felix was distracted, Cole, who had been coughing on the ground, leaped up and grabbed Jessica and Benjamin from behind. In his flurry of emotions, Felix had forgotten about him.

Jessica, who had been walking up to Felix with Benjamin in her arms, screamed. But before Felix could run to her, Cole struck

Jessica hard with his gun's grip and yanked Benjamin away from her. Jessica kept screaming, clutching Cole as he viciously grabbed the child by the neck, but he kicked her off.

Jessica crumpled onto the stone ground like a rag doll. At the same time, a gunshot echoed in their ears. Everything unfolded in an instant.

"Freeze if you don't want to die!" Cole spat curses, their ears still ringing from the gunshot. The bullet had narrowly missed Jessica, tearing through her cardigan. She stood frozen in shock, unable to move. Benjamin wailed uncontrollably, as if seizing.

Felix froze mid-stride. His brow creased, and his fists clenched tight. It was his mistake. He shouldn't have underestimated Cole as a dominant alpha who commanded special operations forces.

"Felix, you should remember I'm also a dominant alpha. No matter how strong your pheromones are, I can withstand them," Cole boasted, curling his bloodied lips.

The strain of his actions weighed on his battered body, and his chest heaved with effort. Sweat, streaked with blood, trickled down his temples. He tried to appear composed, but it was obvious he was in a sorry state: his eyes trembled, and his grip on the gun was slick and unsteady.

Felix looked at the face of a man on the brink of death and simply clicked his tongue.

Cole raised his gun and shouted, "Drop your gun and step back while I'm telling you nicely. If you don't want to see them both die now, scram!"

"Put him down."

"It's all your fault." While he was shouting, Cole reloaded his gun. "Everything is ruined because of you!"

Watching him, Felix couldn't handle his murderous intent and clenched his fists tighter. Felix raised his hands and dropped the Colt. It clattered to the ground and spun out of his reach. "Cole, there's something you're forgetting."

Cole watched the gun with tense eyes, then smirked. "I'm

forgetting something? What could it be?"

"I'm a hyper-dominant alpha, and I can always overpower a dominant like you anytime."

Cole's ailing face darkened further at his casual statement. "No! You won't! You saw your pheromones couldn't subdue me!"

"Sure, maybe you got lucky once—when I was distracted by my son," Felix said, his tone disinterested. Yet his baritone voice carried a chilling weight, enough to raise the hairs on one's neck.

Cole gulped. Cursing under his breath, he tightened his grip around Benjamin's neck and yanked him closer. But Felix's pheromones struck first, crashing down like a wave.

"You will never escape this place—nor my grasp."

Cole grunted.

"You made the mistake of touching my person and my son, and I won't let it slide."

Overwhelmed by the flood of pheromones pouring into him, Cole spewed blood from his nose and mouth. His eyes bulged, on the verge of tearing, and his limbs trembled uncontrollably.

Felix shot forward, fists clenched, ready to strike.

Soon, Cole lost his bearings, and his hands slipped from Benjamin. His eyes rolled back as he toppled backward. At the same time, Felix caught the falling child and held him close to his chest. The small child fit snugly in his arms.

Secure in his arms, the child buried his face into Felix's neck and began to sob, overwhelmed with grief. His damp breath, tears, and snot soaked his skin with a burning heat.

God.

Felix hesitated for a moment, unsure of what to do, then softly whispered as he buried his nose in the child's downy hair, "Don't cry."

He gently patted Benjamin's back with his large hand. He was copying how Isaac used to hug Benjamin, but when the baby powder scent hit his nose, he tightened his arms around him.

"It's okay. Don't cry." Felix soothed Benjamin in a low voice until the child's sobs subsided.

When he regained his senses, he helped Jessica to her feet. She moved closer to Felix, dabbing at the cut on her lip and her bruised cheek. Her eyes held fear and uncertainty, but the way she tried to compose herself made Felix think of Isaac. He smiled bitterly. It must run in the family.

"Felix! You, you dare?" Cole screamed with hatred. Even as he thrashed on the ground, his brain being eaten away by the pheromones, his eyes were wide open, and his mouth was spewing filth. With his collapsed nose, torn mouth, and wounded arms and thighs, his appearance as he cursed Felix was worse than a demon's.

Felix, about to leave with Benjamin in his arms and Jessica following as Isaac had wanted, directed his cold gaze at the yelling Cole. "Shut up. Do I personally have to teach you not to say such filth in front of a child?"

Felix was popping his knuckles when Benjamin, scared by Felix's low voice, shivered and curled into a tiny ball. At that, Felix slowly lowered the fists he'd been raising with the intent to kill.

No matter the reason, he didn't want his son to see him assault someone else. Besides, he was worried that the child would be traumatized even more and cry harder.

"This isn't the time to deal with you," Felix said, almost to himself, withdrawing.

Cole's eyes flashed maniacally.

"Hah, haha, since you're saying that, you must understand now, huh? You see?" Cole realized Felix wouldn't kill him and shouted triumphantly. "I took Kay for myself! You can't kill me—*Arrrgh!*"

Felix suppressed the urge to draw his gun and blow Cole's head off. Instead, he unleashed a crushing wave of pheromones, pouring it over Cole like a storm, ripping a terrible scream from his throat.

"Isn't this the kind of thing you like? Suppressing someone

with your pheromones?" Felix mocked while wrapping his arms tightly around Benjamin to avoid alarming him.

"Stop!"

"It's your turn to have a taste."

The moment the words left his mouth, Felix's pheromones spilled over Cole—almost cruel in their force. Saliva mixed with blood dripped from Cole's mouth as he crawled across the floor, eyes rolling back.

That was the power of a superior alpha, one capable of subduing and conquering the minds of others. Hyper-dominant alphas were extremely rare. A dominant alpha like Cole would usually go unchecked, overpowering both omegas and ordinary alphas. That was why he found betas—immune to pheromones—so unbearably dull.

"Weren't you curious to feel what it's like to be on the receiving end? I'm generous enough to let you know, so enjoy." Felix continued to pat Benjamin placatingly on his trembling back as he spoke to Cole. Not that Cole could understand anything, what with him choking and rolling on the ground.

Felix watched the grim scene with detachment before lifting his wrist to check the time. He frowned. It had been too long since he left Isaac alone.

The image of Isaac in his mind, drenched with pheromones, wearing an incomplete mark, destroyed his patience. Felix turned his head. Tony and his men had caught up to him and were waiting with their rifles aimed at Cole. Should anything happen, they wouldn't hesitate to shoot him dead. Of course, Tony would have told them not to act until Felix was finished. The fact that Tony was personally leading the men down here meant the situation upstairs was resolved.

Good timing, Felix thought with a smirk, and nodded toward Tony, who stepped forward immediately.

"The chopper's ready. Take Mrs. Parker and Benjamin to the hospital right away. Leave that pile of trash in the gutter for now.

Oh, but he can't die, so put a sock in his mouth or something."

"Understood."

"And get everyone out of the house. Now."

Tony looked back at Felix with a questioning glance while guiding Jessica, but Felix had nothing else to add. He just hurried out of the hallway.

Chapter 11

Isaac couldn't stop the moans escaping from his torn lips. His hot breath kept spilling out. He didn't understand how this came to be. All he remembered was being overwhelmed by Felix's pheromones and enduring an eternity of pain as if his muscles had been torn apart.

With Cole's pheromones flooding his system—and then Felix's—Isaac was overwhelmed. A wave of nausea surged through him, and he threw up. Blood dripped from his nose, and a blinding migraine left him screaming, eyes clenched shut in agony.

It was an awful torment. He hugged his shivering body, bit his busted lip, fainted, and kept waking up. When he finally woke up after some time, his feelings had become uncontrollable.

Cole's pheromones had almost vanished, and instead, Felix's overwhelming pheromones were surrounding him. Additionally, his pheromones were acting independently, making his body burn. The sensation was strange yet familiar. Four years ago, his first and only heat cycle. The heat spreading through his body right now was just as intense as that unforgettable night.

"Hah…That can't be."

He tried to figure out why his heat cycle was happening here of all places, but the answer escaped him. He felt dizzy and unfocused. He tried opening and closing his fists and airing out the front of his shirt, but his cursed body continued to produce heat nonstop.

"Ah, fuck!" Unable to contain his frustration, Isaac whacked the sofa carelessly. It only kicked up dust clouds and did nothing else. Gasping for air, Isaac yanked off the buttons of his shirt. They scattered and rolled across the floor.

His hands moved shakily over his stomach and chest, both mottled blue with bruises from Cole's assault, until they found his nipples. Slowly, they trailed lower—until he pulled down the zipper of his pants and reached for his dick, his back arching involuntarily.

God. What was he doing?

His vision was dark, but his hand betrayed him—gripping his stiff cock and stroking. Yet no matter how he rubbed or jerked the restless flesh, it did nothing to ease the burning heat inside him.

Overcome by dizzying desire, Isaac flipped onto his stomach and burrowed into the sofa. He rubbed his feverish forehead, cheeks, and bare chest against the cushions. With his hips raised and his erection twitching uncontrollably, he rocked helplessly, but the boiling heat refused to subside.

Tears of frustration welled in his reddened eyes.

Of course, he knew all too well what his body craved. His underwear was damp with slick, the wetness between his thighs tragically undeniable. He ached to shove his fingers inside himself, but couldn't bring himself to do it. Instead, he bit down on the hem of his shirt, trembling, trying to ride it out.

He had no idea how much longer he could last before losing consciousness. This wasn't the time for this. He didn't even know what had become of his mother and Benjamin—yet here he was, deep in heat.

Desperate to suppress it, Isaac bit hard into his already split lip. But all he tasted was blood. It wasn't enough. It couldn't stop the relentless pull of his heat.

"Ah!" He felt wronged and mortified, especially from the fact that his heat cycle came out of the blue and his body couldn't stop squirming with need, and his traitorous flesh continued to burn.

Isaac curled into himself and shivered. Cold sweat mixed with blood dropped from his chin. The shirt he'd been pulling at fell

apart. He moaned readily, groping his body. At last, letting go of the last pieces of his sanity, he brought his hand to his rear.

Just by sweeping the tip of his finger along his wet entrance, his stomach tightened. His chest heaved, and he expelled a strained breath. Licking at his bleeding lip, Isaac spread his hole.

"Felix!" The name slipped from his lips before he realized it.

Isaac pressed his cheek into the sofa and paused, licking his lip as a sob broke free. It hit him—this wasn't what he needed. Not even close. No amount of rubbing or probing with his fingers could satisfy the aching thirst that tightened his throat.

This wasn't it.

What his body craved now was something more, something hard, something that could thrust deep and powerfully into him.

"Felix. Fuck me, please!" The words slipped out before he even realized. He was painfully aware of how shameful he must look—ass exposed, trembling—yet he felt powerless to get what he needed.

Then he heard a deep voice. "Isaac, I almost exploded waiting for you to call my name."

Isaac flinched, turning his reddened eyes. Felix was there, leaning against the open doorway. He started to walk toward him, his movements silent and stealthy as always.

"W-when?"

As he stared at him with rounded eyes, Felix wore a pronounced smile and came right up to the sofa, where Isaac was huddled.

"Since you tore off your shirt, cursing?" His tone was light, but his gaze sweeping over Isaac's disheveled form was shivering dark. And still, the touch on Isaac's bloodied lips was tender. What a strange contrast.

"Oh God, why were you just standing there?" Isaac's face burned with shame at the thought of Felix seeing him like this—pathetic and exposed. He turned his gaze away, afraid his expression might betray the humiliation and the growing sting of disappointment.

But Felix's response caught him off guard. "I was waiting to see when you'd call for me."

Isaac was unmoved by his calm, even brazen-faced response and stared at him. "And if I didn't call for you?"

"I would have waited, wouldn't I? Seeing as Cole's pheromones are almost gone," Felix muttered flatly and examined Isaac's neck carefully.

On a part of his neck not visible to Isaac—the back of his left ear—Cole's mark was almost completely gone. However, on the back of his right ear, the mark Felix's pheromones were leaving was becoming visible.

Confirming this, Felix chuckled silently. Isaac narrowed his eyes at him, annoyed that he had been left alone in this state.

"It won't do for you to look at me with such sexy eyes," Felix spoke in a melodic tone that put his desire on full display. "I warned you I might explode, didn't I?"

Isaac sighed at his antics, but Felix only brushed away Isaac's sweat-soaked hair.

"Has your anger toward me subsided?" Isaac looked up at him with a flushed face.

Felix reacted as if he had just remembered and made a complicated expression. "Ah, that happened. Shit, this is why it's so unfair. I get excited the moment I see your lewd face. It's a bad bargain on my part."

His words were complaints, but his voice was soft. Unlike before, when he'd left the room furious and angry, now he was gazing at Isaac as he always did, as if all that was water under the bridge. Inwardly relieved, Isaac leaned into him.

"But you can't rest assured already. I remember you said you'd take everything I had to give."

"Anything," Isaac whispered, burrowing his forehead into Felix's chest.

A helpless laugh sounded above him. Was it because of his pleasantly deep voice, or his soft brushing of his hair? The heat

spreading within him came to a boil. He was going out of his mind. He wished fervently for Felix's hand, which was rougher than it looked, to touch his skin and his soaked lower half.

Yet his groans and wriggling motions against his chest didn't last long. In the middle of his stupor, Isaac's eyes suddenly snapped open. He had briefly forgotten his mother and Benjamin because of the overwhelming heat, but now he remembered.

"Mother, Benjamin…" His voice trembled. "What happened to them?"

The very thought of Benjamin made him tense enough for his heat cycle to briefly subside. But he knew Felix being here meant everything was wrapped up. He knew from Felix's usual arrogant demeanor that his mother and Benjamin were safe. Still, Isaac couldn't hide his anxiety as he waited for Felix's answer.

"You don't have to worry. I found Benjamin and your mother, per your wish, and had them taken to the hospital by chopper."

Isaac calmed down at Felix's reply, but widened his eyes again at the mention of a hospital. "Hospital? Are they hurt?"

"Mrs. Parker suffered minor abrasions, but she's not injured. Benjamin's in shock but only needs to be soothed," Felix explained surprisingly patiently. "Don't worry too much."

He was trying to calm Isaac's worries, but honestly, he was a little annoyed. It was normal for Isaac to be concerned, as he was Benjamin's maternal father…

"Is that all you can think about even now? I don't know whether to praise your mental strength or your love for your family."

"What do you mean?" Isaac asked without a clue as to why Felix was grumbling.

Felix clicked his tongue at how Isaac took quick, heated breaths. In his current state, Isaac shouldn't be in the right frame of mind. The claim was halfway done, he was saturated with pheromones, and he was in the middle of his heat cycle. He should be spread out and helpless against the flames of his lust.

Until a minute ago, when Felix returned to the room, Isaac had been half-mad and pleasuring himself. He looked up at him with reddened eyes and a needy expression. But as soon as his family was mentioned, he settled down.

Anyone else would have given in to the chaos in their mind and the heat burning through their body—would've jumped him without hesitation. But Isaac didn't lift a finger, even as he lay there, panting.

His body had to be on fire, yet all Felix saw on his face was worry—not for himself, but for his mother and Benjamin.

Felix could hardly approve. "I told you to take care of yourself first. Who are you to worry about anyone else when you might go into shock at any moment?"

"But—"

"Man, this is annoying," Felix muttered to himself and didn't bother to mask his disapproval. "Or maybe I'm jealous."

He didn't stop brushing back Isaac's hair or wiping the dried blood off his cheeks and lips as he spoke.

"You're jealous?" Isaac blinked and stared at Felix. Contrary to his usual demeanor, his reddened eyes were so erotic that Felix's urge to devour him shot up.

Shit, Felix swallowed the profanity and gripped Isaac's chin. "You're going to make me jealous of your family at this rate. You think only about them anywhere you go."

Isaac was surprised by Felix's honest admission of his feelings. He hadn't known he felt that way. "That's—They're my family. My only family."

"I don't worry about mine too much." Felix smiled bitterly at the conviction in Isaac's reply as he stroked his chin. Uncomfortable, Isaac didn't know what to say and ended up sighing loudly instead. Everyone's feelings and attitudes toward their family were shaped by their circumstances.

"For me…my only family was my father. After he died, I was alone. Always. I was alone in the world." Isaac palmed

his burning forehead as he let the words out like a sigh. "Then Benjamin came to me, and I found my mother after losing contact with her for so long."

He knew he didn't need to make this kind of confession, but he found himself rambling on. It was difficult to tell if it was because the heat was loosening his tongue or because he didn't want Felix to be concerned with such trifles.

"How precious my family, my child, are to me, because they remind me I'm not alone in the world. You might not understand."

Isaac wasn't blaming him, he just wanted to let Felix know that his mother and Benjamin mattered to him for reasons beyond Felix. Seeing Isaac strive to maintain his sanity and answer through his flushed face and scalding breath, Felix had no choice but to shrug.

"Yeah, that's true. I don't fully understand your deep feelings for your family, but I'm going to learn. And I kind of want to become one of the people you care so much about."

"I can't stay jealous forever, yeah?" Felix added nonchalantly, but Isaac still didn't know what he meant, and blinked his blank eyes at him without answering.

It was then that Felix bent down and kissed Isaac's lips. He gently sucked on the cut lip before grabbing his chin, easily opening his mouth, and going straight to wrapping his tongue around his. He was overwhelmed by a deeply intense kiss. Felix consumed not only Isaac's lips but the entire cavity of his mouth like a ravenous predator. But as if he'd been waiting for this moment, Isaac opened his mouth wide enough to clench his jaw and welcomed the kiss.

The wet sounds of their tongues rubbing together, the saliva swallowed during the passionate kiss, were like fuel to the flames rising from his body. His mind became blank. Isaac couldn't think clearly, and his vision blacked out as if smoke filled his view.

Panting, Isaac reached out and grabbed Felix by the neck with a sudden jerk. Felix, who had been exploring every inch of

Isaac's mouth—his tongue trailing deep, almost to the back of his throat—pulled back slightly and let out a low chuckle.

"Isaac, I'm going to claim you for good now. You'll follow my lead without complaint, right?"

"Whatever, fine. Just hurry!" Isaac couldn't stand the sudden emptiness after Felix's hungry yet sweet kiss left him. He held his neck tightly and coaxed him, craving to be in contact with Felix in any way possible.

Felix seemed intent on teasing him, his gaze fixed on Isaac's parted lips, unmoving. Though his eyes burned with lust, he held still.

Desperate, Isaac licked his lips.

Only then did Felix let out a low sound in his throat, his brow drawing into a tense furrow. "Don't be difficult. You're going to be in trouble."

"You said you wouldn't let me."

At Isaac's firm response, Felix tutted in resignation. Still, he was lost in thought, touching Isaac's neck where the mark was faintly visible and doing nothing else. Isaac grabbed his shoulder. Felix had warned him not to be difficult, but he couldn't help himself.

He'd been going crazy before he entered the room. His pheromones were overtaking every part of his body, and his body was reacting with a heat cycle. Isaac couldn't believe he'd been able to maintain a rational conversation with Felix.

Now that Felix was right in front of him, the scent of sweat and pheromones thick in the air, Isaac's cock had long since gone stiff, leaking precum. His front was soaked, but his rear was worse. Had he been in his right mind, he would've been mortified to let Felix see the mess he'd become.

All he wanted was for Felix to thrust into him without hesitation. Just like the night they first met. He was in heat now, just as he had been then, but the overlap of past and present felt surreal. Strange, how nothing had changed, yet everything had.

"Felix, hurry," Isaac moaned.

However, if there was one difference, it was this.

He called out his name first and reached for him first. Isaac wanted no one else but this man to soothe his heat. He only wanted this man to open up and indulge in his body. The very thought excited Isaac, and he tangled his fingers in the back of Felix's hair. His gold-colored hair coiled and fell around his fingers in whispers, sending a shiver through him.

"When the claim is complete and we're out of here." Felix followed Isaac's lead, bending his waist and kissing him on the cheek. He spoke quietly, "Promise me you'll be my partner."

The whispered voice that reached his ear was unexpected. Isaac looked up in confusion. He didn't understand the request.

A claimed pair was supposed to lose awareness of anyone else's pheromones, weren't they? According to Cole, they would become addicted to each other's pheromones, which could get serious. But be his partner? Was there something else left?

"Legally, I mean. I want to be your partner and Benjamin's father."

Isaac was speechless.

"Though I'm his father biologically, I know you're registered as Benjamin's only parent. So give me a chance to become Benjamin's real dad."

As Isaac stared at Felix uncomprehendingly, Felix added one last sentence, embarrassed, "I want to be a member of your precious family, too."

Felix's voice was unusually thick with nerves, but his deep blue eyes remained piercing. Isaac rubbed his spinning head. Felix was serious about this, but it only added to his headache. It was unsettling to see him act so abnormally, but it had to happen here and now.

"Are you proposing?" Isaac lifted his reddened eyes after organizing his thoughts.

"Well, yeah?" Felix answered like it wasn't a big deal.

"Here, in these circumstances?"

"I can't?"

"Without a ring?" Isaac teased, and Felix, who clearly hadn't thought it through, froze. No one dared speak. Especially Felix.

He would be shocked to know Isaac had been convinced it could only be this man the whole time. Of course, Felix wasn't the slightest bit aware and blushed with mortification. "Ah, I have my work cut out for me if I'm to live with you."

In the end, Isaac let out a snicker despite himself. He couldn't help it. He found this arrogant yet absurd man, devoid of awareness, simply adorable.

He was a goner.

"So, you don't want to?" Isaac had a severe case of rose-tinted glasses, but Felix had no idea. His eyebrows went droopy like a child disappointed he didn't get his candy. Ironically, irresistible excitement burgeoned within Isaac at the sight.

Unable to resist his desire to embrace him, Isaac brought down Felix's head with his hand tangled in the back of his hair and captured his lips. Like a starving man, he nibbled and sucked at those sculpted lips and clenched his belly.

The soft, plush sensation and mellow fragrance overwhelmed him, stoking the heat in his body. His vision darkened in an instant, speckled with black.

"Ah, hah…" He squeezed both sides of Felix's face, extended his tongue to lick his lips, and wrapped it around Felix's tongue—damp breaths, indistinguishable in origin, mixed. Felix let out a low moan in his throat. Isaac lifted his hazy eyes. "I told you, my heat cycle has started."

"So?"

"So, start fucking." Isaac clearly expressed what he wanted.

Felix looked at him, stunned, but Isaac held him tighter and pulled him urgently.

"My answer to your proposal will depend on how pleasing your cock is."

"Oh my God, Isaac—"

Before Felix could say anything in his shock, Isaac yanked him by the collar. In an instant, Felix's body swung through the air, and before he could realize it, he had toppled over the sofa and landed neatly on his back. The sudden tug made Felix look up at Isaac with a flurried expression.

"What the fuck. Using a technique like this is against the rules," Felix pouted.

Isaac didn't even pretend to hear and straddled his hips.

"Then, isn't it against the rules to leave me high and dry right as I'm about to go crazy from my heat cycle?"

Isaac yanked off the bulletproof vest Felix was wearing with quick yet skilled hands. It hit the floor with a loud thud. Then he removed his shirt and pants, throwing them aside as well. He made sure to take off his own pants, which were still hanging on his legs, and toss them onto the pile.

Felix watched Isaac do as he pleased and stripped him of his clothes, and he only let out a helpless laugh once he was completely naked.

"Isaac, to tell you the truth, I wasn't completely done being angry before I came here."

"You weren't?"

Felix grumbled again, but Isaac let it pass through one ear and out the other as he bit and sucked at his neck. In his lust-fueled haze, groping Felix's firm chest and breathing in his pheromones made his vision spin.

At this rate, he'd fall into a drunken stupor.

"But see, I forgot all about it when I saw you wiggling your finger in your ass by yourself. Now that's against the rules, isn't it?"

Felix continued to pout like a child, but Isaac barely heard a word he said. Still, Felix made no move to stop him, letting Isaac lick and grope his body as he pleased.

"So, you kept me in suspense on purpose?"

Isaac sucked hard at Felix's neck and collarbone, leaving marks that would surely bruise. Then he reached behind himself, grasping Felix's cock to fondle it.

Despite Felix's lax expression and half-hearted complaints, his erection was anything but relaxed—rock-hard and intimidatingly large.

Isaac's breath caught. It was too big to hold with one hand, and the thought of it entering him again sent a chill through him. He couldn't understand how his body had taken it before.

Yet, despite his unease, his body was already responding, and his hole twitched with anticipation.

"Not exactly," Felix answered, staring up at him while Isaac rubbed his dick. "But there's such a thing as scandalizing someone."

So, he kept him in suspense on purpose.

"Of course, I got jealous when you suddenly went from a vixen in heat to being concerned about Benjamin and your mother."

"Uh. You really don't know anything."

Felix remained outwardly calm, though his erection throbbed hard enough to burst a vein. In contrast, Isaac panted heavily, dragging his perineum across the sensitive tip. When he lowered himself, letting his slick, dripping entrance hover and tease the glans, a moan escaped him.

Felix frowned and clicked his tongue in disapproval.

"You just keep provoking me, don't you?" He growled and grabbed Isaac's ass with one large hand, squeezing it hard, like he meant to make it burst. "I'm trying to go slow. What am I supposed to do if you incite?"

"Why?" Isaac said, panting heavily. "Why do you have to go slow? I'm telling you I'm going crazy. I'm going to die if I don't have your cock inside me now! *Ah!*"

Just as Isaac turned on him with blazing eyes, Felix spread his cheeks and drove his cock into him—sudden, unannounced, and impulsive.

"Ah—Ugh!"

His hole was already as loose and wet as it could be, yet when Felix's blunt cock spread him wide, Isaac stopped breathing at the sheer oppression. Not even half of it was in yet, but his body was already at its limit.

"Fuck, Isaac! You're really going to be in trouble."

Felix's face was just as much of a mess as Isaac's, and his breathing was as labored when he called his name darkly. Isaac barely managed to open his eyes, which had closed in rapture. His hole burned from the impalement, and his stomach felt numb, but his ass shook at the sparks of pleasure.

"You don't get why I was trying to go slow."

Isaac couldn't answer. Felix, taking advantage of this, smiled devastatingly and yanked Isaac's waist into a sitting position. His brutal cock pierced even deeper.

A scream escaped Isaac. "Ah. Felix, it's too…deep!"

Sparks flew across Isaac's eyes. The biggest problem wasn't how he penetrated his gaping entrance and inner walls in one go, lighting them on fire, but that he was full of joy despite his head feeling like it would explode.

"The omega pheromones of yours that I wasn't aware of before are now so distinct, it's a problem. It was driving me crazy this whole time."

"Ah—"

"Once I mark you, I'll be taking your pheromones even deeper. Hah! I don't even know what I'll end up doing then. It's kind of scary." His ocean blue eyes reflected his dangerous desire. "But it's too late now, don't you think?"

Felix licked his red lips and gazed up at Isaac's shivering form. The hungry, animalistic glint of his gaze made his shoulders hunch. Felix reached out to grab Isaac's neck and pull him back. Isaac didn't have the chance to resist before he was dragged and sprawled on top of him, chest to chest. Without preamble, Felix sank his teeth into his neck where the mark was growing darker.

"Ah, ugh—!"

His sharp teeth gnawed at his skin as if to break it. Isaac screamed, but Felix didn't hear, too busy nibbling and sucking on his neck. It felt like he was determined to absorb all the pheromones that had broken out since the suppressants were nullified.

All the while he ravaged Isaac's neck, Felix kept thrusting, relentless and unyielding. One hand pressed down on the back of Isaac's head, the other gripping the ass that clung tightly around his cock as he pounded away at a frenzied pace.

The lewd sound of slapping flesh rang out in all directions. Thrown flat on Felix's stomach while the man lay on his back on the sofa, Isaac couldn't move an inch and could only surrender his neck and ass to him.

"Ah. Felix, Felix. Ugh—!"

Isaac was on top of Felix's supine form, so how had he ended up caught in his clutches? Felix lay flat on his back, hips moving with brutal precision, and yet somehow he was driving into Isaac just as hard as if they'd switched positions. Isaac couldn't understand how, but the question didn't linger.

His mind went blank. He couldn't catch his breath, couldn't match the rhythm of Felix's violent thrusts. His body was rocked back and forth, completely at his mercy.

It hadn't even been a few minutes, and already his vision spun. Every time Felix's mouth latched onto his neck and bit down, and every time that merciless cock slammed into him, Isaac broke into helpless cries.

His mouth hung open, drool trailing down his chin.

"Isaac, fuck! How did you manage to conceal this for so long? Huh?" Felix paused in the process of leaving a huge hickey on Isaac's neck to berate him. "How were you hiding this sweet scent?"

Then he grabbed Isaac's chin and smothered him with a greedy kiss. When Isaac couldn't take the suffocation anymore

and opened his mouth wide to breathe, Felix's tongue took the chance to insert his smooth tongue and disturb his inflamed tissues as he pleased.

They gulped their combined saliva down their throats. The kiss was never-before-seen levels of obscene, but Isaac swirled his tongue around Felix's without resistance. Indeed, what resistance? If anything, he was sucking on his tongue like a man thirsty for its too-sweet sweetness.

"Isaac, you're so fucking sexy," Felix shouted, overcome, squeezing Isaac's ass and snapping his hips up. "Ah, what do I do? I'm going crazy!"

The sound of flesh slapping against flesh grew louder.

Isaac was a wreck atop Felix's chest, teeth sinking into his shoulder in a surge of unbearable ecstasy. His mind was already gone from the relentless pounding inside him, but when his cock dragged against Felix's firm abdomen, the sensation pushed him over the edge far too quickly.

"No! I think I'm going to come—"

"Yeah? You don't have to hold it. Just come."

Felix ran his tongue slowly over Isaac's tear-streaked face, down his jaw and neck, before pulling him into a tight embrace. His hips bounced in a steady rhythm, coaxing Isaac to move with him. With each erotic thrust, Isaac's cock slid helplessly between their pressed bellies—slick and overstimulated.

The sensation was too much to bear.

Isaac let out strangled cries and came without even being allowed to lift his hips. Milky ropes of cum splattered across their overlapping stomachs, the sharp scent hitting his nose as the warm fluid trickled down their chests with slick viscosity.

"Ah, ugh. Felix, wait—"

Isaac went limp, resting his forehead on Felix's shoulder and breathing deeply. But he wasn't granted the leisure to enjoy the release. Regardless of whether Isaac had climaxed, Felix's cock was unstoppable. It rammed into his hole, and Isaac moaned

hoarsely anew.

"Isaac, we haven't even started yet. It's your heat cycle. You can say such weak things already. Do you want me to remind you how it went four years ago?"

"Hah, but…Ah—!"

"Not only that, we're claiming each other. You drove me to insanity with your pheromones, so you should take more responsibility."

Felix curled his lips into a crooked smile, gazing up at Isaac. His expression was arrogant, mean, and lascivious enough to make his hips tremble all at once. Isaac wondered if he was looking at an incubus and licked his lips, his throat burning with an unquenchable thirst.

"We can't have you distracted at a time like this, can we?"

Felix, quick to catch the drift of Isaac's wandering thoughts, clicked his tongue in disapproval. He grabbed Isaac's waist and yanked him back, driving his lethal cock deep inside.

The pressure was unbearable, as if his insides might burst.

Isaac's vision spiraled.

"Huh, ugh—"

"And I'm saying it now, but I don't like having someone on top."

Felix crushed his balls into Isaac's ass, still gripping his hips, and made an unexpected comment. Isaac gasped out the breath brimming up to his chin and raised his pleasure-hazed eyes.

"Ugh. What…What do you mean?"

When their gazes met, Felix affectionately brushed back Isaac's sweaty black hair before lowering his eyes. His smile was sunny and fresh, contrasting with someone who had just been having wild, nonstop sex, but his words were far from cheerful.

"Basically, I don't like it when someone looks down at me from above. Even if it's during sex, I hate having someone sit on my stomach."

Isaac was left speechless once again.

"You made me do it in a position I hate, so shouldn't you give me a nice reward?"

"You really are…"

Awful.

Isaac swallowed back his honest impression and let out a lengthy sigh. Felix smiled brightly and licked Isaac's neck. He rolled his pointed nipples between his fingertips as if to tease.

"Then, what position…is your favorite?"

Unable to bear the electrical current coursing through him, Isaac asked the question as he squeezed Felix's wrists. He lifted his ass to take a brief respite from Felix's cock, which was deep inside him but had yet to ejaculate once.

"My favorite, huh?" Felix held fast to Isaac's pelvis to prevent him from doing so. "If I tell you, are you going to change positions?"

"Yes."

No sooner had Isaac responded through ragged, heaving breaths than Felix surged upward. Wrapping his arms around Isaac's waist, he flipped him over without even pulling out. In an instant, Isaac was face-down on the sofa, hips twitching uncontrollably. A moan tore from his throat.

"Uh, huh—!"

Isaac's head and shoulders were buried in the sofa. Only his ass was up. Felix trailed a finger along his sweaty spine, and Isaac's back muscles twitched at the touch. The sight was insanely lewd.

"This is the kind of position I prefer."

"You….beast…"

"You don't like it?"

Felix bent one of Isaac's legs and spread his thighs as he asked, his tone cantankerous. Isaac couldn't bring himself to admit that he liked it. His face burned. They'd done it in this position many times before, yet he still couldn't hide his embarrassment.

"I don't see you complaining," Felix murmured in a low voice, then gripped Isaac's hips firmly with both hands. He rammed his

cock deep into his hole. Isaac's scream scattered in the air.

But this was only the beginning.

Felix pounded against his inner walls with a different level of force than when he had been lying on his back. The rhythmic pounding was harsher than that of a wild rutting animal. The sparks flying up Isaac's spine only made him feel dizzy.

"Ah, yes. You told me you'd answer after seeing what my cock can do."

"Slower—"

"But, you really couldn't tell from the other times we did it? I'm really good with my cock. The answer is already decided, right?"

Chapter 12

Isaac couldn't refrain from screaming. He'd underestimated the state of being in a heat cycle. Perhaps he'd forgotten too well the last one he had four years ago.

"So good. Ah, there," he moaned uncontrollably. "A little more—"

He couldn't even tell how much time had passed. They had switched positions countless times. It had indeed been a while, but somehow, Isaac always ended up back on the sofa, smothered with his ass in the air, coaxing Felix all over again.

How strange. The more time passed, instead of diminishing, the more intensely his desire burned. And he'd become so sensitive, he could almost come just from Felix touching him lightly with his hand.

As a result, not one part of him was left intact. The nipples Felix sucked and nibbled on were red and swollen, and expanses of his skin were mottled with bruises. It went without saying for the hole Felix was pounding away at. Both Isaac and Felix had come countless times and were covered in semen.

The fact that Felix, who took a while to come, had ejaculated this much meant their animalistic intercourse had gone on for a lengthy period, but neither of them took notice.

"More! Deeper…Ah, *so good.*" Isaac sobbed, clutching Felix's arm and urging him deeper. "Hah, Felix!"

One of his knees was planted on the sofa, the other propped up awkwardly as Felix rocked him, driving his cock in with a force that felt like it could pierce straight through him.

Then Felix stilled, staring down darkly at the debauched

sight—Isaac lost to the flames of his heat, moaning in mindless pleasure. His sloppy hole twitched, clinging greedily to Felix's cock. Just watching it made Felix's lust surge uncontrollably.

"You're driving me mad, really," Felix growled. "Isaac, you were like this four years ago, too. You're just too seductive. I don't think I'll be able to stop in days. You get me?"

Felix brushed off beads of sweat and slowly rotated his hips. From Isaac's hole gushed out an endless stream of Felix's cum. He stirred Isaac's insides, creating wet noises, and more of the white semen trickled down his thighs. Anyone would think a group took Isaac.

"More! Don't stop. More! Ah!" Isaac begged like a seasoned prostitute. He could not be more different from his usual stoic self. Felix loved that about him. It excited him more than anything. He didn't know if Isaac was aware of that, however.

"Oh dear. You're going to squeeze me dry," Felix complained lightly, all the while pinning his hungry blue gaze on Isaac's messy backside.

But his intention was to tease—so he went still, then slowly pulled out, spreading Isaac's cheeks wide as he did. With his cock out, semen spilled from the gaping hole. It didn't even close anymore, allowing a glimpse of its pink insides.

"I'm going mad," Felix sighed lowly, blatantly inspecting the breathtaking sight. His darkened eyes were raw with cloying lust.

"Hurry, Felix—"

"Don't be difficult."

Isaac begged tearfully, unable to bear a moment without his cock inside him. Felix then gripped Isaac's ass with both hands and shoved his cock in up to the root. He slowly pulled out and shoved it in again, repeatedly.

So forceful were his thrusts that Isaac was pushed up on the sofa and hit his head on the armrest with each one. The cum leaked out of his ass and dripped everywhere.

"Ah, ah! This…is too…Ah—!"

"You asked for it."

Isaac wept, but also took his cock in his shaking hand and rubbed. Unfortunately, after repeatedly climaxing, it wouldn't grow stiff. Felix grabbed Isaac's wrists and yanked them behind him. Isaac's waist was pulled back tight and arched reflexively.

"There's nothing left to come out. Why bother touching it? Cum dry." As soon as Felix spoke, he switched from the routine of pulling out and thrusting back into that of jackhammering his hips. The sound of flesh slapping echoed obscenely through the air.

Isaac moaned, toes curling as the thrill rippled through him. Shivers broke out across his skin, causing his hips to tremble. He couldn't hold back the sobs of ecstasy.

"How come your hole is tightening again when it couldn't even close properly before?"

"Ah, ah, ah. S-stop—"

"How much more do I need to lose my sanity until you're satisfied, huh?"

Felix squeezed Isaac's far-flung arms and drove him to his limit. Isaac couldn't speak; he only screamed, shaking his head and his hips. At this rate, he would easily come dry like Felix had bid.

"Ah, ahhh—!"

No, he didn't even need to, because he felt like he would swoon by this alone. He was an animal in heat in every sense of the word. Isaac couldn't form a single thought, his mind empty, as though he'd become a doll seeking only pleasure.

As Felix's movements grew in intensity, enough to inflame his buttocks where they slapped against him, sparks flew before Isaac's vision. When he purposely prodded a particular spot on his sensitive, puffy inner walls, an electrical current shot through him.

His breaths were up to his chin and expelled quickly to the point of hyperventilation. He couldn't hold out against Felix's

demented demands any further.

"F-Felix, stop. No more, ugh!" A dry climax, wasn't that what he'd said? The moment Isaac thought the overwhelming pleasure would kill him, a scream tore from his throat. Tears spilled down his cheeks as he sobbed uncontrollably, trembling like a leaf.

"Fuck!" He heard Felix's breathless voice behind him just as a searing heat spilled into his slick, pliant depths—a now-familiar sensation that still rocked him to the core.

Felix came with a low moan, and Isaac went limp, utterly spent. His vision blurred. He collapsed onto the sofa with a soft thud and didn't move. He couldn't think. Not at all.

α Ω α Ω

When he blinked his heavy eyelids, it was because of a ticklish sensation brushing his neck. Isaac wanted nothing more than to drift back to sleep, but the roaming hands wouldn't leave him alone. Reluctantly, he opened his eyes.

"Felix?" Isaac saw the shadow in his vision and called his name. He was surprised by how hoarse his voice sounded. Meanwhile, Felix looked at him with a relaxed expression.

Maybe relaxed was the wrong word. He wore a lazy smile, but there was a strange mix of tension and excitement behind it. Isaac opened his mouth to ask what was wrong, but Felix was faster, pulling him into an embrace and kissing his neck.

"Isaac!" he exclaimed. "Oh, God! Isaac!"

"W-What's the matter?"

Isaac tensed at Felix's excited voice. Then Felix lifted his head from where he was pressing into Isaac's chest and licking his neck.

"I was so out of it all this time that I almost forgot."

Felix suddenly spoke into his ear. Isaac blinked, still drowsy.

Then Felix kissed him gently.

"My mark. It's become completely visible on your neck," Felix whispered in Isaac's ear as if sharing a secret, gently stroking his damp hair.

"What?" Isaac's eyes widened at the softly spoken words.

"The claim must have been finished while we were going at it like rabbits."

Isaac lowered his incredulous gaze to Felix's neck. As he had mentioned, behind his ear, Felix also bore a mark the size of a fingernail. The claim had been perfected, and the black-blue mark was clearly visible to everyone.

"This is…the claiming mark?" Without thinking, Isaac reached out and touched his neck, asking in a trembling voice.

Felix shrugged. "Evidently, yeah?"

"It's darker than a tattoo."

"Yeah."

It was a first for Felix, too. In fact, he'd never once been interested in claiming anyone and knew little about it. Both Isaac and Felix had gone through with the claim abruptly. In terms of information, they were equally lacking.

"Fascinating." Through his sleepiness, Isaac continued to caress the mark on Felix's neck. He touched it over and over, stared like he would carve the shape into his corneas, but he still couldn't believe it.

This man, none other than Felix Felice, was his—his alpha. It was almost unreal. As Isaac murmured softly under his breath, staring intently at Felix's neck, the man gently kissed him on the lips.

"It's looking nice and pretty."

"Yours too."

"Wow. Look at you. I can't believe it," Felix spoke out loud precisely what he'd been thinking. "You're my omega."

Isaac looked at him, entranced. "Are you pleased?"

The prodding question made Felix arch an eyebrow at him.

"Am I pleased? Of course, I'm pleased. I almost feel sorry I didn't know you were an omega before."

At his resolute answer, Isaac smiled sheepishly. Felix reined in his excitement and fixed Isaac with darkened blue eyes.

"What about you? You've been hiding the fact that you're an omega all this time. You've lived as a beta without anyone knowing, but you can't even do that anymore. Everywhere you go, people will know you're my omega. Are you fine with that?"

Felix's question caught Isaac off guard. He'd never thought about it until now. "To be honest…I haven't thought that far."

He'd always lived as a beta. He didn't know what would be in store for him otherwise. Many things would change, and many problems might arise. As Felix's omega in particular, he would be the subject of all kinds of gossip.

However…

"I get to have you instead. It's a small price to pay. And, why would I care, as long as you're at my side?" He answered as plainly as ever.

Felix's mouth fell half-open in surprise, before his eyes curved in a dazzling smile. "Isaac, if you were trying to make me fall for you all over again, you succeeded."

His smile was so overwhelmingly beautiful that Isaac stared at him in a daze. He would endure anything if it meant possessing this unmatched beauty, he vowed to himself.

"Well now, my omega. Answer me this," Felix prodded, his fingertips meltingly sweet upon Isaac's neck and still wearing that mesmerizing smile.

"Which is?"

"Were you pleased with my cock?"

Isaac stared at him for a moment. His touch on his hair was gentle, and his gaze on his face was warm. But the inappropriate question, spoken in his sweet tone, threw him off.

"Ah. You really know how to hold a grudge."

"You're the one who said it."

"Yes, I did, but—"

"Then answer me."

Isaac couldn't help but burst out laughing. What was he to do with this man? "I'm tired. Let me sleep for a bit and think about it."

As Isaac deliberately turned his back on him, a sinister voice whispered in his ear. "Isaac. If you're going to be that way, I might just not let you sleep at all."

The light touch on his shoulder suggested a threatening strength. If Isaac didn't come up with a proper, satisfactory answer right now, Felix was sure to keep him awake all night.

Isaac secretly rubbed his trembling chest and looked back. "What kind of answer did you expect?"

His mouth wriggled with the effort to keep from laughing. The arms dealer was associated with the mafia. The man who possessed the power and influence to make others tremble with fear. Who knew such a man had the personality of a pouty child?

"I'm asking because I don't know," Felix grumbled, pouting.

Oh dear.

This truly was the famously oblivious Felix Felice.

Finding it hard to keep teasing him, Isaac reached out and cupped Felix's cheek. It was silky smooth against his palm, free of exhaustion despite not having rested since the previous day. Then he traced Felix's captivating lips with the tip of his finger.

"Isn't it obvious?" Isaac whispered back, pressing his finger harder on Felix's lips. He was preventing him from getting a word out.

The hot air that escaped between his plush lips tickled his finger, but Isaac didn't remove it.

"My answer was decided from the beginning." There was no other answer. "Yes."

The moment he answered, Felix's dark ocean-blue eyes flickered slightly. But soon, they softened with delight, making Isaac's heart race. He would always be weak for this beautiful

man.

"Now, let me sleep a bit," he whispered. "One would think you're the one in heat, not me."

Even as he spoke, Felix kept staring at him intently with dark eyes. Embarrassed, Isaac removed his finger from Felix's lips and tried to turn around again. Or at least, he attempted to if it weren't for the man pressing down on him like a boulder.

"Oh my God. You know what? That was the most heart-racing moment I ever had in my life."

Felix pressed himself against Isaac, forbidding him from turning and softly nibbling on Isaac's earlobe as he whispered. The hot, damp breath that brushed into his ear sent a thrill through him, making Isaac tense his neck and stirring his stomach.

He couldn't help it. His heat hadn't yet subsided, and his body was still hypersensitive from the relentless sex. Even the slightest touch made him react. Still, Isaac pretended not to notice.

"Was it?"

"Isaac. I have a confession to make," Felix said cryptically, wearing a mischievous expression.

"What else is left?" The mood took an unlucky turn, and Isaac instinctively scooted back.

Felix, still wearing his bright smile, pecked his cheek. Not only his cheek but also his chin, nose, and lips. Thanks to his efforts, a slight fever started to rise in his unsettled body. "I think my rut's starting."

The words spoken sweetly into his ear were appalling. Isaac stared up at him with round eyes. "Surely not?"

"It must be a severe reaction to your pheromones." Licking his way up his neck, Felix was fueling the flames that were hotter than before.

"No way," Isaac muttered confusedly, yet all Felix did was hold him captive.

"Your heat cycle isn't gone yet either. There can't be a more perfect match, wouldn't you say?"

Faced with his unwavering sunniness, even as he announced thunderous news, Isaac tensed his shoulders. Not that it stopped Felix from showering him with kisses, his face lit up with joy. Eventually, Isaac gave in and wrapped his arm around him.

The affectionate yet greedy kiss continued endlessly. They remained in a seamless embrace, their bodies burning with the same relentless heat.

Chapter 13

A deadly click echoed through the empty space. The process of loading the semi-automatic pistol—filling it with ammo, releasing the safety, and chambering the round—was quick and precise.

A step away, watching Isaac's skilled hands, Felix tutted to himself. He reminded himself once again never to cross him.

Isaac's face was expressionless as he aimed the gun. His hand didn't shake, and his dark eyes were as fathomless as the deep sea. The sheer absence of emotions was hair-raising. Felix almost doubted this was the same person who had blushed with pleasure beneath him mere hours ago.

After the intense sex, they blacked out, and when they finally opened their eyes and regained consciousness, two days had already passed since the claim was marked. With Felix's rut coinciding with Isaac's heat cycle, the spontaneous mating season had flown by in a haze.

They couldn't tell who was more insane. Both were crazy for each other and had spent the days drunk on each other's pheromones, hearing and seeing nothing else. The fact that it was right after the marking drove them crazier.

In any case, after having sex for two days like a starving animal, the first thing Isaac asked about was Cole. It was unexpected, since Felix had assumed he would run to his mother and Benjamin foremost.

"I can't rest easy with an obstacle remaining," Isaac answered Felix when asked why he was going to see Cole before Benjamin.

"I would feel a bit freer if I ended him with my hands." He

explained as he tucked the Colt he'd borrowed from Felix in the waist of his pants. Felix had no choice but to lead Isaac to where Cole was imprisoned.

The day of the shootout, Felix shut down the entirety of Cole's large and luxurious residence. He wouldn't let anyone get close and banned everyone from entering or contacting him. If he didn't, his uncontrollable pheromones would go wild.

The conclusion, though, was that he hated imagining someone other than him smelling and getting excited over Isaac's pheromones. Sure, no one could fight through his alpha pheromones to reach him, but who knew what kind of crazy people were out there? Felix wasn't going to give an inch to them.

The house felt heavy under the weight of Felix's overbearing jealousy. Of course, it had suffered a battle and been vacated, but it wasn't only Isaac and Felix within its walls. Cole was locked in the basement, unable to move a step. It would have been a bigger hassle dragging him out to another location, anyway.

And so, ironically, the only other person who got to smell his and Isaac's pheromones filling the house was Cole. It irritated Felix to no end, but at least he was soon to be a dead man.

Felix managed to settle his disgruntlement at that and regarded Cole dispassionately. The man was sitting in the middle of a putrid-smelling underground cell; he wasn't in the right state of mind.

His mouth was gagged, his limbs tied to a chair that was nailed to the floor. His many wounds had been left untreated and were rotting as a result, and his eyes were vacant like a dead fish.

But when Isaac opened the door and stepped in, those dead eyes widened in recognition. When they landed on the mark proudly on display, Cole's haggard face twisted bizarrely.

Felix noticed Cole's outraged, yet lustful gaze and had to stop himself from getting his gun and killing him before Isaac could. Though contrary to Felix's clear indignation, Isaac expressed nothing and merely loaded his gun.

"I said I would kill you no matter what." Isaac locked eyes with Cole in a silent standoff before finally speaking. But before any words could leave his mouth, a deafening gunshot rang out. The bullet tore through Cole's knee, and he let out a muffled scream.

It happened so quickly that even Felix, who was leaning on the door with his arms crossed, flinched and squared his shoulders. Isaac remained silent; he stared at Cole, his mouth set in a firm line and gaze cold, as the man squirmed from the pain of his shattered knee.

As Cole's consciousness faded, Isaac whispered his words. "It's a small price compared to the sins you committed against me, my father, and my family."

Then three rapid gunshots sounded. Cole, already almost dead, finally dropped his head.

"My family won't suffer at your hands a second time."

And that was enough.

Isaac said it so faintly that even Felix, who was one step behind him, couldn't hear.

A meaningless, lame death. That was all it amounted to. Felix stood near the door, arms crossed and frowning. If it were his choice, he wouldn't have ended his life so easily. He clicked his tongue, but that was just his way of thinking. Isaac finally got the closure he had been seeking.

Such was his chain of thoughts when Isaac came to him with the gun tucked away. Like when he'd entered this place, like when he'd pulled the trigger, his face was devoid of emotion. Felix studied his face for a while, then made a call to have his subordinates come and clean up the area. Isaac was silent the whole length of the staircase out of the basement.

"Thank you."

It was when they stepped outside the front doors of the house that Isaac's quiet voice broke the silence. Felix looked at Isaac. His face was relaxed. The expression made Felix want to kiss him, but he simply held their hands together. “Don’t mention it.”

It was a clear breezy day.

Isaac found out about it later, but Felix had already reported Cole as dead two days ago. He hadn’t considered reporting him as anything but, since he had no intention to keep him alive. To the public, it was announced that Cole had committed suicide once his widespread corruption was found out, and no one questioned it.

Afterwards, a thorough investigation was conducted into the naval officers who were complicit. For a time, the media headlined their misdeeds, and everything was in a jumble.

When the corruption case that had gripped the nation settled somewhat and things calmed down again, a letter arrived stating that Lieutenant Kaysid Patricks had been cleared of all charges and was approved for reinstatement.

But Isaac, who abandoned his past as a special ops agent and reopened his flower shop in downtown San Diego, tore up the letter and threw it away.

This all happened much later.

Chapter 14

After pulling the trigger on Cole, Isaac showered again, changed his clothes, and left for the hospital. Benjamin and Jessica had already gone through their exams with the doctor's observations showing no particular injuries or symptoms. Still, they were recuperating in the hospital while waiting for Isaac.

Isaac hurried into the hospital and took the elevator up to the suite, impatient. In his hand was a large bouquet of spring flowers for his mother and next to him stood Felix, who was holding something that would make anyone's eyes bug out.

In one hand was an assortment of Mickey Mouse balloons so large a child might float away holding them. In the other was an enormous Mickey Mouse doll. Isaac had quietly told him Benjamin might run away in fright from a doll twice his size, yet Felix was unfazed.

And somehow, he was also carrying a chocolate cake. He looked both ridiculous and unstable while carrying all those things. But the only thing Felix asked Isaac to carry was the bouquet for his mother.

The otherwise silent elevator was filled with the squeaky sound of balloon on balloon. Isaac glanced toward Felix and his pile of presents. "Are you all right?"

"I don't know. I feel nervous enough to die."

"What a strange thing for you to say."

"It's the truth." In an unusual display of nervousness, Felix was staring at the floor numbers in front of him. His eyes stayed focused as he mumbled gruffly, "What if Benjamin doesn't like me? He's going to be confused if I show up as his dad."

"You worry too much."

"Does your mother like me? You didn't say I'm with the mafia, right?"

"What does that matter?"

"It does matter. What would she think? She might think I'm less than an upright citizen."

"Like I said last time, you won't be one unless all the upright citizens die," Isaac responded under his breath and kept a straight face as he looked at him.

The higher the elevator's floor numbers went, the more nervous Felix became. He looked to be on the verge of biting his nails if it weren't for the things in his arms. Isaac eventually burst into laughter. Felix turned to face him, and at the same time, Isaac captured Felix's lips.

His plush lips were as sweet as ever. His breath, mixed with his scent and his pheromones, was also sweet enough to intoxicate. Isaac pushed his tongue between the slightly parted lips to placate him until the elevator dinged to a stop, and he sadly had to open his eyes and withdraw.

"There's nothing to worry about." Isaac lightly caressed Felix's shoulder before exiting the elevator. "You're already a great dad."

Felix followed, his face flushed. But Isaac had taken a step into the hallway when he encountered Tony and his men, and he instinctively stopped in his tracks.

"Ack—" Tony was the one who made the bizarre sound. His eyes went round with shock upon seeing Isaac and Felix. He gaped at Felix and the balloons, the enormous doll, and the cake he was holding. Then, finally, he noticed the marks flaunted on Isaac and Felix's necks, and let out a small, horrified shriek.

"You're in the way, move." Felix unceremoniously pushed Tony aside, who was in such a state of shock that he could only wobble his gaping mouth.

"W-What is the meaning of…" He ran up to them, blue in the

face. "No, let me hold the balloons."

Tony staggered, still reeling, looking back and forth at both of them. Felix callously bypassed him. "It's fine, move."

Tony whipped his head toward Isaac this time, but Isaac evaded him sheepishly, out of guilt. Since he wasn't the first to arrive, Tony would later pester him for answers.

The air in the hallway leading to the suite was heavy, much like the air in most hospitals. With Tony's men in black camped out in front of the room, the scene felt especially grim. Isaac discreetly covered his mark with his hand as he walked past them into the suite. Having everyone's eyes fixed on his neck was a bit more uncomfortable than he had expected.

Unlike Isaac, Felix marched forward, tense with nerves. He appeared completely unaware of the whispers around them. Of course, it might just be due to his careless nature rather than nerves.

"Benjamin?"

In any case, with everyone's eyes behind him, Isaac opened the door to the hospital suite and stepped inside, calling for Benjamin. The room was like a hotel room, spacious and comfortable, with a large bed where a child was playing with his toy truck alongside his grandmother. He looked up.

"Daddy?"

"Benjamin, Daddy is here."

"Wow! Daddy!" Benjamin's blue eyes widened when he saw Isaac. His small frame hurried down the bed and darted into his open arms. "It's Daddy! Daddy!"

Isaac held him tightly and finally let out a long sigh. Only with his nose buried in Benjamin's shoulder, smelling the candied scent and rubbing his cheek against the soft golden locks, did Isaac awaken to this reality. He'd returned. His child had finally come back to him.

"I'm sorry I'm late," Isaac looked Benjamin over and asked worriedly. "Nothing hurts? You're all right?"

Benjamin nodded with enthusiasm. "Yeah! I don't hurt anywhere!"

"That's great. I'm so proud of you," Isaac whispered in the child's ear.

Benjamin only giggled, happy to see his father. His heart raced with the sweet sound of laughter. How fortunate he was to have his child back in his arms. It was enough. With this, he felt like he'd been repaid in full.

Isaac held onto Benjamin for quite some time until the child looked up, saw the Mickey Mouse balloons Felix was holding, and shouted in joy. "Mickey Mouse! Balloons!"

There was no way he could not like his favorite mouse floating in the air as a bunch of balloons. The child's mouth fell open and his cheeks flushed red as he waved his short arms toward them.

Felix had been standing behind Isaac, watching him and Benjamin. He then extended his hand holding the balloons with a strained expression. But at that moment, Benjamin noticed the huge Mickey Mouse tucked under his arm and screamed, burying his face in Isaac's shoulder.

"It's scary!" Benjamin burst into shuddering tears.

Isaac had known this would happen. A Mickey Mouse doll that big, with a tail to boot, of course, he was frightened. Isaac turned to Felix, whose strained expression was turning stony. Then he went and opened the door, threw the enormous Mickey Mouse out into the hallway, and swiftly closed the door.

"Hmm, now, there's nothing." Felix showed him his empty hand and spoke fretfully. "See?"

"Doll…big…" The child still couldn't raise his head, sniffling in fright.

Felix slowly approached him. "I threw it out because it scared you. Look, we only have balloons. No, actually, we also have cake. You like chocolate cake, right?"

"Chocolate cake?" Benjamin was drawn to the mention of chocolate cake and lifted his big eyes. He was afraid of the huge

Mickey Mouse, but he also wanted the balloons and the chocolate cake, and he couldn't take his eyes off them.

"Now, here's your present." Felix extended the balloon string to Benjamin with a charming smile.

Benjamin cautiously grasped the string with his tiny hand. His eyes flicked to Isaac, then to his grandmother, as if seeking permission to take them.

Jessica came to Benjamin's side and encouraged him. "You should say, thank you."

Smiling shyly, Benjamin followed her example and mumbled, "Thank you."

"No problem," Felix answered in a slightly thick voice, staring at Benjamin.

Isaac watched him before asking about Jessica and handing her the large bouquet. "This is from Felix."

"Oh my, how gorgeous. Thank you." Jessica, who appeared in much better spirits than a few days ago, smiled brightly.

"Mother, I'm introducing him to you formally. He's the man who will become my partner, Benjamin's father." Isaac's characteristically placid voice cut through the tranquility of the room.

Jessica's eyes went wide over the bouquet in her arms. She looked toward Isaac and Felix.

"Let me introduce myself again," Felix said politely but with a tense face. "I am Felix Felice." Like before, he had surprisingly impeccable manners.

For a moment, Jessica looked back and forth between Isaac and Felix, confused, before settling into a calm, knowing smile. Then she hugged Felix. "Of course, so you are."

Felix stiffened, himself confused by her response, but when Jessica wrapped her small arms around him and patted his back, he leaned down and accepted her embrace.

Felix finished greeting Jessica and turned his gaze toward Benjamin, who was in Isaac's arms, leaning his head on his

shoulder and gripping the balloons. Once again, Isaac pressed his lips to the child's cheek and whispered:

"Benjamin, now you're going to have two dads."

"Two daddies?"

"Yes. This is your dad. You should say hello to him, right?"

Not quite understanding Isaac's explanation, Benjamin stared blankly at the man who looked exactly like him. In turn, Felix—who on any other day would have said "If you're going to pretend not to recognize me, give me those balloons back" or something typical—stared back.

Maybe his gaze was heavy on him, or maybe the child sensed something too, because Benjamin greeted him softly, "Hello."

Felix watched the child's behavior curiously, since he had expected him to hesitate and cry at the idea of having two fathers. But soon, he moved closer to Benjamin, bent down, and looked him in the eyes.

"Hello, Benjamin." His voice trembled unbeknownst to him. And yet his face was one of joy and happiness, of greeting his son for the first time.

"Hi," the child said again, and Felix reached out and tenderly swept his rough hand over his cheek.

Isaac wore a faint smile as he witnessed the birth of his new family. It was the happiest and fullest moment of his life.

Chapter 15

"Tony, I have to tell you something, but don't be surprised." Felix called Tony to the study the day after he came back to the mansion in San Diego.

Of course, he hadn't come back alone.

After being treated and discharged from the hospital, Felix brought back Isaac, who had been injured in his fight with Cole, as well as Benjamin, who was traumatized by getting involved in the incident. Even Jessica Parker was there!

Time flew by after that, leaving no time to communicate with each other, even if they wanted to. Until this morning, they both struggled to adjust to the chaotic atmosphere of the mansion. It was only in the afternoon that Felix was able to call him over.

The quietness of the afternoon matched the stillness of the study. As always, a large window showed the bright, clear sky and blue ocean waters, while the sun shone into the room, brightening it with its glow. Standing in the middle of this peaceful scene, Felix looked at Tony with a heavy expression.

"Is there something wrong?" Tony couldn't hide his nerves and swallowed loudly. Felix was someone who usually joked around no matter the situation, so for him to be acting serious like this had him stiff before a word was even uttered.

"To tell you the truth—"

"Please tell me."

After bringing Isaac and Benjamin back safely, the mood was as bright as ever, so Tony felt relieved. What could have caused this tension in the mood? Cold sweat dripped down Tony's back as he swallowed dryly once again.

"To tell you the truth," Felix slowly began to speak as he brushed his mouth with his hand, "Benjamin is my son."

The confession Felix spoke with all seriousness was so ridiculous it felt like a lie. It was so unbelievable that Tony, with his mouth hanging open, was left speechless. Felix, being as clueless as ever, kept going with his story.

"Isaac is that rotten—I mean, that omega I was looking for for the past four years. On top of that, he gave birth and took care of my son on his own! My God, does that even make sense? They were right beside me, but I was the only one who didn't know!"

Tony couldn't answer.

"Surprised? Of course you are. I was so surprised I almost fell over. I bet you're very shocked. But that's that, so you have to accept it for what it is."

Felix, who spoke in a fast cadence, patted Tony on the shoulder with a serious expression. Tony held back his need to cry and confess that everyone in the world had already noticed and suspected what was going on, except for the man himself.

No matter how oblivious Felix was, how could he only now realize Benjamin, who was basically just a clone of himself, was his son? And despite having slept with Isaac many times, he never once suspected him as the very same omega?

Though he didn't show it, Tony wondered if Felix still had doubts. Still, he seemed normal, so Tony felt like crying again, seeing Felix break his expectations.

"I see. Congratulations." Tony couldn't just talk about his concerns out loud. He felt something stuck in his throat as he swallowed back his tears and tried to speak. He pressed the bridge of his nose with his fingertips, trying to suppress his emotions.

He thought back to the time he tried to secretly prove Benjamin was indeed Felix's son with a DNA test, only to get caught and severely beaten by Isaac. How could he not want to cry in this situation?

"Why are you crying? That's why I told you before word gets out, so don't go dying on me now." Felix clicked his tongue in disapproval without understanding the full extent of Tony's feelings and inner struggles. His shoulders slumped in defeat. It was his fault for serving a man who didn't care about anyone else's opinions.

"So, that's why you suddenly marked him?" Tony managed to say, suppressing the weight of a never-ending wave of depression. He looked at Felix with pity as the other man simply shrugged.

"That's right. If I knew Isaac was an omega, I would have done it right away," Felix answered. "I wasted so much time."

He walked towards the table and poured himself a cup of hot tea brought by the maid. Tony stared at him in disbelief as Felix casually asked, "Do you want a cup?"

If he knew Isaac was an omega, he would have marked him right away? For a man who hated the idea of bonding or marriage, that was unbelievable. While it was obvious he was head over heels for Isaac, the fact that he went as far as marking him was astonishing.

While stunned, Tony managed to recall the events of a few days after Felix had marked Isaac, who suddenly returned and showed off the mark on his neck. Not only was Tony shocked, but everyone else around was as well, all staring at the mark with wide eyes.

Everyone wore expressions as if possessed. Rumors spread quickly, claiming he'd had no choice because of Benjamin. But even that didn't add up—Felix, who despised marriage and attachments, certainly had no desire for a child.

It didn't make sense for a man like that to mark Isaac just because of Benjamin. There had to be another reason for Felix to have bonded. It seemed that Felix was just deeply in love with Isaac, plain and simple. No, that was 100% the reason why.

Who knew someone, none other than Felix Felice, would become a fool hopelessly in love. Seeing a sight he had never imagined he would see gave him a strange feeling.

"Do you like him that much?"

On a hot summer day like this, a cold beer would've been the

ideal drink. Instead, Felix sipped his tea, eyeing the blank-faced Tony.

"Like what?"

"I mean, Isaac."

"Do I really like Isaac? Is that even a question?" Felix frowned as if he had just heard the dumbest question in the world.

Tony, having realized his mistake, sighed. He really did ask the most stupid question.

"This must be what you call a soulmate chosen by the heavens."

Tony smiled faintly as he muttered to himself, "There is no need to question anything anymore. Felix finally found his fated mate." It was almost amusing that the omega Felix had ground his teeth over was his mate all along—though, perhaps, it was all just fate.

Lost in thought, Felix sipped his tea and raised an eyebrow. What kind of nonsense was Tony talking about? Though the words were not unpleasant to hear, Felix eventually relaxed his brow.

"So anyway, find a jeweler or a gem cutter, anyone will do, and bring them here immediately."

Tony's eyes widened in shock at the sudden request. "A jeweler?"

"You can be so slow sometimes. We've already bonded, of course, we need to get married right away. Find someone who can craft the best wedding rings as quickly as possible. With Isaac's personality, he probably doesn't like anything flashy, so tell them to bring something simple."

"Oh, but there's definitely going to be a diamond on it. I'm going to personally pick the diamond, so bring someone who can show me a wide variety." Felix set the barely drunk tea down as he quickly made his request.

"I see…so it's for a wedding ring?" Dumbfounded, Tony could only repeat his words back to him like a parrot. To adjust to this new Felix, who had a 180-degree transformation, he would need some time.

"So then the wedding venue—" To suddenly get married like this, the amount of time and work it will take will be no joke. Tony was brought back to reality from imagining all the future events that needed to be meticulously planned at Felix's blunt response.

"Don't need one."

He looked at Felix in confusion. What did he mean he didn't need one?

"Isaac said he doesn't need a wedding ceremony. We're just going to do it at the County Clerk's office."

How unbelievable.

"T-The County Clerk's office? No matter how simple he wants it, the County Clerk's office?! At the very least, have a small wedding—"

"No, it's too much of a hassle," Felix spoke about his wedding with indifference. "I feel the same way as him."

Tony, as always, could not understand the man. If anyone could have a grand wedding, it would be Felix Felice. With a high-ranking mafia boss as his grandfather, and not only that, but he himself was a powerful arms dealer with significant influence over the military.

The wedding of someone of that caliber would definitely grab the attention of the world. It could probably even become a huge social event as well. But after everything, he just ignored it all and wanted to register his marriage at the county office? How did any of that even make any sense?

Of course, many people get married at county offices. Many couples, for various reasons, opt to skip formal weddings and register their marriages simply, then hold a ceremony at the same location.

The county office was a small building that handled marriage, divorce, birth, and death certificates. Beside this peanut-sized building was a small room that could fit around six people, a place where people were allowed to host a small wedding ceremony.

The city hall employee simply acted as a witness and helped

with a short ceremony. Usually, it was just the exchange of rings and vows, a very straightforward affair. Since it was still a wedding, some people came in wedding dresses and brought guests with them.

A wedding like this would be beneficial for people with limited time, or with no money, or those who require a modest wedding due to specific circumstances. But Tony had never imagined such a wedding would be held for Felix Felice.

"Then what about the guests?" Tony asked with a pale face.

"Guests? What the hell? Only Isaac and I will be going, so please refrain from spreading unnecessary rumors. Wait, that's not right. Mrs. Parker and Benjamin are planning to come, and Noah is insistent on coming as well." Felix hummed as he rubbed his prickly chin. More guests were attending than he initially expected.

"Were you not going to inform Mr. Felice?" Tony carefully asked. Hearing that made Felix turn his head towards him and narrow his eyes.

"I'll tell my grandfather later. After the ceremony is over."

"He will probably get upset."

How could he tell that old man that his favorite grandson, a wedding he had been looking forward to, was just registering it without a proper ceremony? And not only that, but telling him after everything was over? What was he even thinking?

"That's why you shouldn't spread nonsense and just keep your mouth shut. I'll take care of the rest."

Now that he thought about it, throughout his whole life, Felix did whatever he wanted. Tony could only let out a curt sigh. Whatever happened to the future of the Felice household, he could do nothing about it.

"Yes, sir." With his head bowed, Tony quietly left the room.

Only then did Felix gulp down his cold tea and walk toward his desk. Time had passed since the discussion about Isaac, and now he was left with a mountain of work to do.

Chapter 16

As soon as Felix turned into the hall on the second floor, he frowned at the sight before him: in front of Benjamin's half-open door, a deranged-looking guy was peeking inside. That crazy guy was none other than his cousin, Noah.

Felix silently walked up behind his cousin with a death glare. Without a thought in the world, Noah failed to notice him as he continued to stare into the room.

Was this crazy bastard for real?

Felix ground his teeth as he pondered the mental stability of his cousin. Previously, no matter how much they urged him to come out of his workroom, Noah would stay inside with his computer and gadgets glued to his side. Why in the world did he come all the way over here?

Furthermore, his appearance only accentuated his deranged look— with his long, messily tied-up hair, a baggy shirt, pants that revealed his skinny arms and legs, and slippers on his feet. He truly looked like a pervert creeping into Benjamin's room. It also didn't help the situation that he was occasionally sniffling.

If he properly took care of himself, he had the potential to be a charming omega. But in this state, looking like a crazy freak in front of his son's room, of course, Felix would be displeased.

Felix glared at Noah's unpleasant, sniffing face as he opened his mouth to scold him. His eyes wandered in the direction where Noah was staring, which dissipated the words of anger he was about to release.

In the middle of the Mickey Mouse-themed room was a red car-shaped bed, where Benjamin was sleeping with Isaac, holding onto him from behind. They must have dozed off.

Under the long rays of sunlight, the peaceful sight of Isaac and Benjamin sleeping caused Felix's lips to curve into a gentle smile. It was a truly lovely moment that tugged at his heartstrings.

Felix gazed at them gently, eyes full of love, having completely forgotten about Noah. But as Noah crept closer to the doorway, sniffling, Felix's attention snapped back to reality. His expression shifted—he frowned, and his sharp gaze cut back to Noah.

"What are you doing?" Felix growled softly.

Only then did Noah turn his head to look at Felix without any sign of surprise on his face. It seemed he knew who was behind him all along. "Damn…there's no other angel but him. How could a devil like you have such an angelic son? People might think you adopted him somewhere. Though you both do look too alike to say that. Anyway, my nephew is so cute I can't take my eyes off him!"

"What are you even saying? Crazy bastard."

Noah's grumblings were ridiculous.

"Your personality is absolute dog shit—but I'll admit, you're good-looking. My precious nephew looks just like you, and yet he's somehow even more adorable. Honestly, I wouldn't mind if he were shoved into my eye sockets, I'd still be pleased. I just pray to the gods he doesn't turn out to be a useless bastard like you. I swear, I'm going to pray every single day."

Felix's face contorted more with each of Noah's wild words, but nothing could be done since Noah was already completely captivated by three-year-old Benjamin, shifting his gaze from Felix to the sleeping boy. Felix instinctively raised his hand to strike, but changed his mind as he shoved his fist into his pocket, shook his head, and let out a sigh. Turning his gaze to the drowsy boy relaxed him again.

"He is beautiful," Felix muttered to himself.

"Hmph, I guess you at least have eyes." Noah clicked his tongue as if he had witnessed something disgusting.

Felix ignored it and continued to gaze at Isaac and Benjamin. A smile formed on his face. With bright tousled hair, mouth half open, and making cute noises, Benjamin was indeed very cute. The person Felix was focusing on and complimenting, unbeknownst to Noah, was Isaac.

Isaac was sleeping quietly, with no sign of emotion on his face. It was different from when he had been lying under Felix, eyes filled with tears and moaning. Even his peaceful look still made Felix's blood rush to his cock.

He is driving me crazy, Felix thought as he continued to gaze at Isaac, leaning against the door. Suddenly, Benjamin woke up and opened his bright blue eyes. With sleep still clouding his eyes, he looked around the room, looking as pretty as a doll.

"Ah, he woke up!" Noah exclaimed. "Whose adorable nephew is that? I swear I'll die from cuteness!"

Noah shoved his fist in his mouth, holding back his sobs. He exclaimed giddily how unbearably cute and adorable Benjamin was. Annoyed by him, Felix smacked Noah, who turned and glared at him. It didn't last long as Noah went back to waving his hand at Benjamin, looking like a fool.

Benjamin merely stared at Noah, unmoving. Whether it was due to lingering sleepiness or the fact that he'd only met Noah a handful of times and still wasn't used to his presence, but he seemed to have no motivation to approach him.

To counter that, Noah had a secret weapon he pulled out. Unknown was the source from which he had purchased such an item, but from his pocket emerged a massive lollipop that he shook in front of Benjamin. With newfound determination, Benjamin slowly climbed down the bed and waddled over to Noah.

Benjamin was curious about the lollipop and had approached Noah, but he wasn't sure whether to get closer. He looked up at Felix to find an answer. He could see the questions Benjamin had just by looking in his eyes, *Can I get close to Noah? Can I take the lollipop?*

"Go ahead." Felix gave a small nod. "He's your uncle."

At the same time, Noah, crouching by the door, smiled sweetly and spoke charmingly to coax Benjamin into approaching him.

If there was one thing the family had, it was exceptionally good looks.

Persuaded by Noah's gentle demeanor, Benjamin let his guard down. "Uncle?"

With an adorable voice clumsily mimicking his father's words, Noah's heart melted as his hands trembled with joy, handing over the lollipop. Benjamin's eyes widened in awe as he grabbed the gigantic lollipop with his tiny hands.

"Candy," Benjamin mumbled delightedly. With his white cheeks flushed, he was captivated by the large piece of candy.

"Benjamin, do you like candy?" As soon as Noah asked, the child nodded vigorously.

"I see, then your uncle will buy you a box of candy! Wait, not just candy, I'll buy you anything you want! What else do you like? Hmm?"

"A box of candy? His teeth will all rot," Felix grumbled.

Noah pretended not to hear, fluttering his eyes innocently. He was prepared to give Benjamin anything he wanted, even if it was all the stars in the sky.

Benjamin, who had been staring blankly at Noah, tilted his head and slowly replied, "Horsey."

"Horsey? Did you say horse? Damn it, just a horse wouldn't be enough! Of course, I'd have to buy an entire stable for my nephew who likes horses!"

"Enough, I already bought one for him."

"Already bought one? No, Felix, with your crappy tastes, you probably got a shitty one! Your uncle will buy you a top-tier horse! Let's go!"

Just as Felix was about to tell his cousin to shut up, he decided against it to avoid saying something inappropriate in front of his son. Meanwhile, Noah, who had won Benjamin over with candy and horse talk, tightly held his hand as they walked down the hall.

Benjamin, who was usually not shy around strangers, soon got excited and started following Noah. To Felix, he looked like a kidnapper luring an innocent child away with candy, which made him furrow his eyebrows. He decided to tell his son later that he should never follow someone just because they offered him candy.

Felix waited until the pair was out of sight and earshot before turning his head away. In the Mickey Mouse-themed room, Isaac, who had been lying motionless on the bed where Benjamin had been, was already awake and silently staring at Felix.

His obsidian black pupils remained fixed on him. Felix smirked and chuckled. With all this noise, there was no way he could have still been asleep. In fact, was he even truly asleep to begin with?

"I'm worried that he'll end up becoming spoiled," Isaac muttered in a concerned tone.

It wasn't just Noah, but the whole household that was crowded with dark-suited men, and they were utterly at a loss for how to react to the appearance of a doll-like, adorable child wandering around the mansion. Even Jack, who was still wounded from being shot, was limping around, insisting on watching Benjamin.

"Would his behavior really get worse just because of that? He deserves at least this much affection, so don't worry about it and come over here." Felix thought it was no problem, casually leaning against the doorframe and signaling Isaac over with his fingertips. Only then did Isaac start to get up from the bed.

"I was trying to sleep with Benjamin for once, but I never got a chance," Isaac murmured calmly, approaching Felix.

Felix stood before him, brushing through Isaac's slightly tousled black hair. "Still, you managed to get some sleep today."

Although it was only the second day since they arrived, Benjamin naturally slept with his grandmother. Even when Isaac, who rarely had the chance to spend time with him, coaxed him to sleep together for just one night, Benjamin remained firm in wanting to be with his grandma.

It wasn't that he disliked his father. Benjamin, who spent the entire day with Isaac, feeling more content than ever, would still look for his grandmother when it was time to bathe and go to bed. This was a natural routine for the child and a habit that was hard

to break.

After Benjamin was born, they had to move every couple of months. He had to inevitably frequent unfamiliar environments. Each time, this grandmother would soothe Benjamin to sleep whenever he was feeling anxious, leading to the habit of always sleeping with her.

Now that things were settled, Isaac had the opportunity to spend more time together and sleep beside Benjamin without much concern. Benjamin still insisted on sleeping next to his grandmother. While he fully understood his son's preference, he couldn't help but feel a little hurt.

In the end, Isaac settled for trying to take naps with Benjamin, lying beside him every day. This was also a challenge as his son, who was now over three years old, no longer took long naps. He often ran away, not wanting to sleep, and even when he did nap, he would wake up quickly.

"I know it's childish to want to turn back time, but I just regret missing the moments when Benjamin was a baby."

Those precious moments that would never come back passed in the blink of an eye. Being chased by Cole, Isaac missed the chance to spend more time with baby Benjamin, and by the time everything settled down, his child had already grown. It was a sad matter.

"Is that something to say in front of the person who hasn't seen Benjamin from birth to now, not even once?" Felix laughed bitterly, gently stroking Isaac's cheek with his fingertips.

Isaac, who had let out a soft gasp, stared blankly at Felix. The unexpected response briefly revealed his embarrassment.

"It's regrettable, but it's not like you can turn back time. Instead, let's focus on making the most of the countless moments to come."

"Felix."

"I'm just glad I did find you and Benjamin, even if it is a bit late. That's how I like to think of it," Felix whispered gently, his faint scent brushing Isaac's nose, sending a shiver through him.

In that moment, Felix lightly bit his lower lip, distracted by his pheromones. He swiftly gave Isaac a light peck, a gesture that passed by in a blink of an eye, but still left a lingering sensation.

"And think about it," Felix whispered as he licked his wet lips. "How much of a dutiful son Benjamin is."

"What do you mean by that?"

Felix lightly bit his lip again and promptly released it before continuing. "If Benjamin suddenly wants to sleep with you, I'll be stuck in a situation where I'd have to sleep alone, right? How lonely would I be sleeping without you? Don't you think so?"

"That's—"

"Such a great son, yes, a great son indeed. So, you should just sleep next to me, because I need you several hundred times more than Benjamin does," Felix muttered and, before Isaac could protest, quickly pressed his lips to his in one breath.

As if everything up until now had just been child's play, he locked on Isaac's jaw, straining his mouth and pushing himself in without hesitation.

His tongue explored every crevice, as if he intended to melt and consume the mucous membranes in his mouth. Suddenly, his breath caught, rising to the edge of his throat. Swallowing the excess saliva, Isaac reached out and wrapped his arms around Felix's neck. A soft, involuntary moan slipped out.

"Mmm—"

They say once you are bonded, you can no longer sense other pheromones, and you become addicted to the pheromones of your partner.

It seemed that saying was true, Isaac thought. Seeing how his body helplessly became hot and bothered just with one kiss, it was clear that it was indeed the case.

"Isaac, the sun hasn't even set yet. If you keep teasing me, it's going to be a problem."

It was Felix who was testing his patience, which was about to break. Isaac lifted his hazy eyes and looked into Felix's deep blue ones. Those eyes, like a vast ocean pulling him in, always

attracted him effortlessly.

"You're the one who started it."

"Well, that may be true," Felix whispered between kisses. "But what can I do when my hands just move on their own whenever I see you?"

"That's a rather poor excuse."

"An excuse? It's because my omega is just too irresistible. Besides, aren't we still newlyweds?" Felix simply responded with his usual composure, even if Isaac pretended to complain.

"Newlyweds, huh?" Just hearing the word made Isaac feel embarrassed.

Felix, whose shamelessness was unmatched, nibbled on Isaac's earlobe and whispered to him, "If we're not newlyweds, then what are we? It hasn't even been a month since we've bonded, we're still a fresh couple."

"Ah…"

"Also, if we're newlyweds, it's only natural for us to fuck like animals, all day and night."

As Felix nibbled on Isaac's earlobe, he traced it with the tip of his tongue. The obscene act drew soft moans from Isaac, unable to suppress the sounds spilling from his lips. Even the warmth of Felix's breath against his ear sent a tingle down the base of his spine. To be honest, whether the sun was still high in the sky or not, the desire to drag him straight to the bedroom was very high.

If they were alone, of course, they would have done just that and more…

"You tell me not to provoke you, but who's the one actually provoking here?" As Isaac shot him a slightly annoyed look, his breath somewhat ragged, Felix finally straightened his back and gave an awkward smile.

"See? I'm telling you, whenever you're around, I lose all self-control. It's a real problem."

Felix gently brushed Isaac's wet lips with his fingertips and closed his eyes. Isaac felt as if he might fall for that radiant smile all over again. No, it was probably already too late. Still, he had lost the will to argue further. To believe someone could make him so weak was nothing short of cheating.

Felix suddenly grabbed Isaac's hand and started walking down the hallway. With one hand in his pocket and the other firmly holding Isaac's wrist, he kept a cheerful expression.

"Come with me. I came here to show you something, but we got a bit distracted."

"Show me something? Can you at least tell me what it is beforehand?"

"You'll know when we get there."

Even as he asked the question, Isaac vaguely sensed that Felix wouldn't give him a proper answer anyway. So, he stopped asking and decided to follow him obediently. Felix's demeanor reminded him of a mischievous child eagerly anticipating a reaction from a surprise party, which felt oddly innocent. It was even somewhat cute. Besides, as Felix said, he would find out once they got there anyway.

"Looks like we've arrived."

Shortly after, they stopped in front of a reception room. Inside was a space typically designed to welcome guests, and faint sounds suggested that someone was already there, waiting.

Just as Isaac was wondering if a guest had arrived, Felix pushed the door open without hesitation. Inside the reception room, Tony and a middle-aged man whom Isaac didn't recognize stood there. The man politely greeted them as soon as Felix and Isaac stepped inside.

"Nice to meet you, sir. I am Christopher, a jeweler." The man's appearance was immaculate, with no flaws to be found. His attitude, expression, and even his accent were flawless. He looked every bit like a merchant who dealt solely with the wealthy.

A jeweler? Isaac looked at Felix in confusion, but he decided to just listen to what the jeweler had to say. After a brief introduction, Christopher opened three suitcases in front of Felix.

Each of the opened suitcases was lined with luxurious black velvet. In one case, various types of rings and gemstones were

displayed, while the other suitcase contained a set of women's necklaces, bracelets, and rings. The third held small bracelets and various other accessories, all with sophisticated designs and top-tier gemstones that were enough to leave one in awe just by looking at them.

To bring three suitcases like that… Felix must really be something, Isaac thought to himself, but his gaze shifted to wonder where his guard might be. After all, a jeweler wouldn't bring such expensive items and casually stroll in alone.

Even though Felix didn't noticeably turn his head, only slightly shifting his gaze, he immediately picked up on Isaac's mood and told him off. "Isaac, stop worrying about unnecessary things and look at the rings first."

Usually, the man would miss even the most obvious hints, but when it mattered, he was surprisingly quick to notice.

"Are you, by any chance, buying a wedding ring?" Isaac asked casually, absentmindedly glancing at the case with dozens of rings lined up.

"Of course I am. Who was it that criticized me for proposing without a ring in the first place?"

Isaac couldn't help but chuckle softly at his complaining voice, which kept grumbling. As he always thought, Felix was a man with a long-standing grudge.

"Well, in that case, a design that's comfortable to wear would be best. Something that's not too large, heavy, or flashy. Since I probably won't take it off once I put it on, it should be something that won't interfere with my daily life." As Isaac calmly explained what he wanted, he stopped when he noticed Felix staring at him. The gaze that lingered on him was intense.

Before he could even ask why, Felix lowered his head and pressed his lips to Isaac's ear. "If you keep choosing to say such cute things, it might become troublesome."

"The sun will set soon, and I've made plans to listen to you cry all night long."

The voice, filled with laughter, lingered in his ear. The secretive whisper sent a shiver down his spine.

"That has to be the most terrifying threat I've ever heard."

"You heard me, right? Choose a design that's as comfortable and simple as possible. However, ensure that you can add at least one diamond." Felix, ignoring Isaac's complaint, picked up a platinum ring designed with a flat shape and space in the center to set a gemstone. "Oh, this one isn't half bad."

It was a simple yet elegant design, with delicate engravings along the edges. Christopher praised Felix for his good taste and continued with a detailed explanation about the ring, while Isaac simply stared in silence. Not only was the ring Felix had chosen impressive, but all the rings on display were luxurious and refined, to the point where they failed to evoke any emotion.

To be honest, anything would have been fine, whether it had gemstones or not, platinum, gold, or silver; it didn't matter. Just being able to wear the same ring as Felix was enough for him. Any design that he could wear comfortably all day long was fine, but it seemed Felix didn't feel the same way.

Instead of choosing a ring, Isaac simply watched Felix. It was better to match Felix's taste rather than his own, which was more basic. He preferred observing Felix carefully examine and select the ring, rather than focusing on the unfamiliar rings and gemstones.

Isaac had been watching Felix, but suddenly realized there were two more cases, and he shifted his gaze. "What are those over there for?"

Felix, who had been carefully trying on a ring on his left ring finger, looked up at him. Then, as he glanced over the cases Isaac was examining, he huffed "Ah. I'm going to get a bracelet for Benjamin. And for Mrs. Parker—actually, I should start calling her 'Mother' now, right? I'm thinking of giving her a jewelry set. I'm not sure about her tastes, so recommend something for me."

The answer was incredibly simple, yet Isaac still found it hard to grasp.

"There's no need to go that far," Isaac replied indifferently,

furrowing his brow. He had never wished for such luxurious gifts. He also knew that his mother was not the type to wear such extravagant accessories.

Despite his protest, Felix stayed firm. “Giving gifts is my freedom and decision; you have no right to stop me.”

Isaac, suddenly speechless, let out a quick sigh.

“A GPS will be embedded in Benjamin’s bracelet. Just in case, so we can find him anywhere.”

“That’s not a bad idea.”

“If it’s hard for you to pick out a gift for your mother, I’ll handle it myself. Again, there’s no need to feel burdened. I have enough money to enjoy a lifetime of luxury, and of course, half of it will be yours.”

Felix’s sudden remark left Isaac dumbfounded.

Money? It was something he had never even considered in his life. As always, Felix kept speaking casually.

“While we’re living together, there’s no doubt you will have money, and if I die first, all my assets will go to you and Benjamin.”

“Though it will never happen, if we got a divorce, half of my assets would go to you,” Felix explained lightly, as if joking, but Isaac still just stared at him with a confused expression. “So, whatever I do for you, just think of it as me spending your money. There’s no way you’d think I’m a waste of your money, right?”

Suddenly, it occurred to him that, for someone like Felix, marriage could be more complicated because of his wealth. Maybe that’s why wealthy people tend to marry others from similar backgrounds. Various thoughts swirled in his mind.

Sensing Isaac’s inner turmoil, Felix let out a short sigh and said, “Isaac, it seems like you’re getting the wrong idea again, so I’m telling you this in advance.”

“What is it?”

“You can deny it all you want, but I know you’re filthy rich now even without me.”

“I make enough to not starve, but rich? That’s a bit—”

“You are rich.”

He was a former Navy lieutenant. Additionally, as a DEVGRU special forces operator who faced daily life-threatening risks, his hazard pay was significant. The country offered various benefits to its soldiers, and even after death, pensions were provided to their families.

Although he had been discharged from the military, that issue was expected to be resolved soon, so he didn't have to worry about making a living. Still, he wasn't at the level of what Felix called filthy rich. Isaac stared at him, looking utterly confused.

"Sorry, but Noah did a little digging around," Felix confessed, shrugging his shoulders slightly, feeling a bit awkward.

"Dig around? What do you mean?"

Felix smiled faintly, facing Isaac's puzzled expression, as if he had anticipated this. Then, lowering his voice, he continued, "He said he looked up what happened to Cole Patricks's assets. I guess that guy must have been really bored. Or maybe he was dying to know."

Cole Patricks.

Felix mentioned a name Isaac hadn't expected to hear. Without realizing it, Isaac narrowed his eyes. It was a subject about someone he no longer wanted to hear about, so he tried to stop him, but Felix kept speaking without a care.

"To cut to the chase, they said his entire fortune in the U.S. will be seized by the military. It was a predictable outcome."

Given the vast scale of the corruption he committed within the Navy, seizing all his assets wasn't really surprising. It was just the expected course of action. But just as Isaac thought there was nothing new in what Felix was saying, the man continued.

"But no one knew that he had hidden assets in a Swiss account."

"A Swiss account?"

"He acted like a dog and did unsightly things to secretly save up lots of money. I don't understand why he hoarded it so desperately when he wasn't even going to take it with him when he died. Maybe his dream was to make you filthy rich?" Felix's sarcastic words weren't easy to understand.

"What are you even..."

"Kaysid Patricks. Did you forget that you're legally Cole's son? There's no one else legally related to Cole, so that means you'll be the only heir who can inherit Cole Patricks's fortune."

Isaac's mind couldn't seem to sort itself out. He was simply dazed. The inheritance from Cole was something he never expected. It was as if money just fell from the sky.

However, it wasn't necessarily a good feeling. The fact that it was the inheritance money of Isaac's adoptive father, whom he had killed with his own hands, didn't sit well with him. Moreover, the money was gathered through harming many people and corrupt actions, which made it unsettling.

"Maybe he gathered his wealth to at least pay off some of his sins after death. Think of it as that."

Once again, Felix, with scary accuracy, sensed the discomfort and gently stroked Isaac's cheek to comfort him.

"Noah will handle the preparations. You just need to sign later," he whispered sweetly, trying to reassure him that everything would be fine, that it was money he truly deserved.

But Isaac couldn't hide his discomfort. "The money I receive, I could donate it, right?"

"Hmm? Well, what you do with the inheritance is completely up to you."

"In that case, I'll use part of it to reopen the flower shop that Cole destroyed, then donate the rest." For someone who appeared to be lost in thought, Isaac made a surprisingly quick and straightforward decision.

Felix raised an eyebrow, looking surprised.

"I have no reason to accept dirty money, and I refuse to take the inheritance without seeing how tainted it is. I just need enough to reopen the flower shop."

"Do you think I can't help you open a flower shop and really feel the need to use Cole's money? If you feel uncomfortable about taking it, just donate all of it."

"It's not that. Since it was Cole who destroyed the shop, it's better to reopen it with his money. I deserve at least that much compensation," Isaac replied stubbornly while Felix shrugged.

"Whatever you want," he said calmly. "Though I didn't know you were thinking of reopening the flower shop."

Isaac couldn't hide his awkward expression at Felix's remark. "It's my dream."

"Well, it's good to have dreams, whatever they may be," Felix said. "I'm actually relieved. I was worried you might want to go back to the military."

"No way. I have no intention of returning there. The reason I enlisted in the Navy was because of Cole. If it weren't for him, I wouldn't have even entered the Academy."

A faint shadow crossed Isaac's face as he unconsciously remembered the past. Felix gently stroked his shoulder to bring him back to the present. Then, with a glance, he directed Isaac's attention to the rings and accessories still spread out on the table.

As the conversation with Felix dragged on, Isaac had momentarily forgotten, but across from them, the jeweler and Tony were still standing, waiting for them. Isaac quickly rubbed his cheek with his palm, his face flushing with embarrassment, and cleared his throat.

"It seems I've taken up too much of your time. I apologize," Isaac mumbled.

"No, it's fine," Christopher answered with a kind smile.

Shaking off any personal feelings, Isaac gathered his thoughts, determined to wrap up the matter quickly. Even if he planned to leave the ring selection to Felix, he figured he should at least pretend to show some interest.

Felix, unusually cheerful today, eagerly began picking out rings and various other jewels, his eyes gleaming with excitement. Isaac, making a token effort to browse the contents of the suitcase, quickly lost interest. Instead, he found himself watching Felix—whose blue eyes, he thought, sparkled far more brightly and beautifully than any of the gems.

Chapter 17

"Felix!" Isaac's voice rose before he even realized it. While drying his hair with a towel after his shower, Felix, who barged in like a thug, suddenly hugged him from behind.

After moving into Felix's mansion, they had been sharing a room and bed for just over a week. Even in that short time, Isaac often felt uncomfortable about living with someone else.

It wasn't just the discomfort of sharing his space with someone else, but there were times when Felix's presence made him uneasy. Felix would definitely get upset if he knew, but unfortunately, it was the truth.

For example—getting tackled while changing clothes without warning, lying down for a moment to rest only to be suddenly overwhelmed with intense kisses, or, like now, being hugged the moment he stepped out of the shower…

"How many times have I told you not to do this? Stop acting like some horny animal. Ugh—!"

"Sorry to disappoint you, but I am a horny animal."

No matter what was said, it was useless against an alpha in heat. Felix gripped Isaac's chest tightly and pressed his mouth to the nape of his neck, sucking deeply on the spot where his mark lay.

"Isn't it partly your fault for coming out of the shower in front of me so defenselessly when I'm this horny, hmm?"

His voice was a blend of playfulness and laughter, but he clenched his teeth so tightly it looked downright painful.

"Defenseless? So, does that mean I should be on guard from the moment I step out of the shower?"

"You should never let your guard down."

"Then, would it be alright if I start being cautious now and switch my stance?" Isaac retorted sharply, tightly gripping Felix's wrist, while he continued to grope his chest.

In response, Felix grabbed Isaac's chin, turned it, and lightly kissed him.

"No, that's not it," he whispered, licking his wet lips. His voice sounded sickeningly sweet.

It was so sweet and intoxicating that it immediately calmed the slight panic and rush of emotions Isaac experienced, to the point that even he was surprised.

"Isaac, didn't I tell you repeatedly that even if I have you again and again, my thirst for you will never be quenched?" Felix whispered, then gave him another, more urgent kiss. "It's driving me insane."

Once Isaac's head turned back, he sucked on his lips, and without hesitation, he slid his tongue into his parted mouth. The sweet, lingering kiss quickly became passionate. As the kiss filled with blatant desire continued, a warm heat rose from Isaac's lower abdomen. A moan also unconsciously escaped his throat.

Perhaps it was now a reflexive response. Like Pavlov's dog, the moment the kiss began, it felt as if a hidden switch somewhere in his body had turned on, and inside, it seemed as though a heat was boiling.

Overwhelmed by heat and desire, Isaac let out a ragged breath as Felix moaned into their interlocked lips. Their heavy breathing mingled in perfect sync, creating a moment of raw intimacy. Felix, who had been tightly holding Isaac from behind, bent forward and laid him face down on the sink. His chest remained pressed firmly against Isaac's bare back, not leaving even an inch of space between them.

The weight of Felix's body made Isaac's breath catch. He stayed where he was, obedient and still, only turning his head slightly to glance up at Felix. In response, Felix twisted one of Isaac's arms behind him and pinned it to his waist.

Suddenly, Isaac remembered that most suspects are arrested in

this position. They often hit their heads on the hood of the police car while their hands are being cuffed...

"Ah, this is a bit—"

Isaac, who had mostly been the one capturing or killing enemies rather than being captured himself, let out a low moan at the unfamiliar position. Seeming to notice Isaac's discomfort,

Felix, while still holding his arm down, pressed his lips to Isaac's ear and whispered darkly. "Isaac, I'm telling you this now because I might lose control, and I don't want you to fight me. Can you stay still, no matter what I do to you, hm?"

"Hmm. I don't know what you're talking about, but you could just not do it?"

"But I want to do it, that's why."

Even when he argued, Felix maddeningly acted as if he didn't hear a word. Isaac couldn't tell what he was planning. He let his chest and cheek rest against the spotless, gleaming sink countertop, lightly biting his lip.

He hadn't expected to be pounced on at the sink the moment he stepped out of the shower. And hadn't they just been together this morning? No, that wasn't it. Ever since they bonded, they'd been having sex relentlessly, every single day, to the point of exhaustion.

Like he said, they were in the honeymoon phase, but was it really okay to do it this much? At this rate, Isaac felt as if his body would turn into mush and he wouldn't be able to keep going. After all that, you'd think he'd had enough and started waiting in bed like a good boy, but for some reason, Felix just kept pouncing on him more and more, like a hungry beast.

Even now, it was the same. His tongue was greedily licking the droplets still left on his shoulder that he hadn't had a chance to wipe off yet.

"Did you know? Since you stopped taking your suppressants, your pheromones have been getting stronger. Just being near you has become unbearable. I'm starting to worry about someone else catching your scent."

Felix, licking and biting at Isaac's damp shoulder, slowly trailed down the curve of his spine. He nibbled and sucked hard enough to leave vivid kiss marks in his wake. Heat flared across Isaac's skin, and a dizzying current surged through his nerves, rippling through every inch of his body.

Even though it happened every day, the intensity of it never faded.

"In that case, it seems like it would be better for me to start taking suppressants again."

Felix bit down hard on Isaac's waist. So hard that the marks of his teeth were clearly visible. Isaac let out a short groan, flinching as his body trembled.

"Why do you keep spouting nonsense? You've been living with the suppressant all this time, and now you're thinking of taking it again?"

"Then—*Ah!*"

What can I do?

The words dissolved on Isaac's lips before he could speak them. Felix took his finger into his mouth with a wet, squelching sound. As if mimicking oral sex, he deepthroated it, licking and sucking greedily, his tongue sliding between each finger with deliberate care.

Lying face down on the sink, his hands and arms hidden from view, the sensation of having his fingers sucked sent a chilling electric current coursing from his fingertips to his toes. It felt as if his entire body were being drawn in, the intensity making goosebumps rise across his skin.

Oh God, when did his fingers become such a sensitive erogenous zone?

"Learn to control it," Felix said firmly, watching as Isaac grew more and more dazed.

Then, with his breath becoming heavier from the rising heat, he gently ran his fingers down Isaac's back. His fingers, slowly tracing down as if counting each vertebra, eventually reached the bath towel wrapped around Isaac's waist.

As if he'd been waiting for this moment, he grabbed the towel and yanked it off in one swift motion. The sound of it hitting the floor echoed through the room—loud, careless, almost obscene.

"To control my pheromones…" Isaac paused, then suddenly exclaimed, "Ugh—n-not there, Felix!"

Isaac, who had been breathing heavily, suddenly raised his voice when Felix unexpectedly bit his ass with his sharp teeth. No, it wasn't just biting. Felix blatantly grabbed his ass, spreading it apart and sliding his wet tongue down the middle.

An uncontrollable cry tore from his lips, but Felix paid it no mind. He traced slow, deliberate circles around the swollen, slick entrance—already hot and hypersensitive. A helpless moan escaped as Isaac's shoulders trembled again and again.

"F-Felix, wait!" Flustered, Isaac called out to him in urgency. But the grip on his arm—twisted behind his back—only tightened. With no other choice, he clutched the edge of the sink with his free hand, holding on so tightly that the veins in his arm bulged. If he didn't, it felt like the strength would drain from his body and he'd collapse entirely.

And yet, those wet, obscene sounds kept filling his ears. The sound of Felix—of all people—licking and sucking between his ass.

It was unreal.

"Come to think of it, I've been in and out of here countless times, but I've never actually tasted it, have I?"

As soon as Felix's deep, husky voice pierced his ears, all doubt vanished instantly. With each whisper, his hot, moist breath sent shivers down his sensitive skin. The sensation of his blunt tongue rubbing against every fold was vivid. It felt like his head was about to explode.

"Ah, stop…"

"If I had known it was this delicious, I would've eaten it sooner. Well, I guess every time we did it, I was so desperate to get inside you that I lost all patience."

Inside the entrance where Felix was greedily sucking and

pulling, fluid pooled, so much so that even Isaac could feel it. His waist trembled uncontrollably as Felix mindlessly licked the fluid that seeped out, treating it as if it were sweet honey. His vision darkened, his mind spun, and yet his body burned with an unbearable heat.

Isaac's panting grew more frantic. This was because Felix's tongue, which had been sucking and biting as if determined to melt every tender part of his entrance, had begun to push into the now thoroughly dampened hole.

The sensation was nothing like when Felix's cock entered him. This was entirely different. A hot tongue rubbed and swirled against the inflamed inner walls, while sharp teeth occasionally grazed the skin, leaving behind faint marks. It was strange—utterly foreign—and it sent violent shivers down his spine. It felt as if some unknown creature were writhing inside him. Moans, almost like screams, burst from his throat without warning.

His legs, barely holding him up, visibly shook. He couldn't even find the words to beg Felix to stop. No language would come. All he could do was gasp through parted lips, his breath ragged and uneven.

On top of it all, Felix's pheromones had already begun to affect him—subtly, insidiously—before Isaac even realized it. The scent of a hyper-dominant alpha, and more than that, the very alpha who had marked him, was intoxicatingly sweet. It was like inhaling a potent stimulant. His body burned with such intensity that his vision began to blur and flicker.

Each time Felix's thick tongue slid against his inner walls, pressing deep, Isaac's back arched in response, trembling uncontrollably. His cock had long since hardened, flush against his stomach, and precum now dripped steadily to the floor below.

"Hah, ugh! Felix, please!"

His hand, still twisted behind his back and held by Felix, twitched nervously. However, Felix showed no sign of letting go, so Isaac anxiously clenched and unclenched his sweaty palm, growing more agitated.

"Ah, ahhh—!"

How long was he planning to keep this up?

Isaac feared his entrance might melt before this maddening act was over. Or maybe that had been Felix's intention all along: to break him down completely.

The obscenely wet sounds, the relentless movement of the tongue swirling inside him, and the way his entrance twitched in response… everything felt disturbingly vivid, as if he could see it happening right before his eyes.

It was so vivid, it was almost terrifying.

He felt like he was going to die. Yet despite being fully aware of Isaac's state, Felix feigned ignorance continuing to suck him in mercilessly while his free hand gripped Isaac's throbbing, rock-hard cock.

A moan escaped as his back arched instinctively. But Felix's hand showed no mercy. The moment he wrapped his fingers around him, he began stroking fast and hard, as if determined to push him over the edge right then and there.

"Ah, no, Felix, u-ugh, you c-can't anymore!" Isaac's hunched shoulders trembled like a leaf.

Saliva dripped from his half-open mouth, too slack to close, and tears streamed from his reddened eyes. The stimulation was overwhelming—far beyond what he could endure. At last, a choked cry escaped him as he came, his release splattering in thick, obscene streaks across the sink and floor. Dazed and drained from the climax, Isaac slumped forward, utterly spent.

But Felix didn't stop.

His hand, now slick with semen, continued to work Isaac's cock, stroking and squeezing despite its softening state. And all the while, his tongue kept moving inside him, relentless and unyielding.

Isaac's face was flushed red, his breath ragged and uneven, unable to even register the lingering waves of his climax. From head to toe, his body was drenched in Felix's pheromones. The entrance—and inner walls—that Felix continued to devour felt

like they no longer belonged to him, as if they were melting away entirely.

His mind was a blank, white haze, teetering on the edge of collapse. Amid his frantic panting, a flicker of anxiety broke through:

Would he be able to keep himself from going insane from this stimulation?

"It's strange, isn't it? Even though I'm with you every day, I'm always hungry for you. The moment I see you, my rationality just flies away," Felix, who had finally lifted his head from Isaac's soaked ass, muttered in a low voice. "Honestly, it really does feel like I've turned into a mindless animal."

His deep, husky tone sent shivers down Isaac's spine. It was a voice dripping with raw, unrelenting desire. Isaac slowly lifted his eyes from his slumped-over state to look back at Felix. His pupils, already dilated, unfocused, and reddened eyes, gave off the seductive appearance Felix always talks about.

It was when Felix's gaze met Isaac's dazed eyes midair that his voice dropped even lower. "Relax, Isaac."

Isaac couldn't even bring himself to meet his gaze. With a firm grip, Felix spread his ass wide—and in one swift motion, thrust his swollen, rock-hard cock deep inside.

A silent scream tore from Isaac's lips. Even though his entrance had been thoroughly softened from the relentless licking and sucking, the pressure was still overwhelming; that feeling of being stretched to the limit, of being completely filled, no matter how many times they did this, never got easier.

"F-Felix…Agh—!"

Isaac clutched the edge of the sink, trembling. It had only just begun, yet the corners of his eyes were already wet with tears. Only wordless, pleading sounds slipped from his lips. His body no longer felt like his own. Overwhelmed by Felix's pheromones—his scent, his gaze, his voice, his touch, the relentless rhythm of his hips—Isaac could do nothing but sob helplessly.

Felix, too, was far from composed. Unlike Isaac, he was

teetering on the edge of madness in his own way. He clenched his teeth, trying to rein in the feverish thrill surging through him, but it was no use. Still gripping Isaac's wrist tightly, he yanked him closer and slammed his hips forward in a single, forceful motion, lifting Isaac's waist as he drove in deeper.

With a thrust, Felix's coarse pubic hair pressed against Isaac's ass as the deeply embedded cock ruthlessly thrust into his abdomen without mercy. Ignoring Isaac's trembling moans, Felix slowly pulled back and then plunged in again, repeating the motion over and over.

"Ah, aah, hah! Felix, stop, stop—"

The sensation of Felix's cock plunging deep inside him felt as if it were carving out a new hole, tearing through his innermost walls with ruthless force. With every sob and shake of his head, beads of sweat dripped onto the sink, and desperate, breathless pleas tumbled from Isaac's parted lips.

But Felix only moved harder, faster—his thrusts growing more brutal and unrelenting. The obscene sound of skin slapping against skin echoed throughout the spacious bathroom, a rhythm too intense for Isaac to endure.

His face flushed red, twisted with emotion, Isaac could do nothing but sob completely undone, unable to contain the flood of sensation surging through him.

Then Felix, who had been watching Isaac intently, suddenly stilled. "Isaac, you can't make a face like that."

As if savoring the moment, he let his gaze linger, eyes heavy with something unreadable. A quiet laugh escaped him as he ran his fingers along Isaac's slick, sweat-drenched back, tracing slowly up the curve of his spine.

A deep smile spread across Felix's striking face; it was dazzlingly beautiful, yet laced with something dark, something dangerous. The sight of it sent a cold shiver down Isaac's spine.

"How can you cry with such a sexy expression? It's like you really want me to become a horny beast."

Despite the words that instinctively stirred fear, Felix smiled

warmly as he bent down to embrace Isaac from behind. With a low, possessive sound, he bit into the marked spot on Isaac's neck, releasing a flood of raw, unrestrained pheromones. The effect was immediate—Isaac was engulfed, his senses stolen by the overwhelming heat, his mind spinning on the edge of unconsciousness.

Perhaps that was why, from deep within the entrance wrapped tightly around Felix's cock, a sudden gush of wet fluid spilled out, streaming down Isaac's trembling thighs. His toes, barely grazing the floor, curled involuntarily as ragged, unfiltered moans poured from his parted lips.

"Isaac, what are you…Fuck, you really—!"

Felix held the trembling Isaac tightly from behind, his jaw clenched. Then, as if he could no longer restrain himself, he began thrusting with fierce intensity. The lewd sound of wet skin colliding echoed loudly through the room, rhythmic and relentless.

It felt like Isaac's mind had completely unraveled. Whatever thin thread of rationality remained had snapped. Drenched in Felix's pheromones and consumed by pleasure, both his body and mind no longer felt like his own, and that was fine. This overwhelming ecstasy, something only Felix could give him, was intoxicating.

Gasping for breath, Isaac spread his legs wider and accepted him without resistance. As if there were no other choice, he offered his body in full—sobbing, moaning, giving in.

And just like every night before, another endless night passed between them.

Chapter 18

Isaac slowly blinked his heavy eyelids open. His vision was blurred, everything hazy. At some point, it seemed he had blacked out. Fragmented memories drifted to the surface—his legs wrapped around Felix's waist, arms clinging to his neck, his own voice whimpering softly in surrender. But right now, none of it made sense. He had no idea what was happening.

The gentle sound of splashing water echoed around him.

He was lying on his back, pressed against Felix's chest in a wide bathtub, but he had no memory of how he got there. It felt like pieces of time had vanished—like he was suffering from some strange memory loss.

"When did you fill the tub?" The voice asking the question was hoarse and cracked.

"Just now." Felix calmly repeated the motion of scooping water with his hand and letting it drip over Isaac's chest.

"If I keep doing this every day, I'm afraid my body won't be able to handle it," Isaac muttered weakly, resting his head on Felix's shoulder. In response, a soft laugh followed, and Felix's cool lips brushed against his cheek.

"I want to take it slow, but it's difficult to control myself every time."

"Excuses."

"Isaac, even when I see you normally, my blood starts to race and I feel like I'm losing my mind," A faint whisper slipped from the lips, brushing against Isaac's cheek. "But when I see you all disheveled, looking like pure sin, I completely lose control."

Isaac tried to subtly turn his head away, but escaping from Felix's firm grip on his chin proved to be a difficult task.

"When you're covered in my cum, and your entrance is melting and dripping, yet you still cling to me and bite down, and on top of that, you sob with those hazy eyes. How am I supposed to stay calm? Look, even now your face is turning red again."

Felix's shameless whispers, filled with embarrassing words, made Isaac blush even more. As his cheeks flushed bright red, Felix, like a beast ready to devour him, licked them with his tongue.

"Who could possibly doubt you're an alpha, saying such beastly things like it's nothing?"

"It's not like you didn't know what I was." Felix smiled as he lightly bit Isaac's ear, as if all the sucking and licking wasn't enough.

In the end, Isaac closed his eyes, surrendering his body completely to him.

Alphas were indeed more instinct-driven than betas. With their distinct rut cycles, one could argue they were closer to beasts, especially Felix, a top-tier alpha even among his kind. That was why, when it came to sex, he was relentlessly persistent and utterly beast-like.

The problem was that Isaac had to bear the full brunt of it alone.

It had been only a little over a week since they'd begun fucking daily, yet Isaac was already exhausted to the point of collapse. Of course, being marked, he was swept away by ecstasy in the moment, his hips moving in sync with Felix's without thought. But once the haze lifted, he was left struggling to move his weakened limbs—a minor complaint, perhaps, but a constant one.

"No matter how I look at it, having sex like this every day is impossible," Isaac said, exhaling deeply, as if making an announcement.

The rough hand that had been caressing his chest paused abruptly.

"What do you mean by that?"

"You heard me. Even now, it's hard to move my limbs. I have things to do tomorrow, and if this keeps up, I might stay in bed or collapse."

He had always been confident in his stamina—more so than anyone else—but being driven to the point of collapse was another matter entirely. Isaac clicked his tongue.

For someone who had endured a whole week of sleepless training as a basic requirement, it was rare for his stamina to be drained so quickly. That alone spoke volumes about how excessively Felix had pushed him. The most frustrating part, however, was that Felix seemed perfectly fine.

"You can't be serious." Felix looked down at Isaac, who was resting his head on his shoulder. His face showed a mix of sadness and hopelessness, as if everything had fallen apart around him.

"Don't look at me like that, it's the truth," Isaac admonished. "So, let's decide now. I can't do it every day. It indeed feels so good, I lose my mind every time, but I can't keep ruining my body like this."

"What do you propose?"

"How about once every three or four days?"

At Isaac's firm decision, Felix let out a low groan, and his already gloomy face turned ashen. But Isaac didn't even glance his way. He couldn't shake the thought that if his body gave out, he'd be the only one suffering.

"Think about it like this, Isaac," Felix said after a moment of brooding silence. Isaac quietly turned his gaze to meet his. "Wouldn't it just be better to do it every day?"

"What do you mean by that?"

"Let's say we do it once every three or four days, like you said," Felix said. "When we finally get down to it, I won't be able to guarantee what I'll do—or how far I'll go—after being pent up that long."

"Just holding back for three or four days won't make much of a difference. We used to do it just once a week, and it was fine…" Isaac ran a wet hand through his hair, muttering the words like a sigh, then suddenly stopped. The memory of when they used to fuck only once a week, as per their contract, surfaced without

warning.

Back then, Felix had stuck to the agreement with unwavering discipline. Once a week, he'd take Isaac up on his offer and fuck him with such intensity it was almost inhuman—relentless, for an entire day without rest. The following morning, Isaac would either show up at the shop half a day late or spend it in a daze, barely able to function.

"You really did fuck me relentlessly," Isaac muttered unconsciously.

Felix curled his lips into a smile, clearly in a good mood. He, too, ran his wet hand through Isaac's hair, water droplets trailing from his forehead.

It was undeniably a difficult situation—being marked and partnered with a hyper-dominant alpha. Maybe doing it a little every day was better than going all out once every three or four days.

Lying still, Isaac drifted into thought.

"There's something that just came to mind." Felix tilted his head as if something had occurred to him and began to speak.

"What is it?"

"Back then, when you proposed the contract. Why did you say that I could fuck you like a whore? You didn't have much experience, so why did you act like that? Thanks to that, I thought you were used to those kinds of things. But when it came to it, I was surprised because that wasn't the case at all."

Isaac, hearing the unexpected question, let out a low hum as he looked into Felix's deep blue eyes. It seemed he also wasn't sure why he had said that back then, either.

"Four years ago, I was struggling because my heat cycle came unexpectedly at a place and time I didn't expect. You found me like that and took me right away."

"Yeah, I used to grit my teeth whenever I thought of that day. You completely captivated me, only to run away after." Felix's gaze as he looked back at Isaac was sharp. "And you even broke my perfectly good arm."

This man, known for holding grudges for life, still seemed bitter just thinking about the past. But Isaac, pretending not to notice Felix's feelings, kept speaking, "Back then, those were the first words you said to me: "Hold on tight. Or you might end up in pieces," Isaac murmured drowsily, recalling the past as if dreaming.

Felix, looking down at Isaac as he dug up long-buried memories, frowned. "Did I say that? I don't remember."

It was unclear whether he truly didn't remember or was pretending not to. Isaac simply chuckled. It didn't matter to him anyway.

"When I was about to offer myself…I don't know why, but that moment suddenly came to mind," Isaac said quietly. "So I brought it up, casually. I guess part of me wondered if you still remembered me. And even if you didn't, I thought repeating your own words might help you recall them.

"Of course, I quickly realized that I had overestimated you. Not only did you not remember, but you didn't even recognize me. In a way, I guess it was a relief, but…" Isaac's expression grew slightly troubled. As he tilted his head slightly and pressed his lips together, Felix's gaze lingered on his wet cheek.

"Did it upset you? That I didn't recognize you right away?" Felix quickly blurted out a pointed question. Isaac rubbed his cheek awkwardly, looking troubled.

"Well, to be honest, I'm not sure myself," Isaac admitted, rubbing the back of his neck. "I think I was both happy and disappointed. I felt relieved that you didn't recognize me, but at the same time, I couldn't help but feel a small sense of anticipation… wondering if you might care to realize who I was right away."

After hearing his confession, Felix held Isaac's chin and lowered his head to kiss him. His damp lips felt soft against his own. He gently coaxed Isaac's lips to part, his tongue carefully tracing the tender flesh inside.

Isaac leaned his back against Felix's chest, resting his head on his shoulder as he closed his eyes and savored the sweet kiss.

Unlike the rough, animalistic kisses that often consumed them, this one was tender, soft, and dreamlike, with a slow, deliberate sweetness.

Already relaxed from the warm water around his body, Isaac felt as if he might melt away completely under the sweet, honey kisses Felix was giving him. A faint sigh slipped past his lips before he shifted, turning to face Felix and pressing his chest against his. Straddling him without hesitation, he wrapped his arms around Felix's neck, drawing him even closer.

"Isaac—"

Isaac ignored the voice calling his name, deepening the kiss instead. Straddling Felix's firm abdomen, he parted his legs and wrapped them securely around his waist. Felix instinctively grabbed onto Isaac's ass with both hands, pulling him towards himself until there was no longer any space left between them. Every subtle movement sent ripples through the water, the gentle splash echoing sensually in the spacious, quiet bathroom.

"Who was the one who complained about being too exhausted?"

"Why are you bringing that up now?" Isaac asked sharply.

Felix then grabbed his ass as if he were about to spank him. Isaac's brow furrowed involuntarily.

"That hurts," he whispered, but Felix's hand never moved away. Instead, it gripped even tighter.

"You're asking me why I would bring that up? It's because you are serving me a delicious meal, you're practically offering yourself up to be devoured."

The growling voice was still as sweet as ever. Isaac couldn't help it and burst into laughter. "You really do seem to pounce at the slightest twitch of my finger."

"Has there ever been a time I wasn't this way? Even from way back, I've always been ready to pounce on you."

"Is that so?" Isaac raised his wet hand and gently cupped Felix's cheek.

"Yeah," Felix pouted, grumbling like a sulky child.

Staring at his flawless, beautiful face, Isaac laughed. Once again, he was struck by the simple truth—he had no way of resisting this man who clung to him so desperately.

"I really am exhausted, so just a kiss for today," he whispered tenderly, lowering his head.

Instead of answering, Felix held him more gently than ever before. Their lips met softly, tongues entwining with familiar ease, sharing the taste of each other's breath. Amid the splashing of water, the occasional wet moan slipped from their locked mouths.

As always, Isaac responded with unrestrained passion to the kiss that melted him in an instant. Yet, he couldn't shake the ominous sense that this wouldn't end with just a kiss—and, as it turned out, he was right.

The seemingly endless night went on.

Chapter 19

The front desk receptionist stared blankly with wide, surprised eyes at the man who had just opened the door and walked in. It had been nearly a year since she began working at this preschool, which was known for its good facilities but high prices. During this time, she had met many parents but had never seen a man like this before.

The neighborhood itself was affluent, and the daycare was luxurious, catering to these wealthy residents. As a result, the parents who brought their children there were naturally wealthy and prosperous. Their jobs were also highly prestigious, including positions like CEOs, professors, lawyers, accountants, doctors, and others.

The man who had just opened the door and stepped inside was someone the employee could say with certainty she had never seen before. Tall and broad-shouldered, with bright blond hair and a chiseled nose and jawline visible beneath black sunglasses, he was striking enough to be mistaken for a Hollywood actor.

Yet, despite his bright and handsome appearance, the moment he entered, the air seemed to grow heavy under an overwhelming pressure. Even dressed casually in a light yellow polo shirt and khaki shorts, the suffocating intensity of his presence made the front desk receptionist draw in a sharp, involuntary breath, almost like a hiccup.

Not only that, but the man following him had a rough appearance. With his massive build, tall stature, rugged face, and piercing eyes, he looked around the room like a bear hunting for prey. If the handsome man who entered first hadn't been carrying a child in one arm, she might have immediately called the police.

The boy, who appeared to be around three years old, clearly seemed to be the son of the striking man holding him, without even needing to ask. With the same bright blonde hair and facial features, it was obvious that he was a miniature version of the man. It was clear that this was a parent who had come to drop off their child.

For a moment, the employee stared blankly at them, lost in thought, then quickly gathered herself and greeted them, "W-Welcome."

Only afterward did the blonde man holding the child approach her and open his mouth to speak, "I was told the registration was already complete and my son would be starting here today."

"I see. And the child's name is?"

"Benjamin Parker," Felix responded, his brow subtly furrowing. He had just been reminded that since he and Isaac had not yet registered their marriage, Benjamin's last name remained the same as his grandmother's.

Felix knew it would take time to get everything sorted out properly. Still, every time he had to say Benjamin's name, he couldn't help but feel frustrated. It was his own son, yet Benjamin didn't carry Isaac's last name, but that of his maternal grandmother's remarried partner, someone with no blood relation to him.

Felix couldn't help but think to himself that he needed to get this sorted out as soon as possible.

"Ah, yes. Benjamin is set to start today." The employee, who had been typing on the computer, flashed a business-like smile and spoke up, waving brightly at Benjamin. "Hi, Benjamin!"

Felix decided to hide his unnecessary irritation. He signed the attendance sheet to confirm he had brought Benjamin, then turned to look at the boy.

"Benjamin, you've arrived at your new school, huh? How about we go inside and see what kind of friends you can make?"

Whenever he spoke to Benjamin, Felix's voice was incredibly gentle, whispering to him while stroking Benjamin's cotton

candy-like hair. It was the complete opposite of the dangerous aura he usually exuded. Just from hearing his voice, one would naturally think he was a doting father who was enamored with his adorable child.

The receptionist's eyes widened in surprise as she looked at Felix. She quickly regained her composure, adjusting her expression, and then opened the door to the hallway leading to the classroom.

"Would you like to come in? I'll show you to the classroom. Initially, it's beneficial for parents to accompany their children and take a brief look around to help ease their anxiety. We don't recommend staying too long, since the children need to learn how to interact with their fellow classmates without their parents around."

"Let's save the explanations for later." It was Jack, standing behind Felix, who interrupted her polite explanation with a dismissive tone. "Please show us to the classroom first, I need to see where our Benjamin will be spending his time."

Jack muttered complaints under his breath, still on crutches because of a wound that hadn't fully healed. He claimed he was nearly recovered and often wandered around alone, insisting he couldn't miss Benjamin's first day of school. He followed along, determined to be there for the occasion.

Of course, Noah also threw a tantrum, insisting on seeing Benjamin settle in. In the end, he couldn't get past Felix's temper and was kicked out. As a result, Jack, who had been assigned as the bodyguard, became even more smug about his victory.

Just like Noah, Jack had become a doting fool for Benjamin. His casual remark made the employee flinch, and she quickly closed her mouth. She soon changed her mind, shot Jack a sharp look, and firmly stated, "Only parents are allowed to enter."

For a brief moment, Jack was stunned, then he started to argue, questioning why he couldn't enter, claiming he was the child's bodyguard and needed to see inside the room. The reasons piled up, but the employee stayed firm. In the end, Jack, with his shoulders slumped, had no choice but to watch Benjamin and Felix go into the classroom while he waited outside in front.

"Please, come in."

The employee, who kindly glanced at Felix, led him to the classroom and told him that it was where Benjamin would be staying. Noticing that no children were in sight, Felix asked why. She explained that the kids who had arrived early were gathered in a separate area to play.

The building was large and spacious, with top-notch facilities. There were many classrooms, likely due to the large number of children, and the walls were adorned with bright, colorful paintings, drawings, and photographs. Toys were neatly organized, making the space seem more than enough for the children to spend their day.

Felix still couldn't hide his displeasure. It would have been the same no matter where he sent Benjamin. Everything just felt unsatisfactory; nothing was good enough for his son. After quickly glancing around the classroom, Felix finally turned his attention to Benjamin. The child, seemingly unfamiliar with the place, was resting his cheek on Felix's shoulder, reluctant to let go.

"Benjamin?" Felix called to him softly, and Benjamin lifted his round eyes to meet his gaze. "Shall we get down and take a look around together?"

Benjamin just gave him a look.

"Why, you don't want to? They say there are a lot of kids your age here," Felix asked, but Benjamin pressed his cheek against Felix's shoulder and kept his mouth tightly shut.

Felix had heard that Benjamin had gone to daycare without any issues back in La Jolla, but now it seemed like he wasn't even considering stepping into the school at all. It was possible that after spending more than a month at home while Felix was looking for a school, Benjamin had become wary of unfamiliar places. Additionally, having been kidnapped by Cole and receiving ongoing therapy and regular hospital visits might have made this

adjustment even more difficult for him.

Felix rubbed his forehead with a worried look before glancing back down at Benjamin. He had been determined to take Benjamin to school himself instead of Isaac, wanting to be there for his first day, but he hadn't foreseen something like this happening.

"Benjamin?" A gentle voice called out. Felix, still holding Benjamin with his face buried in his shoulder, knelt and sat on the floor. He carefully tried to set the child down while gently patting his back.

At that moment, Benjamin suddenly let out a loud cry, wailing uncontrollably, and Felix's face turned pale.

Chapter 20

About a month ago, as soon as Isaac decided to reopen the flower shop, Felix quickly showed him a store near the mansion. The area was lively yet clean, and the shop's size was just right.

Through the large windows, bright sunlight streamed in, making the interior look inviting to Isaac, so he signed the contract without hesitation. Over the past few days, he had been diligently preparing to open the flower shop. There was a lot to do, and the interior was still messy, but the process of getting everything ready carefully was nothing but enjoyable for him.

It had been his dream for years to live peacefully while running a small flower shop, and now he felt like that dream had finally come true. He could run the shop without fearing for his life. Additionally, he could live with Benjamin, his mother, and, of course, Felix.

Sometimes, Isaac did wonder if he was dreaming.

If this were a dream, it was so wonderful that he didn't want to wake up. As he looked out the window, lost in nice thoughts, he soon shook his head, dismissing the idea, and quickly moved the potted plants around.

Inside the shop, where the dazzling morning sunlight beamed in, every time he moved, the sound of his footsteps echoed. It seemed to blend perfectly with the quiet music playing from the radio. Though the heat from the weather had already caused beads of sweat to form on Isaac's temples, it was a rather peaceful morning. That is, until someone suddenly entered the shop without a warning and pulled him into a tight embrace from behind.

"W-Wha—!"

Suddenly, a strong force wrapped around his shoulders,

causing Isaac's body to tilt backward. In an instant, Isaac grabbed the man's arm, bent at the waist, and hurled him forward. It was an automatic reflex, and the whole thing happened in the blink of an eye.

With a loud thud, the man hit the floor. Lying there, he looked up at Isaac, his bright blue eyes narrowing in a mask of pain. The agony in his gaze froze Isaac where he stood, his body going rigid.

"Felix?"

"Well, isn't this just great? I can't even mess around a little." Felix let out a soft grunt as he slowly got back to his feet.

Isaac stood there, frozen, staring at him as he brushed dirt off his clothes. Honestly, who would have guessed that the person who snuck up on him like a thief and grabbed him would be Felix?

"Why didn't you block me?" Isaac muttered with a sigh, running a hand through his hair and ruffling it.

It had been a reflex, but since he had outright slammed Felix to the floor, he couldn't help but feel a little guilty. "I wasn't trying to attack you, so how could I?"

"Then you should've just come in normally. Why are you acting like some kind of pervert?"

"I just wanted to surprise you." Felix raised both hands in surrender at Isaac's firm tone. "Alright, alright, I won't do it again."

Only then did Isaac let out a short sigh. What a way to start the morning.

Sometimes, Felix could conceal his presence so perfectly that it was almost eerie. He could get close without Isaac noticing at all. It was astonishing. Given his line of work, Isaac was usually sharp enough to sense anyone, no matter how much they tried to hide their presence, but with Felix, there were far too many times when he simply couldn't tell.

It had always been that way. So whenever Felix suddenly appeared like this, it was impossible not to be startled.

"I react instinctively…" Isaac sighed. "So it would be better if you didn't approach me so silently. I could have accidentally broken your arm."

"Yup, once was enough for me." Felix shuddered and shook his head. It was clear that the time when Isaac had broken his arm and run away had left a strong impression on him. Judging by his reaction even now, it must have been a significant shock.

Isaac shrugged his shoulders, feeling a bit awkward. Then, as a thought suddenly came to him, he turned to look at Felix.

"Oh, how's Benjamin? Did you manage to take him to school without any trouble?"

Felix groaned at Isaac's question, his shoulders stiffening. Rather than answer, he drew out a long, thoughtful hum—a drawn-out "Hmm…" that marked the start of an elaborate excuse.

"So, are you saying you haven't been able to take Benjamin to school yet?" Isaac asked again, brushing off the dust on his apron. His tone remained as calm as usual, but the sharpness in his black eyes made Felix avert his gaze, unable to hold eye contact.

"About that…" Felix grumbled, looking away. "The kid started crying. What was I supposed to do?"

Isaac, who had been staring at Felix with a troubled look, let out a long sigh. He had thought there wouldn't be any problems since Benjamin had attended just fine when he was with his mother, but it turned out that wasn't the case. Still, he hadn't expected Felix to be the one struggling to send Benjamin off to preschool.

Isaac was often surprised to realize that, even though he thought Felix would be a strict father, he was far from it. Instead of being strict, Felix became a soft-hearted fool who didn't know what to do whenever Benjamin cried.

"I would have left him there, even if he was crying." Isaac, who had been quietly watching Felix, finally spoke up.

"I never saw you as the heartless type," Felix mumbled sarcastically.

Isaac let out a bitter laugh. He wanted to give Benjamin everything and would never hurt him, but he knew he could be quite cold-hearted sometimes.

"It's a relief that you're not as cold-hearted as I am."

"What are you saying? I'm a very cold-hearted person."

Isaac responded with a casual "Sure" as he glanced back at Felix. After all, he knew better than anyone that Felix could definitely be a cold-blooded man in other situations.

"But when it comes to Benjamin, that's not the case."

"Well, he's only a kid…"

Watching Felix mumble in a troubled tone, Isaac drifted into thought again.

"I remember when Benjamin first started school, I felt the same way. I thought it was natural for kids to cry when they went to school and were separated from their parents, so I left without even looking back. I was told that while he cried for a day or two, he gradually got better, and that we had to get used to being apart from each other little by little."

Isaac let out a short sigh as he recalled the day he had first taken Benjamin to school the previous year. He had left the crying child behind, but the uneasy feeling remained clear in his memory. His own situation weighed heavily on him, and as a result, he wasn't able to properly care for Benjamin.

As Isaac reflected on the guilt he felt while dropping Benjamin off so coldly, he suddenly heard Felix's tongue click in disapproval.

"Still, there's no reason to force a child to be separated from you when they're scared and crying. They'll grow up and eventually leave on their own, even if you want them by your side." Felix said nonchalantly in a curt voice, as if it wasn't a big deal. "Isn't that right?"

Isaac looked at him, full of thoughts, feeling an odd tingling sensation in his chest.

Raising a child is difficult. There's a lot to learn, and it takes patience and effort. Yet, there are no definite answers to problems that may arise. Perhaps that was why Isaac was somewhat shocked by Felix's response. He never thought to consider it from that perspective.

"You don't have to be too hung up on rules and regulations,

right? What's the harm in sending him to school a little later? There are plenty of people at home eager to look after Benjamin anyway."

Of course, Felix's opinion wasn't entirely correct. Still, instead of making decisions alone, Isaac believed that consulting and discussing with Felix, who had a different perspective, would likely lead to better conclusions. After all, Felix often helped him notice things he might not have realized or understood on his own.

"I'm glad you're here with me," Isaac softly whispered his confession.

"You're realizing that now?" Felix, who had been hesitant about leaving Benjamin at school, now spoke with a smug expression, as if he wasn't worried just a moment ago. It seemed that the usual arrogant man had finally returned. Isaac wore a faint smile in response.

"It's my first time raising a child, and when I think back to my childhood, I remember my stepfather, who acted like a soldier even at home. I believe that's why I sometimes come across as a bit forceful with Benjamin without realizing it."

The smile that lingered at the corner of his lips slowly turned bitter.

"Even if I sometimes act forcefully, please handle Benjamin gently like you're doing now."

"Isaac."

"Raising a child is really difficult."

As Isaac let out a weary laugh, Felix gently cupped his cheek with his hand.

"Yeah, you're right," Felix spoke to comfort him, but having suddenly become a father overnight, it must be even more difficult and confusing for him. Despite that, he was doing a great job.

It seemed that there would be much more to learn in the future, things that he would have to learn alongside Felix. As Felix gently caressed his cheek, Isaac continued his unspoken thoughts.

As he leaned slightly against his firm hand, gathering his thoughts, a sudden curiosity arose. "So, where is Benjamin now?"

"He's in the car playing with Jack," Felix casually offered in a nonchalant tone.

Isaac quickly lifted his head. "You're saying he's not at home, but here?"

"Yeah, I brought him here because you said you wanted to see him."

Isaac was still trying to process the fact that Benjamin had come along. He looked at Felix in confusion before quickly tossing aside his dirty apron and gloves. He had been in the middle of arranging the potted plants, but that hardly mattered now. Leaving the disorganized shop behind, Isaac quickly spotted Felix's car and picked up his pace.

Watching Isaac's back as he hurried away, Felix clicked his tongue again. Although he sometimes acted cold, whenever Benjamin's name was mentioned, he would drop everything and rush to his side. Isaac, unaware of Felix's jealousy, simply hurried off to find Benjamin.

The window of the spotless sedan was tinted dark, making it hard to see inside. As Isaac bent down to peer through the window, Jack quickly rolled it down. Through the opening, Benjamin peeked out, his face lighting up as he shouted, "Daddy!" His face was as bright and cheerful as ever.

"Benjamin!" Isaac opened the door and swiftly scooped Benjamin into his arms. While he pressed his lips to the soft cheek, still faintly streaked with dried tears, Benjamin let out a gentle, carefree giggle. It was a sound that always made Isaac's heart flutter, no matter how many times he heard it.

"Did you cry a lot today?" Isaac gently pulled Benjamin into a warm embrace and asked soothingly.

Benjamin, perhaps a bit embarrassed, let out a soft "hmm" before replying faintly, "A little."

Isaac smiled softly, a soft chuckle escaping his lips. "I see. I guess I'll have to do my best to make sure my Benjamin doesn't want to cry anymore. We'll have fun and eat something delicious, too."

As Isaac gently patted his son's back and whispered as if sharing a secret, Benjamin became excited and started raising his voice. Isaac listened to the excited chatter about what Benjamin wanted to do and eat.

"Didn't you say you wanted to go to Balboa Park with Benjamin and have a picnic? You also said you wanted to go to Disneyland, right?"

Isaac was briefly taken aback when Felix's question suddenly came from behind him. When was that? It felt like it was a long time ago, he said as a passing remark. He hadn't expected Felix to remember it after all.

"Yes, that's right. My dream was to go on a peaceful picnic with Benjamin, without any worries."

Since moving into Felix's mansion, Isaac had often gone for walks in the nearby park, but both had been busy with their work. They hadn't yet had the chance to visit Balboa Park, the zoo, or any of the theme parks kids would enjoy. It had already been several weeks since they had planned to go.

Isaac felt a bitter taste in his mouth as he reflected on himself. When their circumstances weren't favorable, it couldn't be helped, but now, he was too busy to go, and it made him feel like an inadequate parent.

"Let's go right now."

Felix's sudden suggestion caught Isaac off guard. Still holding Benjamin in his arms, Isaac froze, unable to find the right words. Seeing this, Felix grinned widely, his eyes sparkling with mischief as he looked at Isaac.

"Benjamin, how about we go play at that big park over there?" He bent down to face Benjamin, asking the question in a gentle voice. To anyone who passed by, it was the image of a loving father with his son.

"Yeah! I want to go!" Benjamin eagerly nodded, clearly happy to stay with his dad instead of going to preschool.

Isaac kept gazing at Felix, still lost in thought. He was well aware of how busy Felix had become recently, to the point where

it seemed like he hardly had time for anything.

"Wasn't your schedule packed today?" Isaac asked with concern, but as usual, Felix's reply only made Tony seem more pitiful.

"Tony can take care of that."

How could he be so carefree? Isaac sighed quietly, offering silent comfort to Tony, who likely had no idea what was going on. Come to think of it, Felix's outfit was perfect for a trip, light and casual. Isaac briefly looked him over with a suspicious expression, but it was hard to tell what he was thinking.

"What are you doing? Hurry up and close the shop so we can go."

"Are you sure we can go right now?"

"What's stopping us? We have time now, so we might as well just go. Since we're already heading out, why not pick a nice place, have brunch, and enjoy a little date?"

Felix took Benjamin from Isaac, quickly placing him in the car seat in the back. Benjamin, who didn't even know what Balboa Park was, got excited just hearing they were going somewhere, and he started kicking his feet. He even helped Felix, who was still unfamiliar with the child car seat, by explaining how to fasten the seatbelt.

"No, you have to clip it here. Right here."

"Here?"

"Yeah. That's it!"

Hearing Benjamin's confident voice praising his dad made Isaac chuckle softly. Felix was a man who usually never had time for anything, so Isaac wasn't going to argue with him. "I'll close the shop and be right back."

"Alrighty, come back quick," Felix replied to Isaac, and Benjamin, sitting in the car seat, eagerly waved his hand while repeating the words his father said.

Watching them, it was undeniable how much they resembled each other. As time passed, they began to resemble each other more closely. It almost felt like it would be impossible to hide it now, and without realizing it, a smile spread across Isaac's face.

Like the bright, clear weather, his steps felt just as light and carefree. Everything was going smoothly. Soon, the flower shop would be fully organized and open for business. Benjamin was growing up healthy and bright, and his mother had regained her peace of mind.

Above all, Felix, who cherishes and loves him more than anyone else, is by his side.

With his beloved family by his side, he was going to enjoy a peaceful life. Isaac was sure that he had never been happier than he was at this moment. It felt like the pinnacle of his life, drifting lazily through dreamlike times. He even pinched his own cheek, wondering if he might be dreaming.

Isaac locked the store door and lowered the shutter before turning his head. Under the clear blue sky, Felix stood like a picture, waiting for him. Tilting his head slightly, he looked at Isaac with his piercing blue eyes, mouthing his name.

"Isaac."

Isaac, who had been gazing at him as if dreaming, took a slow step forward to approach him. But as soon as his feet hit the ground, his steps began to quicken without him even realizing it.

Suddenly, from one of the many shops across the street, Louis Armstrong's "What a Wonderful World" began to play.

I see trees of green, red roses too
I see them bloom for me and you
And I think to myself, what a wonderful world

The deep voice, the slow jazz melody, and the lyrics full of happiness.

As he thought that the song playing seemed to be singing about the happiness he was feeling right now, a man as beautiful as sunlight opened his arms toward him. Isaac, with a brighter smile than ever, ran toward him.

Chapter 21

There were several reasons why the day they went to register their marriage turned out to be much later than expected.

First, the diamonds, rings, and other jewels ordered from Christopher, the jeweler, arrived later than expected. After the rings arrived, a series of miscellaneous tasks followed. Last week, Felix had to go on an unexpected business trip, and as a result, the marriage registration kept getting postponed.

Perhaps that was why, last night, Felix, who had returned to the mansion after a week, suddenly opened his eyes in the early hours of the morning and shook Isaac awake, who was still asleep beside him. His face was filled with determination.

"Isaac, wake up."

For Isaac, the morning had been unusually intense. No sooner had Felix returned than he pounced on him like a starving beast, leaving Isaac sleepless, gasping, and crying until dawn. Now, Felix was forcing him awake, even though he had barely managed to drift off.

"What do you want?" Isaac struggled to open his heavy eyes, letting out a lazy sigh. He couldn't understand why Felix, a man who loved his sleep, was acting this way so early in the morning. Felix replied genuinely in a calm, deep voice.

"I can't wait any longer, let's get married right now."

Isaac was completely stunned at Felix's absurd words. It was only natural that he couldn't form a clear thought, still half-asleep and foggy in the mind. But Felix, undeterred by his lack of response, persistently urged Isaac to get up and managed to wake him up from bed.

After a quick, simple breakfast, they went outside. Isaac felt dazed; from head to toe, his body ached, and after barely any sleep, he felt sluggish. It was no surprise, though, since Felix had suddenly dragged him out, insisting they get married immediately.

But who could possibly break Felix's determination?

They arrived at the county office at 9 a.m., right when it opened, and were the first to step inside. Next to Isaac stood Jessica, with a bright smile on her face, and Benjamin, dressed in a cute little suit like a young gentleman, holding her hand.

Of course, Noah also showed up. With his love for sleep greater than even Felix's, he could only be found sitting like a corpse, with a face as pale as a ghost. Additionally, his mismatched outfit, which he had just thrown together before leaving, earned him a disapproving look from Felix. But as always, he remained unfazed.

Among all of them, Felix was the only one carefully filling out the marriage application. A tension lingered around him, something rarely seen in his usual arrogant demeanor and relaxed attitude.

In contrast, Isaac, who stood by Felix's side and simply stared blankly at the monitor, was still sluggish from the wild night they had shared until the early morning. Felix's fingers tapped with purpose on the screen, neat and precise. Isaac liked the tidy appearance of his nails, freshly trimmed and well-groomed.

Isaac´s eyes widened, realizing that he had been thinking about unnecessary things. If Felix found out, he would most likely get scolded for not paying attention. No, what was even more surprising was that, despite filling out his own marriage application, he couldn't focus. It was almost unbelievable.

It felt like he was looking at a stranger's marriage application, not his own. Was it because he still couldn't fully grasp what was happening? Just as the thought crossed his mind, Felix finished filling out the paperwork and, catching Isaac's eye, flashed a bright smile.

"That was simple, wasn't it?"

Isaac looked blankly at Felix, who was as excited as a child.

Meanwhile, the paperwork was processed, and a staff member approached, asking them to follow him to a room.

The small room held only a long bench along the wall for guests and a small platform in front. As Isaac glanced around in confusion, a staff member dressed simply in a robe stepped forward and began the brief wedding ceremony.

They agreed to accept each other as life partners and slid the rings onto each other's fingers. Finally, the staff member, acting as the witness, declared the marriage official, and with that, the ceremony came to a close. It was a simple wedding that ended quicker than expected.

The three family members watched the brief wedding and congratulated the couple with bright smiles. Benjamin, not fully understanding what a wedding was, handed Isaac and Felix a small bouquet. Of course, it was something Jessica Parker had prepared, but the flowers were lovely. Seeing Benjamin so excited and unaware of the wedding's significance made Isaac's heart flutter with warmth that spread from deep inside.

Isaac was still in a daze, an indescribable unease stirring in his chest. Was he truly Felix's legal partner now? Perhaps because it didn't yet feel real, questions kept circling in his mind, leaving him uncertain what to think.

Felix Felice was the partner he would spend the rest of his life with.

Of course, they had already bonded and were living together, but holding the marriage certificate in his hands after completing the official registration felt completely different. Isaac unconsciously turned to look back at Felix.

As if he had sensed Isaac's feelings, Felix met his gaze with an enchanting smile. When their eyes locked, it was as if Isaac finally snapped back to reality. This man, Felix Felice, the hyper-dominant Alpha and notorious arms dealer, was his partner, and that fact hit him with a sudden, undeniable clarity.

"Come to think of it, I haven't really kissed my partner yet, have I?"

Unable to look away from Felix's Prussian blue eyes, Isaac felt himself almost entranced. Before he realized it, Felix had moved closer, whispering softly. The familiar scent, mixed with a touch of cologne, tickled his nose.

Isaac gently cupped Felix's cheek with his hand and shut his eyes. "Indeed."

As they softly whispered to each other, neither knowing who started it, they shared a gentle, sweet kiss. The sound of applause echoed around them again, and Isaac, feeling a twinge of regret, lifted his head.

"Love you." A small confession slipped past the cheers and applause.

Isaac let out a quick, amused laugh. "Love you too."

As he gently caressed Felix's cheek and whispered, Felix firmly grasped Isaac's hand, and only then did they step out of the office. Their steps were light. Once outside the building, the bright sunlight pouring down from above blinded them for a moment, but even that seemed like a source of happiness. The warm breeze, combined with the slightly hot weather, made everything feel pleasant.

As they headed toward the parking lot, Noah suddenly called out to Felix. "Wait, Felix."

Noah, who showed more emotion than expected, had quietly wiped away tears throughout their wedding. But just as they stepped outside, he called Felix. His awkward expression made Isaac wonder if something was wrong.

"What?" Felix, still holding Isaac's hand tightly as if to show off that they had just gotten married, asked indifferently, "What is it, Noah?"

Noah groaned and rubbed his chin, clearly hesitant. There was something definitely fishy about this situation. "What should we do?"

"What's going on? Did you get yourself into trouble again?"

"No, Grandfather called for you urgently." With an awkward expression, Noah handed his phone to Felix.

Felix immediately snatched it from him, and just as Noah said, his grandfather had sent a brief message. It was a congratulatory note for the wedding, followed by a command to come over immediately. And of course, Isaac and Benjamin were expected to come along as well.

"Noah…" Felix read the message and immediately narrowed his eyes, glaring at Noah.

"No, it's just he said he wanted to watch a video or something… I couldn't exactly refuse," Noah, sensing his own fault, subtly backed away as if he already knew the trouble he was in.

Just as they were leaving, feeling good about completing the marriage registration, the tense, sharp atmosphere made Isaac feel like a confrontation was unavoidable. Isaac grabbed Felix's arm to calm him down. "It's only natural that we go to greet him. How long have you been planning not to tell me about this?"

Felix frowned at the question. "I was planning to explain it to you later."

"Did you want to hide Benjamin and me?"

"Of course not!"

Even though Isaac knew it wasn't true, he couldn't resist making a remark. As expected, Felix jumped in surprise, clearly flustered and unsure how to respond. Jessica, who had been walking toward the parking lot, turned around with a puzzled look, and Benjamin, waving his hand, looked back and forth between the married couple.

Realizing that it looked like they had gotten into an argument in front of their family, Isaac let out a small sigh. Just as he was considering whether they should move to a quieter spot to talk, Felix urgently grabbed Isaac's hand and spoke up.

"Isaac, I swear, it's not what you think. With Grandpa's personality, if I had told him in advance, he would've started planning the most extravagant, lavish wedding imaginable right away. That's why I put off telling him." Felix shook his head. Just thinking about it tired him out. Noah, agreeing with him, nodded from the side.

"Plus, he would've invited all kinds of people, which would have made the planning process even longer. And even if we did have the wedding, who knows what would happen during all that chaos." Felix continued his explanation, "That's why I desperately wanted to get married first. I didn't have the luxury of waiting while trying to cater to all of my grandfather's personal preferences."

"In that case, it seems Noah did a good job in reminding us. Tell him we'll go to greet him soon."

"It's far," Felix muttered a faint excuse again, like a child who keeps procrastinating on something they didn't want to do.

His gaze avoided meeting anyone's, and in that moment, he looked like a careless, immature child. The usual intimidating presence he had seemed to disappear entirely. Isaac firmly squeezed his hand, a little harder than usual, causing Felix's handsome face to crease slightly in discomfort.

"I remember telling you the things you don't want to do are the ones you should finish first," Isaac said, his voice calm, as if soothing a child. He watched Felix let out a long sigh.

"Are you really going to be okay with this?"

"With what?"

"Grandfather's personality is a bit..." Felix paused for a moment, as if carefully choosing his words. "Well..."

In the meantime, Noah quickly added, "He's eccentric, to say the least."

Felix's eyebrows furrowed once more.

"It doesn't matter to me. I've dealt with many people in the military, and there were some eccentric ones among them."

"But—"

"Let's just pay a quick visit and get it over with."

Felix nodded as if he had no choice but to accept Isaac's decision. Relieved at last, Isaac took his hand and started walking. "What could possibly go wrong?"

Perhaps comforted by Isaac's calm tone, Felix let out a laugh. "Yeah, you're right."

What could possibly go wrong? Everything would turn out smoothly. There would be no more threats to his family. He wouldn't allow it. Just like this blissful moment, they would keep walking hand in hand, unchanged, for a long time to come—now and forever.

Dreaming of sweeter days, Felix walked beside Isaac, whispering, "I love you" once more to the partner who would always remain at his side.

Together, they moved forward beneath the dazzling sunlight.

Chapter 22

"Trick or treat!"

The children's voices rang out loud and lively. Isaac scooped handfuls of candy, chocolate bars, and caramels from the large pumpkin-shaped basket he had prepared beforehand and handed them into the bags of the children gathered in front of him.

The children held tightly onto their candy-filled bags with their tiny hands, squealing with excitement. The scene was chaotic and loud, but Isaac wore a bright expression on his face as he handed out candy to the children, who swarmed around him like little chicks rushing toward scattered feed.

Among the children was Benjamin, his flushed cheeks and sparkling eyes showing just how excited he was. It was no surprise, since he rarely got candy or chocolate because he was often told it would ruin his teeth and spoil his appetite. But now, with a basket overflowing with sweets in his hands, how could he not be overjoyed? Isaac couldn't help but chuckle watching Benjamin already sucking on a lollipop, his cheeks puffed out like a hamster.

In the mansion's courtyard, the Halloween party for the children was in full swing. The children were dressed in a variety of costumes, and although Elsa and Anna remained popular, there were also plenty of fairies and superheroes. Some families had even coordinated their outfits with each other. Star Wars and Harry Potter-themed families stood out, but what truly caught everyone's eye was an adorable group dressed as ketchup, mayonnaise, a hamburger, and a hot dog.

This year, Benjamin's costume was surprisingly not Mickey Mouse but Captain America. Since he started talking, he had been obsessed with Mickey Mouse, but after he began school, he gradually fell into the world of superheroes. His most treasured toy had shifted from a Mickey Mouse plushie to a Captain America shield. And so, after years of insisting on wearing a Mickey Mouse costume, he chose Captain America this time.

It was an astonishing development, and proof that Benjamin was growing up—a realization that left Isaac with a tangle of emotions. Benjamin, meanwhile, was simply overjoyed, proudly wearing his Captain America costume without a care in the world.

The three-and-a-half-year-old, who barely reached Isaac's knees, wore his Captain America costume, mask, and shield while striking what he believed to be a cool pose. In reality, he was more adorable than imposing, leaving the mansion's staff utterly smitten. Not that Benjamin noticed. He seemed convinced that they were collapsing because of the "pew pew" sound effects he made when firing his toy gun.

For days leading up to Halloween, Benjamin had been running around in his costume with excitement. When the big day finally arrived, he joined his friends in trick-or-treating. The route was simple—they would visit a few neighboring houses around the mansion. Acting as the children's guardians, Jack, dressed as Winnie the Pooh, and Tony, in a Tigger costume, followed close behind, keeping a watchful eye on them.

And at the very end of the group, Noah followed stubbornly, despite everyone's efforts to stop him. Dressed in a mad scientist costume with white clothes splattered with fake blood, he insisted on going with Benjamin. Many pointed out that his costume wasn't much different from his usual look and warned him he might scare the children, but Noah paid no attention and proudly stuck with his choice.

Along with them, several of Felix's subordinates had taken it upon themselves to protect the children, quietly watching over them from both visible and hidden locations. Surrounded by this unseen protection, the children cheerfully went around shouting "trick or treat!" Having just returned to the mansion and received

their last handful of candy from Isaac, they were happily enjoying the party in the backyard.

The mansion's backyard had been transformed into a charming Halloween party venue for the children. Tables were piled high with cookies and cakes shaped like bats, spiders, and ghosts, while small pumpkins glowed warmly all around. The party Benjamin had invited his classmates to was filled with adorable, whimsical touches, creating a festive and age-appropriate atmosphere.

When they planned to host the Halloween party at their house and send out invitations to Benjamin's school friends, Felix wasn't particularly excited about it.

It was to be expected—after all, this was no ordinary estate. Beneath it lay a state-of-the-art intelligence room that could rival any major agency, along with a fully stocked armory. From the outside, it appeared perfectly ordinary, but in truth, it could be called a fortress. And yet, here they were, hosting a Halloween party for children.

Isaac, oblivious to the true nature of the mansion, cheerfully invited Benjamin's friends to the party, but it put Felix in an awkward position. It wasn't that he didn't want to explain, there was just no easy way to do it. In the end, unable to find a good reason to stop Isaac, he reluctantly let it happen, though he couldn't shake the feeling of discomfort.

Tony subtly reassured Felix, indicating that it shouldn't be an issue since the kids weren't even going inside the house—just playing in the backyard for a little while. In fact, with the government still watching them, hosting a party for the kids could actually help create a more normal, family-like atmosphere.

While Tony was insistent that he wasn't particularly interested in going to the Halloween party himself, he confidently backed Isaac's side, assuring Felix that it would be a win-win situation. He stressed once again that the reason he supported Isaac wasn't that he was eager to attend Benjamin's Halloween party.

After glaring at Tony, Felix reluctantly relented and told Isaac to do as he pleased. His once-elegant and grand backyard had turned into a chaotic Halloween party, with children running around, shouting, and tripping over one another.

The hyperactive three-and four-year-olds, fueled by an overload of candy, cookies, chocolates, and juice, tore around in an uncontrollable frenzy. Loud, flashing lights and gratingly childish music blared in the background, making it nearly impossible to think. As if that weren't enough, activities filled every corner—a balloon artist shaped whatever the kids desired, while simple games like balloon-popping and ball-tossing added to the noise and chaos, heightening the already hectic atmosphere.

Additionally, his normally tough, imposing subordinates, who were dressed in cute Disney character costumes, were hopping around in a completely out-of-character way, playing with the kids and even taking photos. Occasionally, the mad doctor Noah would appear unexpectedly and scare the children, causing ear-piercing screams. It was utter chaos.

The large yard was lively, resembling an amusement park, with joyful sounds echoing everywhere. Among the crowd was Isaac. As the party host, he casually conversed with Benjamin's friends' parents and occasionally grabbed some snacks. He walked around, making sure everything was in order, all the while keeping an eye on Benjamin, who was running around energetically with his friends.

However, instead of joining the party, Felix stood by the window in the study on the second floor, looking down at the backyard. His blue eyes, usually calm and composed, were now filled with discomfort as he watched the chaotic scene unfold below.

"That's just way too lewd," Felix muttered to himself, his voice filled with irritation.

Isaac, who was busy running around among the children, was dressed as Benjamin's second-favorite hero, in a Spider-Man costume that was a bit too tight and left very little to the imagination. The clingy outfit was certainly not helping Felix's mood.

While Spider-Man costumes were traditionally skin-tight, covering the body from head to toe, he couldn't help but feel that there was no need for it to look exactly like the one in the movies. But Isaac's costume? It was eerily identical to the one worn in the film, down to the last detail. Felix grumbled under his breath, wondering who in their right mind would design such a thing, and who would even buy it.

The form-fitting Spider-Man costume left little to the imagination, outlining every curve of Isaac's lean frame—from smooth calves and toned thighs to his firm, round ass and narrow waist. The tight fabric showcased his flat stomach, sculpted chest, broad shoulders, and defined arms. Felix couldn't help feeling a surge of irritation, thinking how absurd it was for Isaac to be walking around in front of all those people looking so… *exposed.*

Felix glared at him as he downed his wine, his eyes narrowing in frustration. The tension in his gaze almost seemed threatening, as if he was ready to snap at any moment. Yet Isaac, unaware of Felix's intense stare, casually placed his hand on his slim, triangular waist and tossed his mask onto the ground. With a quick motion, he ruffled his dark hair with his fingertips, completely unaware of the storm brewing in Felix's mind.

The mask he had been wearing was quite stuffy, but Felix, completely smitten, didn't seem to notice. The way he removed the mask and shook out his hair seemed like a scene from a movie, and the way he exhaled deeply and smiled at the children with his calm face was incredibly seductive. No, it wasn't just seductive, it was downright lewd. Enough to make blood rush to his groin and throb just from watching.

Under the sparkling lights, Isaac looked more magnificent than ever. Usually so stoic, his face appeared unusually relaxed today. Had he eaten something different? His affectionate eyes and the soft smile on his lips made it hard to look away.

If someone had been beside him, they might have looked at Felix with disbelief and clicked their tongue. But Felix, completely infatuated with Isaac, couldn't hide his anxiety and furrowed his brow. After staring at Isaac for a while, Felix attempted to quench his burning thirst by sipping from the wine glass. However, the gaze fixed on Isaac didn't ease. Instead, it grew more intense. It was a stare that seemed ready to devour him alive if given the chance.

"That cheeky Spider-Man. He can't be left alone. He needs to be taught a lesson," he muttered, the words scattering into the quiet space as he licked his wet lips.

After finishing the last drop of wine, Felix set the empty glass on the table and turned away. It was almost time to go to the Halloween party.

Chapter 23

Isaac rubbed the back of his neck and let out a long sigh. The Halloween costume he was wearing for the first time was much more uncomfortable than he had expected. Especially since the Spider-Man suit clung tightly to his entire body, making him feel self-conscious about how much it revealed.

But even though the Spider-Man costume was designed to cling to the body, something felt off. Looking around, no one else's costume clung as tightly as his. The way his Spider-Man suit hugged his body seemed a little excessive.

When he went out trick-or-treating with the kids, he ran into a Deadpool whose suit also clung to his body, but wasn't excessively tight. So why was his Spider-Man suit so unusually snug? Was the size too small? Various thoughts crossed his mind, but he couldn't figure it out. Feeling both frustrated and embarrassed, Isaac finally removed his mask and exhaled briefly. He tousled his messy hair and looked around before quietly turning to leave.

The Halloween party was nearly over. Since it was for kids around three or four years old, it made sense for it to end a little early. It was time for the children to go home, wash up, and get ready for bed. So removing the costume a bit early shouldn't be a problem. Benjamin might cry and be disappointed that Spider-Man had vanished, but outside, Pooh and Tigger were there—along with the mad doctor who was busy scaring the kids.

Isaac slipped unnoticed into the mansion. Inside, it was very quiet. Maybe it felt even quieter due to the lively chaos outside. In the kitchen, the maids and servants were bustling around for the party, but since they used the back door, which led directly from the kitchen to the backyard, the living room was naturally as silent as an empty house.

Walking through the spacious living room where his footsteps echoed unusually loudly, Isaac headed straight for the stairs. The first floor consisted of the main living room, a conference room for guests, a small reception area, the kitchen, and the dining room. However, all the private rooms were located on the second floor.

To change his clothes, he had to go upstairs.

Thinking about how exhausting it was to maintain such a large house, he stepped onto the stairs. Just then, as if on cue, the lights near the entrance clicked off with a faint sound. Isaac stopped and turned his head. Was someone there? He couldn't sense a presence. Maybe a power outage? But only the lights by the entrance were out; the rest of the living room still glowed. Perhaps the bulb had simply burned out. Deciding to change his clothes first and call someone to fix it later, Isaac resumed his climb up the stairs.

Then, as if meticulously planned, the lights in the hallway leading to the kitchen went out. Isaac flinched, freezing in place as a wave of tension ran down his spine. He turned his head, eyes narrowing, just as the lights in the spacious living room began to flicker out one by one—like a scene from a horror movie. Soon, only the light above the stairs where he stood remained; the rest of the house was swallowed in darkness, making it impossible to see beyond the shadows.

This might be trouble, Isaac thought.

Clicking his tongue inwardly, Isaac slowly clenched his fists. If it was a prank, it was a nasty one, and if it was a real burglar, that was just as troublesome. And of all times, during the kids' Halloween party…

Though it wasn't a crazy coincidence, Halloween was the night with the highest number of crimes in the United States. With everyone wearing masks, it was easy to conceal identities, and with parties happening everywhere, crimes fueled by alcohol and drugs were common.

That's why Halloween was a day when the police focused especially on security. But even beyond that, Isaac had never imagined that a crime would occur at Felix's mansion. What kind of daring thief would even attempt to rob Felix's place? It seemed impossible unless someone was determined to target Felix himself.

"Show yourself."

As Isaac calmly spoke into the darkness, something moved from within the shadows. The figure had a black body and wore a white mask—the ghostly appearance that could make anyone faint from surprise. It was the famous Scream mask.

The costume that portrayed Munch's *The Scream* with a mask was a must-have item for Halloween. That classic ghost mask, made even more famous by the movie "Scream," and this intruder showed up wearing it?

Isaac forced a smile. As soon as he realized that the pale ghost who had deliberately attacked him was wearing a Scream mask, the figure vanished into the darkness like a real ghost. It seemed like things were about to escalate. It was a tense moment as he sensed something ominous.

Suddenly, something lunged out of the darkness. Isaac instinctively raised his hand to defend himself, but his opponent's movements were faster than he expected. Not only was their speed unmatched, but the strength and technique behind the attack were flawless, delivering a barrage of strikes without hesitation.

"Ugh—"

A stifled groan escaped his mouth. The incoming fist was precise and swift, with no sign of hesitation. Struggling to turn his head and avoid it, Isaac could feel cold sweat sliding down his back. It had been a while since he unexpectedly faced an opponent like this. Was this petty thief he had underestimated, not someone to take lightly?

Isaac, unsure of what to do, clenched his teeth and launched an immediate counterattack. *Thud, thud—!* The exchange of fists and kicks between them was relentless. The fight started on the staircase where some light was still visible, but soon they moved into the dark living room to continue. Before he knew it, a lot of time had gone by. Despite this, the fierce battle showed no signs of stopping and only grew more intense.

Though they were only exchanging punches and blocking attacks, every move during their fight was so controlled that anyone watching would think it was a professional match. The attacks were sharp, fast, and precise, and the defense was flawless. The fight showed no clear signs of an outcome, and before long, sweat began to trickle down the side of Isaac's temple.

The skin-tight costume made fighting more challenging for Isaac. The opponent wore a mask, but oddly, their movements appeared completely normal. Additionally, every time Isaac attempted to knock the mask off, the opponent skillfully evaded with ghost-like agility. He couldn't help but wonder who they were.

After exchanging punches for a while, both Isaac and his opponent were gasping heavily, maintaining their distance from each other. Still, they kept cautiously circling each other, their steps slow but deliberate. Isaac didn't know who this person was, but he couldn't shake the feeling that he had finally met a worthy opponent. Wiping his sweat-soaked hand on his thigh, he got ready. If things took a turn for the worse, he planned to escape and call security, but for now, he had no intention of backing down. Moving his body again after so long was surprisingly satisfying.

Isaac steadied his breath and sized up his opponent, curling his lips into a smirk. This time, he stepped forward and launched the first attack. With a sharp whoosh, his punch shot out quickly and precisely. Caught off guard by the sudden strike, the ghost let out a brief groan and tilted their head to dodge it. Isaac's follow-up attacks were so fast they were nearly impossible to see.

The opponent focused only on dodging, starting to show signs of panic. Isaac noticed their changing balance and took the chance. *Thud—!* He punched the side, making the ghost lean forward and groan in pain. Isaac quickly followed with a kick, extending his leg and hitting their back hard. The ghost nearly fell to the floor but managed to grab the table, steadying themselves and cursing softly.

The ghost was definitely skilled, but as time went on, they started to lose their composure, and Isaac didn't miss the chance. As the ghost staggered backward, Isaac quickly closed the gap and threw a straight punch aimed at their face. With the speed behind it, the mask, along with their nose and face, would have shattered if it connected. The ghost, clearly flustered, stumbled back with a sharp click of their tongue, visibly frustrated.

In that moment, a sharp, cloying scent hit Isaac's nose. The pungent sweetness slammed into his senses with overwhelming force, making his head spin. His vision blurred, and his body locked up as if the smell were a powerful drug. It wasn't merely a fragrance—it was like an electric shock, a jolt to his system.

A pheromone—familiar, yet impossible to make sense of.

How?

Isaac's punch faltered as the question flashed through his mind. That brief hesitation was enough for the ghost to strike back instantly. Grabbing his unsteady arm, the ghost twisted it sharply, then grabbed his shoulder and threw him down. With a loud crash, Isaac's head and body slammed into the wall. A low groan escaped him, but the ghost didn't miss a beat. Still disoriented, Isaac found himself pinned, with the ghost's arm pressing hard on the back of his neck, preventing any movement.

With his back exposed to the ghost, his forehead and shoulder pressed against the wall, Isaac's vision blurred. Whether from the lingering, provocative pheromones or the shock of being caught off guard, he couldn't regain his focus. In that moment of disorientation, the man in the Scream mask yanked his arms behind him and bound them tightly. There was no doubt—the ghost had planned this from the start.

"Who the hell—!"

Isaac couldn't even finish his question. The flood of pheromones engulfing him from head to toe left him utterly overwhelmed. So this was a 'pheromone shower'—an act meant to assert dominance, a way for an alpha to mark their omega by releasing their scent to drive others away. He had never experienced it before. Caught in the sudden, overpowering wave, he could only tremble, his body shaking under the relentless assault.

Of course, Felix had used pheromones on him before, even before marking him. Isaac knew that Felix had tried it several times, though unknowingly. At that time, he had been regularly taking suppressants, which made him almost like a beta. Because of that, he could handle the pheromones to some degree, even when Felix released them.

But since being bonded, nothing seemed to work anymore. Even a small trickle of alpha pheromones would send a sharp, overwhelming sensation through his head. How could he possibly endure a flood of them, pouring down like a waterfall? Grinding his teeth in frustration, Isaac finally couldn't take it anymore and collapsed weakly to the ground.

Isaac's vision blurred, and his knees buckled beneath him. The only thing that prevented him from collapsing was the man behind him, who held him up firmly. His body hung limp like a soaked rag, unable to move. Sharp breaths involuntarily escaped him, while cold sweat streamed down his body like rain. Without hesitation, the man effortlessly lifted Isaac onto his shoulder and strode toward the conference room, kicking the door open.

The room was dimmer than the living room because the curtains were drawn. It was furnished with a long meeting table and chairs, a TV and phone for remote conference calls, and a neatly arranged short bookshelf with books and documents. The interior resembled a typical office conference room. Directly across from the table was a fireplace, with two plush sofas facing each other, creating a surprisingly cozy atmosphere.

The man wearing the Scream mask threw Isaac onto the armrest of the sofa like a sack of potatoes. Isaac couldn't believe the situation he was in, completely at the mercy of this man. His face was pressed into the sofa, his lower abdomen draped over the armrest, and his hips lifted uncomfortably. The position was humiliating and unbearable.

Isaac tried to push himself up, forcing strength into his legs sprawled on the floor, but the man pressed down on his back and bound his arms, making his resistance useless. Then a hand slid over his ass. The tight suit stretched even further as he lay prone, and the touch tracing the clear curve of his rear grew rougher, more insistent.

A chilling sensation ran through Isaac, and he held his breath, his limbs going rigid. Noticing his reaction, the man grew even more depraved, kneading his ass before gripping it hard with one hand, as if trying to crush it.

"Ughh—!"

The grip was strong enough to send a sharp jolt of pain through him. Gasping under the heavy haze of pheromones, Isaac couldn't hold back a cry. Yet, ironically, it wasn't the pain that rattled him, but the warmth spreading through his body. With pheromones this suffocating, heightened sensitivity was inevitable—but that didn't make it any less infuriating. Damn pheromones.

Damn...

"Felix!" Isaac shouted angrily.

Omegas and alphas who bond can only respond to the pheromones of the ones who marked them. Additionally, Felix is an exceptionally rare hyper-dominant alpha; there wouldn't be any pheromone in the world that could elicit such an intense reaction from him. In other words, the shameless person who, pretending to be a thug, failed with brute force and then used pheromones to suppress and bind him while continuing to harass him without hesitation could only be Felix.

But why? He was always a man who was hard to understand, but this time, he was even more challenging to grasp. In the middle of a Halloween party for the kids, he suddenly approached him like a creep and even drenched him in pheromones.

Isaac's eyes were red, his gaze clouded by the haze of pheromones. He glared at Felix, whose behavior was nothing short of insane. Yet Felix showed no sign of removing his mask, entirely absorbed in groping Isaac's ass. Worse, he was already grinding his hard cock against Isaac's thigh—a beast completely consumed by lust.

"Are you crazy? What the hell are you doing?"

Felix growled deeply but remained silent. After emitting such strong pheromones, was he trying to act like nothing was going on? What kind of bullshit was this?

Isaac, still lying face down on the sofa's armrest, gritted his teeth and twisted his body. But Felix, as if amused by Isaac's resistance, pressed down hard on his bound arms and continued to pour out pheromones.

With a groan escaping his throat, Isaac slumped onto the sofa. It was unbearable. Ignoring the feverish heat spreading through his body, the tingling sensation in his lower abdomen caused blood to rush to his penis, pressing painfully against the sofa's armrest. It felt like his head was about to explode.

His entire body felt hypersensitive, as if his heat cycle had started; his breathing quickened, and his hole was already dripping wet. It was a natural reaction—this was the first pheromone shower he'd experienced since their bonding—but the sudden rush of arousal still shocked him. Isaac had to swallow back the curses on his tongue and gasp for breath.

The man, openly groping Isaac's ass as he watched his reactions, suddenly pulled a pocketknife from his pocket. Catching the glint of the blade, Isaac stiffened, alarm jolting through him. In the next instant, the man sliced cleanly through the fabric covering Isaac's rear. The sound of tearing cloth in the dark, silent space was eerily obscene.

The thin fabric that was already clinging tightly and stretched from the position of his raised behind, tore easily and fell on either side. As the cool air touched his bare skin, Isaac shuddered and let out a moan. He couldn't even imagine how he must look, with only his ass exposed through the torn fabric.

"Felix..." Isaac murmured faintly. "Stop—"

A cool finger brushed his twitching entrance, his body intoxicated by the pheromones as if he'd taken a heavy dose of

stimulants. The long, rough digit traced over the sensitive folds, drawing out wet, sloppy sounds. Hearing just how slick he already was made Isaac squeeze his eyes shut.

Isaac's shoulders tensed. Then the fingers finally parted his entrance and pushed inside, two at once. The already slick heat offered no resistance; if anything, it clung to them, as if begging for more, drawing them deeper. Soon, his ass was flush against the man's palm as the fingers began to work his inner walls, thrusting slowly, deliberately, and rubbing along every sensitive spot. The teasing touch was maddening—tickling, yet leaving him aching for something more.

"Are you satisfied with just my fingers?" he asked in a low voice, watching Isaac tremble and press his forehead against the sofa.

When he finally spoke, his voice was rough and cracked, betraying just how aroused he was. Isaac turned his head, glaring at him through reddened eyes.

"What are you trying to do? You suddenly attack me, and when I fight back, you use your pheromones to reduce me to this state? Isn't that too self-centered?" Isaac growled, his voice sharp with accusation, and Felix responded with a low hum.

"I had to bring you down somehow. And I'm naturally self-centered. I'm the type who needs to win at all costs, no matter how dirty or unfair the methods are."

"So, *hah*," Isaac asked between heavy breaths, trying to ignore the lewd sounds that came with every movement of his fingers. "Why are you doing this to me?"

The man behind the Scream mask tilted his head slightly as he stared down at Isaac.

"It's Halloween. My costume is similar to a robber's, so think of it as a kind of robbery game."

"Are you seriously trying to justify this nonsense with—!"

"Also, Spider-Man's ass looked so tempting, I couldn't just stand by while everyone was eyeing it up."

"So that's it? You just didn't like this outfit?"

Isaac had always known that Felix Felice, despite his notorious reputation as an arms dealer, had a petty and childish side. But he never imagined that a simple costume would push him this far.

"Yeah, I wanted to tear it to shreds," he added, immediately grabbing the slightly torn fabric and ripping it apart. "Like this."

A sharp sound echoed as the clothing ripped from his waist to his thighs. Still wearing the Spider-Man suit, Isaac's perfectly shaped ass was now fully exposed.

"Y-you pervert—ugh—!"

Isaac raised his voice but never finished the sentence. Felix yanked his fingers out from inside him and, without pause, drove his fully erect cock deep into him.

It felt like an auditory hallucination. The thickness of his cock—so different from his fingers—stretched Isaac's entrance, plunging in all at once and crushing his inner walls. His breath came ragged, his vision flickering black, yet the pleasure that surged through him like an electric current was intoxicating. What had been missing with just fingers was finally there, filling him completely, and the sensation was achingly satisfying.

"Ah…huff…"

The heat simmering in his body since being drenched in pheromones now surged like a raging flame, threatening to consume him. No—more than that—it felt as if his body would melt under the tingling electric current coursing through him. The tips of his bound fingers trembled, and his ass, wrapped around Felix's massive cock, twitched uncontrollably, intent on taking him in completely. *Deeper. Further. Harder.* Words he couldn't bring himself to say churned in his mind.

"Felix, Felix. Ah, huff…"

Thrust, thrust, thrust.

Even as Felix relentlessly plunged into him, gripping his ass tightly, Isaac was restless. Saliva dripped from his open mouth, soaking the sofa, and his vision blurred as his focus dissolved. His body, drenched in pheromones, no longer felt like his own. Even in this embarrassing state, with only his ass exposed and

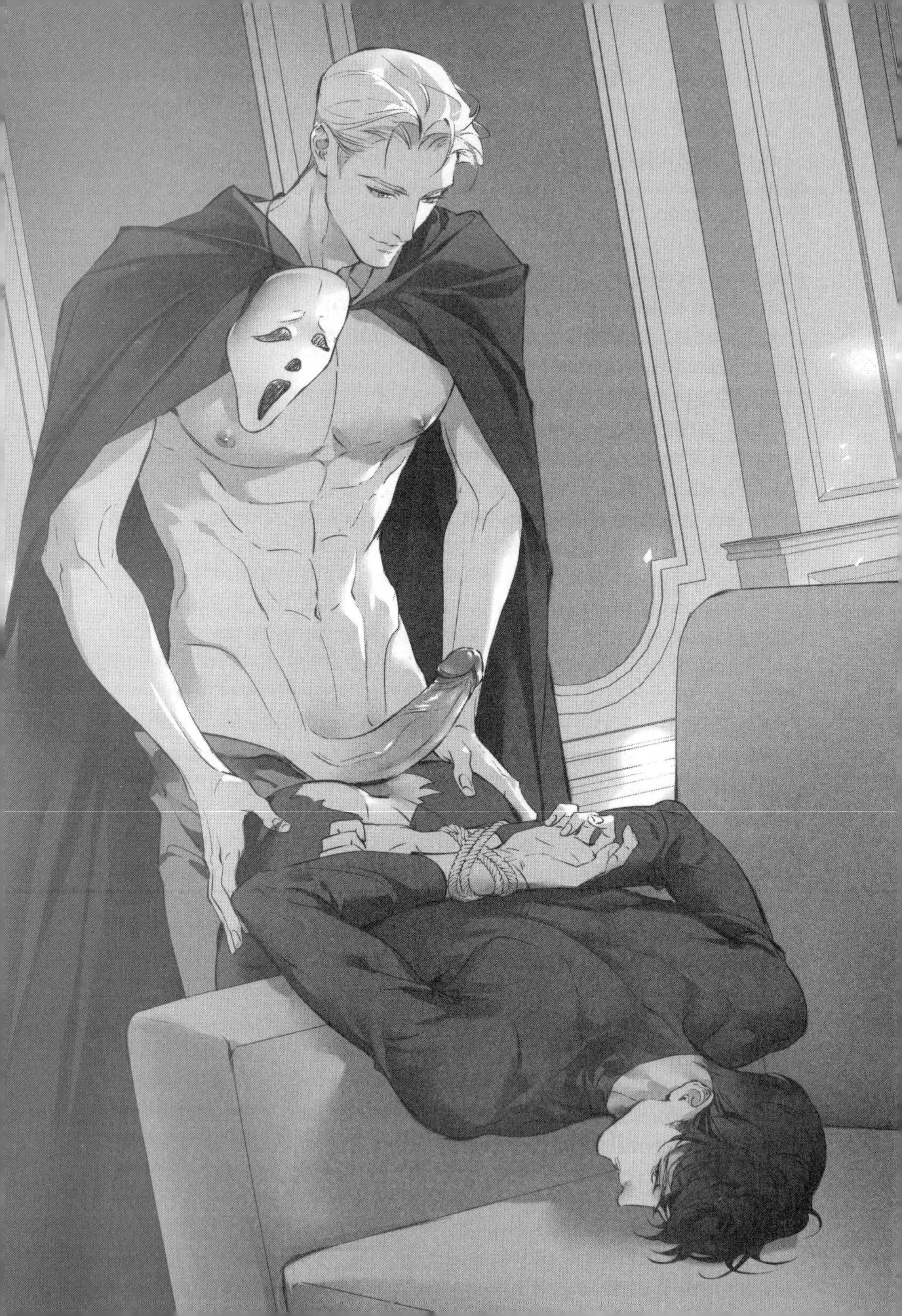

pounded relentlessly, it felt overwhelmingly good. It seemed that his mind was also thoroughly soaked and weighed down by the pheromones.

If his arms weren't bound, he would have clung onto Felix, but lying sprawled like a ragdoll on the sofa, shaking senselessly, was all he could manage. Whether he understood how he was feeling or not, Felix continued to grope and squeeze his exposed behind while thrusting. Then, just as Isaac unconsciously clenched around him, he suddenly slapped Isaac's ass.

"Isaac, stop clenching. If you get too excited and clench like that, you know you'll have to get punished, right?"

"Ugh, ugh—!"

"You're really going to cut my dick off."

Muttering in dissatisfaction, Felix slapped Isaac's ass again. Isaac, his vision swaying, stared blankly at him. Wouldn't hitting someone's ass make them clench even more? He wasn't entirely sure, but that's what he'd always thought. Felix's words and actions didn't seem to match.

Maybe the slaps were meant as punishment, yet every time Felix left a red mark, Isaac twitched and reflexively clenched. That only seemed to annoy Felix, who would slap him again for clenching. It was a vicious, endless cycle.

Yet he couldn't bring himself to tell Felix to stop, not with the dizzying pleasure spreading through his body to his fingertips. Each time Felix's rough hand came down in a slap, the sharp sting mingled with a tingling bliss that made his toes curl. The chilling rush left him wondering if he'd just discovered a sexual preference he'd never known he had.

"Isaac, your ass turned red," Felix muttered after a while of slapping him and thrusting at an overwhelming pace, suddenly slowing his movements.

Only then did Isaac feel the burning sensation, heat rising over the swollen skin. Isaac couldn't bring himself to say it hurt, biting his lips and swallowing his moans. Then, as if teasing, Felix rubbed the thoroughly wet behind and let out a sharp laugh.

"You're not, by any chance, enjoying being punished, are you?" Felix whispered through the mask, leaning in close to Isaac's ear. "You're completely soaking wet down here."

Only then did Isaac realize that, still trapped in the costume, his groin was damp, just as Felix had said. How was this possible? Embarrassment reddened his cheeks. He was speechless, biting his lips.

Suddenly, Felix roughly pulled off the mask he had been wearing and threw it on the floor; the Scream mask rolled across the floor with a clatter. But Isaac didn't hear it. His attention was fixated entirely on Felix's face and his piercing blue eyes, leaving him unable even to blink.

His sweat-drenched blond hair was swept back as he laughed like a mischievous boy, seeming to radiate light even in the darkness. He was beautiful and captivating. And that incredibly alluring alpha was now staring at him with darkened eyes, filled with raw desire, as if he wanted to devour him whole right then and there.

"Untie my hands," Isaac said, calming his rough breaths as the thought of falling for him all over again crossed his mind. Felix, who had been casually unbuttoning his shirt as if it had all been a game, tilted his head.

"Why? I'm still not done being angry."

The blunt response seemed almost innocent. Isaac let out a sigh. His resentment was truly deep.

"So, what more do you plan on doing?" Isaac asked in a resigned tone, face slumped down on the sofa.

Felix's hand gently caressed Isaac's reddened behind, continuing to thrust slowly, burying himself deep and then pulling out to the tip before plunging back in.

"Hmm. Honestly, I'd love to marinate you in my pheromones—" he murmured, "let my scent seep into every crevice of your body, so no matter where you go or what you do, my pheromones will waft off you."

"I'd probably die before that happens."

"Do you not know how much I love you? There is no way you can think I'd ever kill you? I just want to see you lose yourself and become a horny dog that desires only me."

As soon as he finished speaking, with a sly smile, Felix released another wave of pheromones. The reaction was immediate. Isaac's entire body trembled, and a sharp moan, almost like a scream, burst out. His vision blurred into darkness, then flashed with light.

"Ah, aah—! Felix, that's enough, stop!"

His already hypersensitive body felt ready to explode. Isaac sobbed, unconsciously tightening around the cock buried deep inside him. The sheer sensation of being filled was enough to push him over the edge. He couldn't hold back. Shaking his head and gritting his teeth, he finally came, his release bursting forth like a dam breaking, soaking the sofa's fabric and his clothes. Watching him lost in pleasure, drenched in tears and saliva, Felix let out a faint, breathless sigh.

"Oh my God, Isaac, Isaac..." Felix moaned. "Why are you so fucking hot? Huh? Everything you do is just so damn sexy. And now you're sticking your ass out, making it even worse for yourself."

Felix gently stroked Isaac's black hair, smiling with an expression overflowing with love for his partner—his omega. But his actions told a different story. He bit down hard on Isaac's cheek, leaving a mark while driving his cock into Isaac's gaping hole with all his strength.

Isaac let out a short scream and arched his back, but Felix held him tightly from behind, refusing to let go. The beast-like thrusts continued, each deep plunge echoing with wet, obscene sounds. Felix's hand rubbed Isaac's cock through his soaked clothes with rough insistence, while his other hand gripped Isaac's chin, forcing his mouth open to push his tongue inside.

His thick, hot tongue moved as if it owned the place, exploring every corner, sucking, and tugging at Isaac's tongue. His head, his body, his stomach, his ass, every part of him was being claimed and violated. Though it was impossible, all he could do was offer

his mouth and his entrance, swaying in a dizzy haze.

At some point, Felix—thrusting like an animal in heat—released his hot cum deep inside Isaac, yet the relentless pounding didn't stop. As if he hadn't just come, the rough movements continued, each thrust forcing slick heat to spill out and splatter, the wet squelching growing louder as Isaac's reddened ass throbbed harder.

With his head buried in the sofa and his body trembling nonstop, his vision began to blur. He wished he could just black out, but Felix kept flooding him with pheromones, again and again, making it impossible. It felt like suffocation. The cruel part was that, despite his will, his pheromone-soaked body was surrendering to the pleasure that crashed over him like a storm.

His body betrayed him, climaxing over and over, drenching his lower half and the entire sofa. It was also he who, without thinking, greedily sucked on Felix's tongue and rhythmically clenched and released around his cock.

"Ah, aah, Felix, there, keep going, don't stop, more, more—*ugh, ugh—!*"

"Isaac, do you know that every time you make that erotic face when you come, it drives me completely insane."

Felix seized his thigh and drove in to the hilt. The deep, unyielding stimulation made Isaac sob and shake his hips. The harder Felix pounded, the more Isaac's ass burned from the slap of skin against his thighs. Just as Isaac was about to collapse from exhaustion, Felix let out a breathy moan and went still.

One hand clamped tightly on Isaac's ass, Felix furrowed his brow, cursed under his breath, and buried himself even deeper, as if he couldn't hold back. Heat flared inside Isaac again, spreading from deep within his belly, scorching and vivid.

Gasping like a fish out of water, Isaac closed his eyes, thinking it was finally over. But from behind came a sharp click of the tongue—disapproving, almost knowing—as if Felix could see right through him.

"You do this every time," Felix muttered in dissatisfaction.

"You get so fucking sexy that it drives me crazy."

He thrust into Isaac once again, a wet sound echoing as if he hadn't just finished moments ago.

"Ugh—!"

Wrongfully relieved, Isaac felt his thighs tremble with spasms. Through his sweat-drenched hair, his black pupils—still clouded with lingering pleasure and lust—were a stark contrast to his usual calm, indifferent demeanor.

Felix seized a handful of his hair and kissed him, licking his chin and cheeks slick with saliva before drawing in a deep breath of his omega's scent. More precisely, it was pheromones laced with his natural body fragrance. The moment it filled his lungs, blood rushed to his already aching cock. Intoxicated by the sweet, unfamiliar scent, Felix greedily sucked at Isaac's lips and kept thrusting.

"Uh, ugh…Felix, my arms…untie them."

The plea slipped out between their locked lips. Felix looked down at him through narrowed eyes. It was the first time he had restrained Isaac's arms, and the fact that it thrilled him so much was undeniable. The rush of having such a strong man bound and utterly at his mercy was intoxicating. A part of him wanted to keep Isaac tied up and locked in his embrace forever.

"Don't wanna."

With a mischievous smile, Felix thrust hard. Isaac, who had been moaning loudly, turned his head toward Felix. His eyes, still red and wet from crying, held a pleading expression that he had never seen before.

"My arms hurt a little," Isaac whispered, furrowing his brow slightly.

"Shit, did I keep them tied for too long?"

Felix, flustered, immediately reached for his pocket knife and, without hesitation, cut the rope binding Isaac's arms. Isaac hadn't expected to be freed so easily. He clicked his tongue as he stared blankly at the rope that had fallen to the floor.

Still lying face down on the sofa, Isaac let his arms hang limply, unable to get up right away. His arms, having been twisted behind him for so long, were numb and hard to move.

"Are you okay?"

Seeing Isaac—who never faked anything—lying there unable to get up, Felix rubbed his arms slowly and asked with concern, wondering if his attempt at a new kink to punish him had gone too far. His expression darkened as he anxiously looked him over. After catching his breath, Isaac slowly shifted, propping himself up on his arms and lifting his upper body.

"No," Isaac replied shortly, the word slipping out in a sulky tone.

Just as Felix was about to ask if it still hurt, Isaac suddenly turned, seized him by the collar, and hurled him onto the sofa. The plush cushions shook violently as Felix landed where Isaac had been lying moments before. Still gripping his collar, Isaac swung a leg over and straddled his waist. In the blink of an eye, the tables had turned, leaving Felix blinking in stunned silence.

"I really can't let my guard down for even a second."

"Then why did you, even while knowing that?"

Still breathing heavily, his chest rising and falling, Felix looked up at Isaac, perfectly pinned on top of him, and let out a low laugh. Slowly, his hands slid to caress the waist straddling him.

"I'm always amazed when I see you. Just moments ago, you were mindlessly shaking your hips, and now you're completely composed? Even after being drenched in pheromones. It wouldn't have been strange if you were bedridden for days."

"Why would I be stuck in bed for days when it's not even my heat?"

Isaac snapped back, but Felix was right—this wasn't something an ordinary omega could do. He had always been this way, able to resist alpha pheromones, even those of a hyper-dominant alpha like Felix, and regain his composure.

Before, he could at least use the excuse of being a recessive omega who took suppressants. But now, even after being marked and stopping the medication, not much had changed—aside from being far more sensitive to pheromones than before. The fact that he reacted only to Felix's scent, becoming utterly flustered at even the faintest trace of it, was endlessly endearing to Felix.

And yet, when Isaac decided to snap out of it, he could regain his composure in an instant. His mental strength was simply that formidable. Felix had met countless omegas, but none like Isaac, and it always left him in awe. Whether it was a good thing was hard to say. Watching Isaac break free from his alpha pheromones made Felix fall for him all over again—while also leaving him a little frustrated.

"I wanted to see you get more excited and cum for a little longer."

"Haven't I done that enough already?"

"Not enough for me."

Isaac's eyes, red and heated, were still unfocused. It seemed difficult for him to completely break free from the pheromones that had poured over him like a storm. His waist, barely supporting him, trembled as he gritted his teeth and forced himself to stay upright. But to Felix, it felt unfair—insufficient.

"Isaac, I want to fuck like dogs for a little longer."

Felix leisurely licked his lips and rubbed Isaac's exposed ass with his palm. But Isaac's expression remained cold.

"Don't use your pheromones."

"Why?" Felix frowned. "You didn't like the pheromone shower?"

"I don't. It feels like being addicted to drugs, and I really hate that feeling."

Seeing Isaac speak so bluntly about it, Felix felt a twinge of fear that if he unleashed another pheromone shower, the consequences would be severe. He couldn't help but sigh in disappointment, shoulders slumping, but he soon brightened and lifted his head, smiling, as if a brilliant idea had struck him.

"If you hate it so much, why don't you just do it to me?"

"Can an omega like me really shower you with pheromones?"

"Why not? Just drench me in your pheromones. Let them

know I'm your alpha," Felix's eyes sparkled as he egged Isaac on. "Boldly declare me as yours."

He seemed oddly excited, but Isaac, staring at him with a skeptical look, eventually turned his head away.

"I'll pass on that. It'd be like chopping off my own foot with an axe. If I made you more aroused here, I'd be the one suffering. Why would I do that to myself?"

Felix pouted in disappointment at the curt reply. It was tough because Isaac was a formidable opponent who didn't fall for tricks.

"It would feel so good to have your pheromones and scent all over my body."

Isaac dismissed it as nonsense, but Felix couldn't give up and kept trying to persuade him. Isaac leaned over and ran his fingers through Felix's golden hair.

"Even now, you're already really, truly, like a dog in heat. If you became any hornier than you already are, I wouldn't be able to handle it. So it's better if you don't drench me in pheromones or ask me to do the same to you."

Felix looked at Isaac, whose face was slightly flushed, hair damp with sweat, and who exuded a sweet scent, yet spoke so coldly. He couldn't help but let out a laugh.

"I can't tell if that was a compliment or an insult."

Felix smiled with his captivating face. His gaze showed he wouldn't push further, recognizing how firm Isaac was. Still straddling Felix's waist, Isaac studied him. Though he could be petty, underhanded, childish, and sometimes do absurd things on a whim, he responded so honestly to Isaac's words.

If Isaac said his arms hurt, Felix would untie him. If Isaac said no more pheromones, Felix would stop immediately. Though he could throw tantrums like a child at times, especially when they were intimate, he always listened to Isaac's opinions and made sure never to hurt his feelings.

That's why, occasionally—just really, occasionally—Isaac felt both annoyed and proud of him. Maybe that's why he found himself weak toward this man. As he thought about how Felix seemed to have found his weakness, Isaac lowered his head.

"Hmm?"

Felix's dazzling face, unable to hide his surprise, moved closer in an instant. Isaac bent down, pressing his chest against Felix's, and impulsively stole a kiss from his perfect lips. It was a very impulsive kiss. The idea of wanting to kiss this man, who was so childish yet endearing, so eccentric yet gentle, had crossed his mind, and he simply acted on it.

With a squelching sound, his tongue brushed over Felix's lips. As Isaac pushed his tongue into Felix's open mouth, exploring every corner, Felix moaned and closed his eyes. Unintentionally, the pheromones flowing from him grew stronger. The tickling sensation at the tip of his nose made Isaac exhale a warm breath. Heat radiated from his body once again.

This was dangerous.

The moment that thought crossed his mind, Felix's strong arms coiled around him like a snake. The way they tightened, as if trying to crush him, gave Isaac a sense of unease, like there was no way to escape.

"This time, you're the one who provoked me."

"Just with a kiss?"

"If you knew how hot and sexy your kisses are, you wouldn't be saying that."

Really? Isaac wondered what he did that was so hot and sexy. But before he could think any more, Felix quickly pressed his lips to Isaac's, as if to stop any other thoughts from coming up. Isaac simply closed his eyes.

The obscene, intense, yet sweet kiss continued. Naturally, Felix's aroused cock couldn't stay still. Rubbing against Isaac's already slick entrance, it soon slid inside with ease.

Perhaps it was because the pheromones hadn't completely faded, but as Felix's veiny length pressed against his inner walls, uncontrollable pleasure spread through Isaac. His arms were no longer bound, yet they were now locked tightly in Felix's embrace.

A suppressed moan escaped him. The heavy, intense sensation of being filled was dizzying, yet it carried a strange euphoria.

"Didn't we decide, huff... to stop now?"

Isaac gasped out a question, lying against Felix's chest. But instead of answering, Felix suddenly sat up, shifting their position. Without warning, and still thrusting hard, he moved abruptly, making Isaac sway and instinctively loop his arms around Felix's neck, clinging to him.

"As I said, you provoked me first this time," Felix whispered in a sweet voice, sucking on Isaac's nape as he clung onto him.

Though his tone was soothing and gentle, the cock buried inside Isaac moved roughly, a stark contrast to his words.

"Ah, ah, then let's just stop for a bit, no, just slowly, ugh—"

"What should we do? We don't have the luxury of doing that."

The wet, slapping sounds were loud and distinct. Felix had already come twice without pulling out, and Isaac—still fully clothed—had climaxed multiple times, leaving their lower halves drenched and sticky. Yet Felix, as if it were his first time having sex, continued to ravage him mindlessly.

His thrusts grew increasingly violent, until Isaac could no longer keep up. Being on top only drove his weight down harder, forcing him in even deeper. His cock bulged visibly against Isaac's belly, vanishing and reappearing with every brutal thrust.

"A little, more slowly... Ah, ah, Felix!"

Just as Isaac, gripping Felix's shoulders as he pounded hard enough to make his pelvis ache, shook his head, Felix suddenly stopped. As if he had decided to listen to Isaac's plea, he looked up and gently caressed Isaac's cheek. His wet hand slowly trailed down Isaac's cheek, jaw, and nape. The sensation was strange; it was as if Felix were lost in thought while touching him.

Finally catching his breath as Felix stopped, Isaac swallowed against his dry throat. He had screamed and moaned so much that even swallowing hurt. Meanwhile, Felix's fingers wandered over Isaac's chest, still covered by the thin costume.

"Now that I look at it, only your ass is exposed."

Following Felix's inappropriate remark, Isaac lowered his head. He hadn't realized it in his dazed state, but Felix was right; the Spider-Man costume was still clinging tightly around his body. The only difference from before was that the crotch area was now completely soaked. Oh, and of course, the fact that his backside was torn open like a pervert's fantasy.

"I was going to tear this ridiculous outfit to shreds and burn it."

Suddenly, as if recalling something he had forgotten, Felix frowned. No one could match this man's talent for holding a grudge. Although Isaac might have never realized that this style of costume would provoke such a reaction, to Felix, who was glaring down at it, the outfit clinging to Isaac's body seemed like a heinous criminal deserving the death penalty.

Isaac hesitated, unsure of what to say, but before he could speak, a sharp rip echoed as the fabric tore. Like Superman ripping open his shirt, Felix grabbed Isaac's costume and tore it apart. The difference was that while Superman revealed the iconic "S" on his chest, Isaac's nipples were now fully exposed.

Isaac, dumbfounded, looked down at his exposed chest and then up at Felix. He wasn't sure if Felix had intended to tear the costume to shreds, but at this point, he was utterly baffled by the man's ulterior motives.

"Wow, that's hot."

Felix curled his lips in satisfaction, licking them as he stared at Isaac's exposed chest. Isaac clicked his tongue.

"Should I tear the bottom half, too? It's frustrating not being able to touch you properly."

"Might as well just take it all off."

"No. This looks more delicious."

"You really are," Isaac muttered in disgust. "A pervert."

But Felix ignored him, latching onto Isaac's erect nipple. The sudden wet heat against his chest sent a tingling current up his spine, drawing an involuntary moan from his lips. The feel of Felix's mouth enveloping his nipple, nibbling gently, was almost unbearably intense.

"Felix, w-wait—!"

Surprised by the unfamiliar sensation, Isaac tried to push Felix's head away, but Felix didn't budge. Instead, he tightened his arm around Isaac's back and continued greedily sucking on his nipples. To make matters worse, Felix resumed thrusting, causing Isaac's limbs to tremble uncontrollably.

Felix often sucked on Isaac's nipples until they were raw, but this time, they were unusually sensitive. Every time Felix rolled his tongue over them or bit down, sharp waves of pleasure spread through Isaac's body, bringing tears to his eyes. It seemed he couldn't fully escape the lingering effects of Felix's pheromones.

"Ah, ah, wait, wait, just a second—"

Isaac hunched his shoulders and ran his fingers through Felix's hair, tugging at it. It felt like the only way to endure the overwhelming sensations. But Felix, clearly enjoying Isaac's heightened sensitivity, made loud, slurping noises as he suckled on his chest, almost as if to show off.

By the time Felix finally stopped, Isaac's nipples were swollen and red. His face was flushed crimson, tears streaking his cheeks. The unyielding grip on his waist, the relentless sucking at his chest, and the deep, driving thrusts made his vision flicker. He felt as if he were about to die.

"You think if I suck hard enough, milk will come out?"

"Stop saying...*ha, ugh!* Felix!"

But Felix, still latched onto Isaac's chest, showed no sign of stopping, persistently and greedily sucking at his nipples. Isaac let out a sob and arched his back. His groin dampened again, the sharp, pungent scent of semen hitting his nose. Even without removing his clothes or touching himself, he had come again—and he could no longer remember how many times it had happened.

Completely drained, Isaac slumped forward. Felix tapped his shoulder, urging him to lean against him. He was both the cause and the cure to Isaac's pain, and Isaac silently buried his forehead against Felix's shoulder, trying to steady his ragged breathing. A long sigh slipped out before he realized it.

Isaac didn't notice, but Felix seemed exhausted too. The warmth pooling in his abdomen finally registered. The lingering soreness and tingling in his chest, where Felix's mouth had been, left him with no strength to even think about the cock still buried inside him.

"Did getting your nipples sucked feel that good?" Felix asked lazily, stroking the back of Isaac, clinging to him. "Since when did they get so sensitive?"

Instead of answering, Isaac bit his lip and fell into thought. While it was true that Felix's lingering pheromones had left his body extra sensitive, something felt off.

When Isaac raised his hand to touch his chest, a sharp pain shot through him. His nipples felt swollen and erect, and they might even be slightly chafed. But more than that, something felt different. His entire chest felt warm and unusually sensitive, as if every nerve was on edge. As Isaac rubbed his firm chest muscles, lost in confusion, Felix pressed his lips to Isaac's cheek and whispered.

"Think you're pregnant?"

"Are you joking?" Isaac's eyes widened.

"If not, then never mind." Felix chuckled as if it were a joke, but Isaac couldn't bring himself to laugh. A strange, uneasy feeling brushed past his mind. He really had a bad feeling about this. Something felt off.

"Last time, the knotting…"

At Isaac's mutter, Felix looked puzzled and replied with a simple "huh?" It was true—there had been a knotting a couple of months ago. Since the first time, four years earlier, when he and Felix had slept together without even knowing each other, Isaac had always refused to be knotted, even during his heat cycles. But there had been one day when Felix, not in his right mind, had done it anyway. It was the day Mr. Felice, Felix's grandfather, had visited.

"What? Back then?"

Felix scratched his cheek, looking embarrassed. Finally

snapping out of his daze, Isaac sat up suddenly. Reflecting on it, he realized he had been feeling unusually tired lately. He had even experienced chills, wondering if he was just coming down with something.

But still, surely not…

"I need to wash up first." His voice and expression were firm, as if he hadn't been trembling with excitement just moments ago. But Isaac couldn't get up right away. The instant he tried to rise, kneeling on the sofa, a thick stream of semen spilled out of him.

The uncomfortable sensation was hard to bear, and Isaac bit his lip in response. His limbs trembled as he leaned against Felix's shoulders, a low moan escaping him. The semen that had pooled inside him from being pumped and filled over and over was now dripping out, the sensation almost nauseating.

"Hmm, guess I did go a bit overboard," Felix muttered with an innocent expression as he slid his fingers into Isaac's gaping entrance. "I'll take it out for you, so leave it to me."

When he spread his fingers like scissors, another gush of fluid poured out. As he scraped the inner walls, more dripped down his hand. Isaac furrowed his reddened eyes and briefly held his breath.

"You're erotic even when I do this." Despite the embarrassing act, Felix seemed to be enjoying himself.

"Hurry…" Unable to bear it any longer, Isaac urged him on.

Felix, still stirring his fingers inside him, leaned forward and licked the erect nipple before him. It was the opposite side from the one he had been sucking earlier, yet just as sensitive, sending shivers racing down Isaac's spine. The unfamiliar sensation was almost unbearably strange, only deepening his suspicion.

Pushing Felix aside coldly, Isaac got to his feet on trembling legs, steadying himself on the floor. "I think… I need to go to the hospital."

His face was pale, probably from the chaotic thoughts swirling in his mind. The feeling wasn't good. Now, remembering the last knotting incident, he felt even worse.

"Jesus, Isaac, it's nighttime. The hospitals are all closed." Looking confused, Felix tried to explain.

Isaac ignored him, ripping off the Spider-Man costume that now looked ragged and tossing it aside. "If we want to leave early tomorrow morning, we should wash up and get some sleep now. If I spend the whole night in bed with you again, we'll lose track of time."

"But still—!" Felix, who had planned to keep Isaac moaning all night and had already spent hours inside him without pulling out, grabbed at him as he tried to leave, his expression both betrayed and shameless.

Isaac, draping himself in Felix's black robe, crossed the room without looking back. He paused briefly at the curtained window, glanced outside, and let out a sigh. "The Halloween party is probably already over."

It was a situation that made him sigh deeply. He hadn't been able to take care of Benjamin or the Halloween party until the end, too busy fooling around with Felix. And now, with this unexpected realization, his mind was a complete mess.

"Tony probably took care of the party, and your mother probably already put Benjamin to sleep." Felix, still shameless and sulking, leaned his head back on the sofa, pouting like a child.

Once again, Isaac didn't look back, walking to the door and flinging it open. Cool air rushed in, filling the room that was full of lust, excitement, heat, and pheromones, clearing the fog from Isaac's mind.

"If by some chance I go to the hospital tomorrow and get confirmation that I'm pregnant…" Isaac said quietly before stepping out.

Felix jerked his head up from the sofa in surprise. "If you're pregnant, will you produce breast milk?"

Why hadn't he thought of that earlier? Felix finally had the idea, his eyes shining with excitement as he fixed his gaze on Isaac's chest, looking incredibly sinister. Isaac let out a short sigh, knowing exactly what Felix was thinking.

"There will be no sex for the time being."

Instead of answering about breastfeeding, a shocking announcement made Felix's eyes widen to the size of lanterns.

"Isaac! How does that even make sense?" he exclaimed.

Isaac looked at him indifferently as he suddenly got up from his seat and approached him like an angry bear. "Isn't this something you brought upon yourself? You were the one who knotted me, and you were the one who got me pregnant, so shouldn't you take responsibility?"

"No, of course I'll take responsibility, but how is that related to us having sex?"

"If you want a child, there is a responsibility to have that child," Isaac spoke coldly, turning away. "Let's talk to the doctor about the details tomorrow."

The party had long since ended, and even the last of the staff had already gone. Crossing the empty living room of the mansion, Isaac's figure seemed to vanish into the darkness.

At the door, Felix stood in utter despair, exhaling a deep, heavy sigh. Regret still clung to him. Yes, he wanted a second child, and yes, he had unintentionally knotted him…but no sex if he was pregnant? How long was this supposed to last? Where in the world did such an absurd idea even exist?

If he couldn't hold Isaac for even a single day, it felt like thorns would sprout from his mouth—or worse, from… well, *you know*. And now Isaac was saying no more sex? He could endure anything else, but not that. He'd sooner starve than go without holding him! How was he supposed to resist his omega when he looked that irresistible?

"Isaac! Let's rethink this!"

Pale-faced, Felix hurried into the dark living room where Isaac had vanished. No matter how he turned it over in his mind, this wasn't right. His footsteps pounded against the floor, the sound echoing through the quiet mansion—then fading. Within moments, the house, steeped in the depths of dawn, was silent once more. Peace settled over it, as if nothing had happened.

But come the first of November, that stillness would shatter, replaced by the usual chaos.

The End

Thank You

As we reach the final chapter of our very first translated series, we want to take a moment to express our heartfelt gratitude.

To our readers: thank you for trusting us to bring this story across languages and into your hands. Your support, enthusiasm, and passion for storytelling make all the long hours and late-night edits worth it.

To the author: thank you for entrusting us with your words. It's been an honor to carry your voice to new readers and cultures, and we hope we've done your vision justice.

To our translator(s), editor(s), and everyone behind the scenes: this moment is yours too. Without your care, creativity, and dedication, this series would never have made the leap from one language to another.

Publishing this first series has been a labor of love, and we're proud to have taken this journey with you all. Here's to many more stories ahead—thank you for being a part of our beginning.

With gratitude,
BLoved Publishing

Bringing stories across borders

5'9"
5'6"
5'3"
5'
4'9"
ID No.
DATE
40375
07:04:27
ID No.
DATE
POLICE
DEADLOCK
Saki Aida

Deadlock is rated MATURE for language and sexual content, Intense violence, Graphic sexual content, Gambling with real money, Strong language, Horror, Mature themes, Blood, Violence, Nudity, Sensuality, and Adult activities. Reader discretion is advised.

Published originally under the title of Deadlock © Saki Aida

Originally published in Japan by (name of company) through (Company name). This English edition is published by arrangement with (company name).

PROLOGUE

Footsteps approached.

As Yuto lay amidst the darkness, he strained to hear more. The jangling clicks of metal knocking against metal reached his ears. Hope swelled quick and fierce, but he tamped it down with savage force.

Cut it out, he told himself. Over the past two weeks, he'd heard footsteps countless times, only to be met with disappointment.

"Yuto Lennix," stated a voice sharp-edged as a blade. "Get up."

In the narrow space of Yuto's solitary confinement cell, the order echoed mercilessly. He opened his eyes, staring fixedly at the blank wall before him.

"I said get up!" The assistant sheriff's voice had gotten decidedly irritated at his insolence. With casual slowness, Yuto sat upright on the bed, then turned his gaze toward the iron bars of his cell. "Come over here and put out your hands."

Obediently, Yuto rose and approached. He placed both hands through the hole in the center of the bars.

The assistant sheriff immediately clapped cuffs over his wrists, then opened the cell door. "You're getting on a bus in an hour. But first, you're gonna have to go through a pat-down and change your clothes."

"And where is this bus taking me?" Yuto asked calmly, voice soft.

The assistant sheriff's voice was all business when he replied, "Schelger Prison."

A relieved sigh leaked from Yuto's lips. The possibility that a mistake might happen somewhere down the line that caused him to get sent to the wrong place had been haunting him for ages.

"Yeah, you've got some real shitty luck," the assistant sheriff commented, completely misreading his reaction. "But you'll just have to get over it."

It was a natural conclusion for the guy to come to. Most criminals would be horrified to find out they were being transferred to an infamous prison known for its many layered security.

But not Yuto. To him, Schelger Prison represented something else entirely. It was the only place on Earth where he might be able to find a way out of the abyss he'd fallen into.

CHAPTER 1

"Hey. This your first time in prison?" someone whispered.

The words came from the blond-haired Caucasian man seated next to Yuto—he'd boarded the bus back at San Jose, California, and couldn't be more than twenty. There was a childlike innocence about his face, which was currently pale with anxiety. It made the guy look like a carsick highschooler.

"Yep," Yuto said shortly, shooting the kid a quick glance before facing forward once again.

The front and back of the prisoner escort vehicle were both sectioned off with metal partitions. Behind them stood a number of guards armed with shotguns, their eyes on the prisoners within the vehicle.

"Oh, me too! Man, we're so unlucky. I mean, we're getting locked up in Schelger Prison, of all places! I heard that—"

"Hey!" snapped a stern voice from behind them. "No talking on the bus."

The kid's runaway mouth snapped shut.

An oppressive atmosphere settled over the prisoner escort vehicle as it continued onward, carrying its twenty plus red-jumpsuit clad passengers due north. Dazzling rays of summer sunlight beamed through the barred windows, proving quite a contrast to the prisoners' melancholy gloom.

Who knew when they would next be able to step outside and bask in the sun like this? Feeling oddly sentimental, Yuto narrowed his eyes against the glare and stared out at the scenery passing by. "Warden Corning, sir. Is there something I can help you with?"

"No, I'm just doing a routine inspection. It's an important part of my job to know what's going on in this place, after all."

The warden shot a quick look over to where Yuto was standing, then scooped his file off the top of his officer's desk.

"So your name's Yuto Lennix, huh? Twenty-eight years old, from Los Angeles..." He trailed off, eyes lifting from the file to shoot daggers in Yuto's direction. "And I see here you worked for the DEA before your arrest, is that right?"

When Yuto didn't reply, the officer in charge's voice turned sharp. "This man is the warden of Schelger Prison," he growled. "Open your mouth and answer him!"

Giving in, Yuto replied, "Yes, that's right."

"What kind of work did you do there?" the warden asked, prying even further.

"I was an investigator."

The warden's eyebrows rose past his hairline at Yuto's monotone answer, and he shook his head. "For one of the people whose job it is to crack down on crime to become a criminal themself. How depressing. And to kill your own partner? You must not have even an ounce of shame."

Yuto fought to keep his eyes blank and calm, but inside him, rage boiled red-hot. The warden didn't know shit.

Killing his own partner—even being accused of such a thing out loud felt unbearable. He hadn't touched a hair on Paul McLean's head. The man hadn't just been Yuto's brother-in-arms, but also his close friend. Losing him had been just as devastating to Yuto as losing a close family member. He'd valued Paul more than he could begin to explain.

Before Paul's death, the two of them had posed as drug dealers to infiltrate a drug-trafficking ring in New York as part of their investigative work for the DEA. Around a year after they'd initially made contact, they'd been able to penetrate the ring deep enough to successfully arrest the person at the top. But their celebration had been short-lived—just two weeks after they'd come out from undercover,

Paul had been found stabbed to death in his room.

Yuto was four years younger than Paul, and he had a great amount of respect for his more experienced partner both as a person and an investigator. Where Yuto had a tendency to recklessly catapult into danger head-on, Paul had always had a good head on his shoulders. His steadfast nature, coupled with his ability to come up with complex strategies on the fly, had proven invaluable many times over.

He'd been a person who Yuto had felt he could lean on, entrust his life to. But now he was dead.

When Yuto had first received the news, he'd been struck dumb. But that wasn't the end of the tragedy. Somehow, his fingerprints had ended up on the kitchen knife that'd been used to kill Paul, which had led to the police arresting Yuto under the suspicion that he'd committed the murder.

During the questioning, one of the detectives had shoved the murder weapon right in front of Yuto's eyes, and he'd had no other choice but to admit that it'd come from his very own kitchen.

In a desperate attempt to exonerate himself, he'd told the police that someone must have come and secretly taken the knife from his home, but the police hadn't bought it. They'd already received testimony that the night before the crime, Yuto and Paul had gotten into a disagreement at a local bar. In their minds, he had already been guilty.

While it was true he and Paul had fought that night, it hadn't been a big deal. It wasn't uncommon for them to get into heated arguments over how to move forward on an investigation, which was exactly what had happened at the bar. To outsiders, their drunken quarrel had likely looked pretty serious, but neither of them would have held a grudge over a dustup like that.

Yuto had tried to explain that to the police, but they hadn't believed him one bit. And when you paired that with the fact that he'd lived alone at the time and had no alibi, it'd been clear he was pretty much screwed.